WisCon Chronicles

Volume 1

WisCon Chronicles

Volume 1

Aqueduct

Seattle

Published by Aqueduct Press
PO Box 95787
Seattle, WA 98145-2787
www.aqueductpress.com

First Edition, August 2007
11 10 09 08 07   1 2 3 4 5

"Researching WisCon Stories: Revisionist History or Re-visioning the Past with the Future in Mind" by Joan Haran was first published in the WisCon 30 Souvenir Book (2006).
The Delany-Russ interview was first published in *Broadsheet*
(Feb 2007 http://www.broaduniverse.org/broadsheet.html).

ISBN: 1-933500-14-X
ISBN: 978-1-933500-14-0

Library of Congress Control Number: 2007902986

Cover Design by Lynne Jensen Lampe
Book Design by Kathryn Wilham

Fishbowl cartoon, p 36, courtesy Tom Duchamp

Cover images

Credit: NASA/The Visible Earth (http://visibleearth.nasa.gov/) for "Snow and Ice in Wisconsin"

NASA/Aerial of Madison (http://asapdata.arc.nasa.gov/Image.htm)

Front cover clock face and back cover female symbol/clock sign courtesy Jeanne Gomoll

Printed in the USA by Applied Digital Imaging, Bellingham, WA

Dedicated to all the behind-the-scenes ConCom members and volunteers who over thirty-plus years have made WisCon into the vibrant, ever-evolving community it is today.

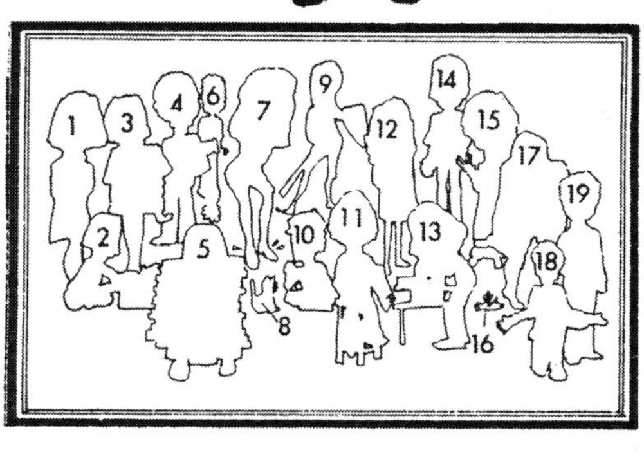

The First ConCom

1. Perri Corrick-West
2. Tom Murn
3. Diane Martin
4. Doug Price
5. Jan Bogstad
6. Pat Simmons
7. Lesleigh Luttrell
8. live cat
9. Richard S. Russell
10. John Bartelt
11. Jeanne Gomoll
12. Rick White
13. Hank Luttrell
14. Jim Cox
15. Lucy Nuti
16. dead cat
17. Phil Kaveny
18. Richard West
19. Greg Rihn

Jeanne Gomoll

Georgie Schnobirch

Table of Contents

Jeanne Gomoll

Introduction

by L. Timmel Duchamp

WisCon, for those who don't know, is a feminist literary festival organized and run by volunteers, held annually in Madison, Wisconsin. Last year at WisCon 30 one thousand people attended.

There's nothing in the world we now have that's quite like WisCon. I've often heard attendees describe it as a feminist utopia, but that's not a characterization that would work for everyone (particularly those who believe that "utopia" is necessarily a bad thing). The fact is, there is no definitive WisCon experience; WisCon has always meant different things to different people. An attempt to represent it, therefore, may seem foolish, presumptuous, and doomed to failure. But as Liz Henry pointed out during WisCon 30's "Feminist Think Tanks" panel, feminist work and activities, especially those performed in connection with ephemeral occasions, have a tendency to slide under the radar and vanish from the historical record. "Document, document, document," she urged us all—which was exactly what she was doing herself at that moment, her fingers flying over the keyboard of her laptop, making a rough transcript as a few dozen of us explored the need for and possibilities of creating a feminist think tank.

In most cultures, women's space is understood as private space, while public space is coded male. WisCon explicitly aims to create a non-separatist "women's space" that is public. A women's space that is also a public space is such a rare occurrence in our world that it *feels* science fictional. The aim of this anthology series is to help document WisCon, to celebrate the continual creation and re-creation of a women's public space in serious but pleasurable pursuit of feminist ends. The opening volume documents WisCon 30, held Memorial Day Weekend, 2006.

I regret that so much of WisCon 30 had to be omitted from this book: but a four-day convention featuring six tracks of programming for one thousand participants made omissions inevitable. I especially regret that I couldn't manage to organize a forum for discussing the post-con reactions to the cultural appropriation panel, a digest of which would have made a significant contribution to this book. Still, I hope the diversity of the materials in this volume will give readers unfamiliar with WisCon some idea of the range of interests typically addressed there even as it exposes those who attended it to parts of that they couldn't manage to experience themselves.

Out of the many papers in the academic track presented by scholars, the anthology offers four. In "Wonder Woman: Lesbian or Dyke? Paradise Island as a Woman's Community," Trina Robbins, an expert on women comic-book heroes who writes comics herself, explores the attractions of a women's community for girls reading Wonder Women comics. In "Lord of the Monsters," novelist Andrea Hairston, who is also a Professor of Theater and Afro-American Studies, vigorously takes issue with the racist subtext of *King Kong*. In "Piercy's Gendered Cyborgs: Hope, Threats, and Blurred Boundaries," graduate student Linda Wight, new to WisCon, considers Marge Piercy's gender-coding of cyborgs in *He, She, and It*. And in "'A Man Is Like a Nut': Gender and Magic in Ursula K. Le Guin's Later Earthsea Novels," Australian scholar and novelist Sylvia Kelso examines the construction of masculinities in Le Guin's Earthsea novels.

Panels, of course, make up the bulk of WisCon's programming. Therefore the volume includes partial transcripts (with post-con annotations) of four panels—"Feminist Think Tanks"; "Is Reading Feminist SF a Theory-Building Activity?"; "Uncomfortable Politics in Feminist Writing"; and "Who Wants a Revolution?"—as well as Micole Sudberg and Yoon Ha Lee's post-con descriptions of and comments on two panels and two post-con essays provoked by panels, Rosaleen Love's "A Think Tank Thing for Feminists" and Nancy Jane Moore's "We Aren't Civilized Yet: Reflections from the WisCon 30 Panel on Women Warriors."

Essays by Joan Haran and Rachel Swirsky look beyond and behind the celebratory. Rachel's "Welcome Back to the Beginning" offers us a sober reminder from a young feminist of just how much work in our genre remains to be done. Joan's "Researching WisCon Stories: Revisionist History or Re-visioning the Past with the Future in Mind," which appeared in WisCon 30's souvenir book, views WisCon as an ongoing negotiated political process that attempts to offer a "broad church feminism" that has not always been successful in eliminating implicit—often unspoken—exclusionary practices.

Much of the WisCon experience involves conversation of diverse sorts. Broad Universe sponsored and transcribed a telephone interview of Joanna Russ by Samuel R. Delany (attended by just about everyone at WisCon not scheduled for programming at the time), and we reprint it here with their kind permission. Although the volume does not include the speeches made by WisCon 30's Guests of Honor, Jane Yolen and Kate Wilhelm, which will appear elsewhere, it does offer Nisi Shawl's "Dry Eyes," describing her experience announcing and presenting the first Carl Brandon Society Kindred and Parallax Awards.

In addition, we asked Eileen Gunn to interview "a coven of WisCon attendees" with one question each; and Julie Phillips, Suzy McKee Charnas, Carol Emshwiller, Mark Rich, Ellen Klages, Ted Chiang, Ursula K. Le Guin, Liz Henry, Lisa Tuttle, Diantha Day Sprouse, Tempest Bradford, Spike Parsons, and Jeanne Gomoll generously consented to make up Eileen's coven. In his essay "A Forty-Year-Old Con-Virgin Goes to WisCon," in dialogue with Samuel R. Delany, Stephen Gold describes his experiences as a first-timer and man attempting to negotiate a feminist-dominated public space, followed by "Sympathy and Power: L. Timmel Duchamp Asks Samuel R. Delany a Question," Chip's gracious answer to an interview question I put to him about men and feminism inspired by Stephen's essay.

Finally, we conclude the volume with a dessert concocted by Rosaleen Love. Original to this volume, "No Man's Land" sends us off with a smile on our lips.

The generosity and cooperation of many people made this volume possible. I would especially like to thank Melanie Madden, Aqueduct's intern, for her editorial assistance and her indefatigable work transcribing the audio recording of the "Who Wants a Revolution" panel. Jeanne Gomoll generously made the graphics she and others have designed for WisCon over the years available to us. Joan Haran encouraged scholars to send me their papers. Diantha Day Sprouse kindly helped me with post-con discussions of the cultural appropriations panel. I especially owe Laura Quilter and Liz Henry a debt of gratitude for their documentation of WisCon 30 on the Feminist SF Wiki as well as their permitting me to use their excellent panel transcript notes in this volume. I'd also like to thank the panelists and audience participants who read over, corrected, and annotated the transcript notes, viz., Vonda N. McIntyre, Janet Laffler, Susanna Sturgis, Laura Quilter, Rosaleen Love, Liz Henry, Karen Joy Fowler, Joan Haran, Laurie A. Selke, Cheryl Morgan, Margaret McBride, Sylvia Kelso, Ian K. Hagemann, Patrick Nielsen Hayden, Lenny Bailes, Susan Karen Kinast-Porter, and Avedon Carol. And finally, thanks to Eileen Gunn, for her good sense and moral support, which have been of inestimable value for the enterprise.

Julie Phillips

Q: WisCon 30 was your first WisCon, wasn't it? What did you expect? Did you get it?

A: Although I'd been hearing about WisCon, and how great it was, for a long time, I was very nervous actually going there, because I hardly knew anyone. But that changed remarkably fast. I've never before met so many people I liked in one weekend, or who were so fascinating to talk to. By the end I felt like I was going to die of talking, and I didn't care.

I was also anxious because I don't actually know all that much about science fiction, but that changed fast too. I sort of knew about panels but didn't expect to learn so much from them. (I've since gathered that the WisCon standard is pretty high.)

I did expect to buy books there, but I didn't expect to buy my new favorite pair of earrings as well. And I definitely didn't expect to see a seven-foot-tall award-winning author tied up in a hot-pink brassiere.

Julie Phillips is the author of
James Tiptree Jr.: The Double Life of Alice B. Sheldon
(St. Martin's Press, August 2006)

http://www.julie-phillips.com

Wonder Woman: Lesbian or Dyke? Paradise Island as a Woman's Community

by Trina Robbins

In his now-infamous 1954 indictment of comic books, *Seduction of the Innocent,* Dr. Frederic Wertham called the Wonder Woman comic book of the 1940s and '50s[1] "The Lesbian counterpart of Batman," whom, along with his young sidekick, Robin, he had already accused of membership in NAMBLA. Using acrobatic leaps of logic, Wertham went on to make the following connection about Wonder Woman's sidekicks, students at the all-woman Holliday College: "Her followers are the 'Holliday girls,' i.e., the holiday girls, the gay party girls, the gay girls."[2]

Later critics would echo Wertham's theory. In the 1970 classic, *All in Color for a Dime*, Jim Harmon describes how Wonder Woman would "exchange hugs and kisses of delight with the readily available Holliday Girls." He adds, "It was a very sick scene."[3]

In a 1996 private phone interview, Robert Kanigher, who took over writing the comic in 1948, after the death of creator William Moulton Marston, who wrote the comics under the pseudonym "Charles Moulton," let me in on what he called the truth about Wonder Woman: the amazons from her home, Paradise Island, where no men are permitted, were all lesbians.

Not everyone agrees. Jules Feiffer, clearly wishing for something closer to *Hothead Paisan*, draws a different conclusion in his 1965 memoir, *The Great Comic Book Heroes*. "Wonder Woman," he writes, "wasn't dykey enough. Her violence was too immaculate, never once boiling over into a little fantasmal sadism."[4] In her introduction to the Bonanza Books 1972 collection *Wonder Woman*, and again in her introduction to Abbeville Press's 1995 collection of Wonder Woman covers, also titled *Wonder Woman*, Gloria Steinem avoids the issue entirely, preferring to write about "sisterhood." And in the 2000 Chronicle Books production, *also* titled *Wonder Woman,* writer Les Daniels, hired by D.C. comics, writes off the accusation in one short sidebar of the 206 page book: "[Wertham] saw innuendo everywhere, and...managed to work himself into a lather because he thought Wonder Woman contained 'Lesbian overtones.'...as Robert Kanigher later pointed out, surely some inhabitants of Paradise Island must have had Sapphic tendencies. Not in the comics, however!"[5]

So, are the amazon princess Diana, her home-town amazons, and her Holliday girl sidekicks lesbians? And is this a *bad* thing? William Moulton Marston was a successful pop-psychologist and also happened to be the inventor of the lie detector. The man knew what he was doing, and if there is lesbianism in the Golden Age Wonder Woman,[6] he put it there. What hints does he give the reader?

Well, there's the hugging, but, as previously mentioned, women *do* hug.[7] What about lovers? Marston occasionally hints that Wonder Woman might be in a Xena and Gabrielle relationship with another woman. In *Sensation Comics* #19, 1942, Wonder Woman's amazon best friend, Paula, is called in to help when the princess runs amok because her bracelets have been removed.[8] Stopping Wonder Woman in the act of strangling a suspected fifth columnist, Paula says, "Easy, darling—it's your Paula!"

Another story[9] deals with Marya, a beautiful eight-foot-tall "Mexican mountain girl," who definitely has a crush on Wonder Woman. She calls Wonder Woman "brave princess" and "beautiful princess." When the two women are captured in nets, Wonder Woman, ungraciously considering only her dumb blond "boyfriend" Steve Trevor, tells her, "I'm sorry for you, Marya, but at least we've saved Steve…" Marya, with the selflessness of true love, replies, "I care not what happen to me if I help save your friend, Preencess!" Finally, Marya is encased in cement up to her chest. But when the amazon princess is about to be killed, "Driven desperate by her great love for Wonder Woman, Marya wrenches savagely at the solid cement which encases her legs." Leaping from the cement she shouts, "My preencess—I **come**!" Finally, Wonder Woman freed and the villains vanquished, Wonder Woman declares, "The credit goes to the biggest girl and the bravest—my little friend Marya!" Marya kneels at the amazon's feet, clutching her hand rapturously, saying, "Oh Preencess!"

Getting in the way of Wonder Woman's relationships with other women is always Steve Trevor, the Token Boyfriend.[10] The Lois Lane to Wonder Woman's Superman, he seems to exist only to be rescued. She always puts him off when he asks her when they will marry, with statements such as, "When justice has finally triumphed over wrong!" or "When evil and injustice vanish from the earth!" In other words, it'll be a cold day in hell, buster. Her reluctance to marry Steve may have had nothing to do with her interest in other women, but rather, her reluctance to spend the rest of her life with someone so stupid that he constantly fails to make the connection between the amazon princess Diana and her alter ego, army nurse Diana Prince.

It is generally accepted that Marston created Wonder Woman for girls as an alternative to the male-oriented superhero comics of the time; however, I could find no actual statement on his part saying that. In her introduction to the collection of Wonder Woman covers, Gloria Steinem writes, "…[Marston] had invented Wonder Woman as a heroine for little girls, and also as a conscious alternative to the violence of comic books for boys."[11] Of course, Steinem was not there, nor did she ever interview the good doctor. The statement I have found by Marston that comes closest to reflecting Steinem's conclusion is from an article written by Marston in *The American Scholar.*[12]

> It seemed to me, from a psychological angle, that the comics worst offense was their blood-curdling masculinity...it's smart to be strong. It's big to be generous, but it's sissified, according to exclusively male rules to be tender, loving, affectionate... "Ah that's girls stuff!" snorts our comic reader, "Who wants to be a girl?" And that's the point; not even girls want to be girls as long as their feminine stereotype lacks force... strength. (35)

I have also found no statistics that show just how many girls *did* read Wonder Woman,[13] so my only evidence is anecdotal. Obviously, as she tells us in her writings, Gloria Steinem read, and was strongly influenced by, the amazing amazon. In her introduction to the collection of Wonder Woman covers, she describes the origin of *Ms Magazine*: "Since Joanne Edgar and others of its founding editors had also been rescued by Wonder Woman in their childhoods, we decided to rescue Wonder Woman in return (by putting her on their first cover)." On the back cover of my book, *The Great Women Superheroes*, author Jane Yolen writes, "I was one of the legion of young girls who adored Wonder Woman back in the 1940s..." In her article, "Looking For Wonder Woman,"[14] Lillian Robinson writes of "devouring monthly installments of Wonder Woman." She continues, "I didn't know she was an icon, of course. But she was certainly the apotheosis of the female hero I...sought..."

And of course there's my own memory. When I was a young girl, my girlfriends and I all read and loved Wonder Woman.

Much information can be gleaned from the letters pages of a comic. The original Golden Age Wonder Woman comics had no letters pages, but as late as the early 1960s, when Robert Kanigher was writing and editing the book, the letters page reveals the demographics of his readers. The April 1962 issue contained letters from two girls and one boy, the May 1963 issue had letters from five girls, and the October 1964 letters page was another all-girl affair, with letters from five girls. Judging from their letters, the writers were all young, and they wrote to Wonder Woman herself, rather than to the writer or editor (in this case, the same person), as later, older male fans would do. In her letter from the 1963 issue, Linda Parson, from White Castle, LA, wishes to actually visit Paradise Island:

> When another reader begged you to take her to Paradise Island with you, you answered that Paradise Island is imaginary. Well, how about taking me on an imaginary trip there?

In asking to go to Paradise Island, Linda Parson is expressing a desire to go to a woman-only world, the world of Golden Age Wonder Woman comics. Steve Trevor is not only the Token Boyfriend in these comics, but often the Token Male in stories that otherwise feature only women. Any other males in these stories are usually villains, like Mars, god of war and sworn enemy of the amazons.

Many Golden Age Wonder Woman stories, especially the ones that take place on the all-woman Paradise Island, do not include even Steve, because men are not allowed on Paradise Island. Some of the women in these stories are butch to an extreme. In *Wonder Woman and the Coming of the Kangas,*[15] male cat-headed alien invaders turn out to be women in disguise. "We're amazons like you," says the beautiful redhaired leader, after she has been defeated, "We have no home. Won't you let us join your nation?" In *Villainy, Incorporated!*[16], the evil "Hypnota, magician of the Blue Flame," is a mustached and bearded woman with breasts. Another of the villains in this story is the cross-dressing "Byrna Brilyant, the Blue Snow Man."

Even off Paradise Island, in what Marston referred to as "Man's World," the amazon princess mostly interacted with women. In *A Human Bomb,*[17] Suzan Patience, "the famous woman penologist," wants Wonder Woman to help her convince the governor to make her warden of the new woman's prison. Steve Trevor, whose imagination is on par with his I.Q., says, "Impossible! Whoever heard of a female prison warden?" Of course Wonder Woman agrees to help, and she starts by giving the prisoners new outfits. As they toss off their gray uniforms and try on the colorful dresses, the prisoners exclaim, "These clothes aren't like prison uniforms at all!" "Cute!" and "We don't look like convicts anymore—all the uniforms are different!"

For at least a few years after Marston's death, Wonder Woman continued, in the spirit of her deceased creator, to interact with women. In the 1950 story, *Hollywood Goes to Paradise Island*, the amazon puts together the "first all-girl crew in cinema capital history," including a "directress," "The only woman director in Hollywood!"[18]

Even Wonder Woman's birth, as related in the very first issue of *Wonder Woman*, is an all-woman affair, without even the aid of a turkey baster. In a feminist reversal of mythic hero birth stories, in which a virgin mother is magically impregnated by a male deity,[19] the virginal amazon Queen Hippolyta, desiring a baby, is instructed by the goddess Athena to mold one from clay. Then Aphrodite bestows the gift of life upon the statue, who becomes the baby princess Diana. Thus, like Heather, Diana has two mommies.[20]

The world of boys and men can be threatening to girls.[21] In *The Reader's Companion to US Women's History*, Marie Wilson has this to say about adolescent girls:

Sexual comments, jokes, and threats become more intimidating as girls develop an understanding of sexuality and as boys, on average, become physically bigger and stronger than girls…they begin to realize that good looks are necessary for certain kinds of success, and that good looks lead to being looked at, which for young adolescent girls can seem threatening.[22]

In the 1940s, sexual harassment in the workplace and in schools, although never approved of, was accepted as an unavoidable evil, as was domestic violence, which was not then illegal. At home, young girls saw their mothers being hit by their fathers, and accepting it.[23] In school, it has only recently been understood by educators that traditional teaching has focused on boys' interests and behaviors. Teachers have traditionally called on boys more often than girls. They have accepted that boys tend to act out and disrupt the classroom in various ways, meanwhile encouraging girls to be passive and quiet.[24]

Girls have needed, at least in their fantasy lives, a safe place to be with other girls, where they could express themselves without being threatened by boys. British girls' magazines seem to have recognized this need more than American comics. In my study of four British girls' magazine annuals, from 1956, 1958, and 1963,[25] I found comics in which the protagonists, usually students from all-girl schools, interacted with other girls, and any male in the stories is usually a villain. In a typical story from 1958, three school girls dress up as "The Silent Three," in hooded robes and masks[26] to help a younger girl whose dog has been stolen by a wicked man, who hopes to use the dog to retrieve a hidden paper that will lead to treasure.

In "Staunch Allies of the Swiss Skater," from 1956, two British schoolgirls, vacationing in Switzerland, befriend a young Swiss ice skater, buying her a dress to wear for a skating contest. When the girl's cruel uncle locks her up, forbidding her to enter the contest, they free the girl and find a paper proving he is an impostor, masquerading as her dead uncle "to steal the legacy her mother left her!" One of the contest judges knew the real uncle and would have recognized him. In the end, a British girl hugs the skater and says, "Your troubles are over, Odette dear. You're free—free to skate!"

American girls' comics from that period are very different. Instead of the sisterhood themes of the British comics, the American comic stories usually revolve around the theme of the eternal triangle—two girls, one of which is the protagonist, fighting over the Token Boyfriend. Patsy Walker and Hedy Wolfe fight over Buzz Baxter, Betty and Veronica fight over Archie Andrews, and so on. Although the comic books were aimed at and read predominantly by girls, the message seems to be of the importance of boys in their lives. Perhaps the publishers, using Wertham's logic, feared that without boys in the stories, they might be interpreted as promoting lesbianism?

In the women's community of Paradise Island, girls did not *have to* have boyfriends; they could be "free—free to skate!", or free to be themselves and to interact with other girls.

Marston's message to girls lasted for at least twenty years after his death, although it was progressively watered down. By 1968, however, as comics grew more and more male-oriented, new creators started aiming Wonder Woman at the new larger male audience by disempowering her, thus making her less intimidating to men. Writer Denny O'Neill divested the amazon heroine of both her powers and her costume, putting her instead into a mod jumpsuit. Worst of all, he sent Paradise Island off to another dimension. Without her community, Wonder Woman was alone, and had to turn for help to a man, an old Chinese martial arts instructor with the unlikely name of I Ching.

This unhappy state of affairs lasted three years, during which time the books continued to lose what female readers were left. Although Wonder Woman regained Paradise

Island and her old costume in 1971, the costume slowly shrank over the years as her bust size increased. After disempowerment came hypersexualization. By 1994, when the amazon was drawn in her most sexually provocative style, her starry shorts shortened to thong size, by Brazilian artist Mike Deodato, sales of the books skyrocketed, but the new readers buying it were men. As for Paradise Island, it had become a place of conflict, where a vicious, minimally clad amazon named Artemis battled with Diana for the title of Wonder Woman. Sisterhood was a thing of the past, and the safe place for girls was long gone.

It will never be known if Wonder Woman's creator really intended any hidden lesbian agenda in his comics, or if suspicions of Sapphism were simply products of Wertham's McCarthyist mentality, but for over ten golden years, William Moulton Marston provided a haven for girls in the pages of his comics, away from Man's World.

Endnotes

1 Comics from these years are referred to by collectors as "Golden Age."

2 Using this same kind of logic, one might question the gender preferences of actor/comedienne Judy or singer Billie, not to mention the subversive hidden agenda that must be concealed in the classic film, "Holiday Inn."

3 Page 186. Actually, although Wonder Woman is indeed seen hugging her friends and her mother in the pages of these comics (women *do* hug!), she doesn't kiss them. She's never even depicted kissing her "boyfriend," Steve Trevor!

4 Page 45. Feiffer also refutes Wertham's argument that Batman comics were producing gay youth. He writes, "If homosexual fads were certain proof of that which will turn our young queer, then we should long ago have burned not just Batman books, but all Bette Davis, Joan Crawford, and Judy Garland movies."

5 Page 103. Daniels also writes, of Wonder Woman, "No overt eroticism of any type was present in these comics..." Yet he devotes eight pages in the first chapter to bondage and domination scenes in Wonder Woman. D.C. comics, for whom Daniels wrote this book, has courted a male audience to the exclusion of females since at least the late 1960s. Possibly the D.C. theory is that descriptions of kinky sex will interest the boys in reading Wonder Woman, but that God forbid they should mention lesbianism!

6 For purposes of this paper, I have defined Golden Age as the 1940s and early 1950s. Even though Marston died in 1948, he left some scripts behind, and as late as the early 1950s, certain Wonder Woman stories seem to bear the Mark of Marston.

7 With the exception of the French, Russians, and Italians, white heterosexual men, fearful of being considered gay, do *not* hug.

8 Removal of Wonder Woman's bracelets cause her to become "**Too Strong.** The bracelets bound my strength for good purposes—now I'm completely uncontrolled! I'm free to **destroy** like a **man!**"

9 This comic book is coverless and bears no dates, but is probably postwar, because a character says to the villains, "You—you are Nazis! But Germany...is licked—"

10 Possibly so that readers will not suspect them of lesbianism, fictional American heroines for young girls always seem to be given Token Boyfriends. Nancy Drew had Ned Nickerson, and Barbie, of course, has Ken. In the early 1990s when I was one of the writers on Marvel's *Barbie*

Comics, I did some research with two young girls who were playing with their Barbies at my local photocopy center. They told me that they each had five Barbies and one Ken, but that they did not play with their Ken doll much. I asked them what they used their Ken doll for, and the answer was that when they dressed Barbie up and played bride with her, they needed Ken so that she would have someone to marry.

11 Page 11.

12 "Why 100,000,000 Americans Read Comics," *The American Scholar*, Winter 1943-44.

13 Obviously, neither does D.C. comics, or Les Daniels would have quoted them in the 2000 Wonder Woman book when he makes the dubious statement, "It's an open secret, however frequently acknowledged, that Wonder Woman's readers have always been predominantly male" (page 33). Gloria Steinem refutes this in her introduction to the collection of Wonder Woman covers: "Wonder Woman did attract some boys as readers, but the integrated world of comic book trading revealed her true status: at least three Wonder Woman comic books were necessary to trade for one of Superman." On the other hand, in recent times, as Wonder Woman's bust size has grown and her pants have shrunk, and girls no longer read comics because there are no comics for them to read, her readership has become predominantly male. In the mid-nineties, when Brazilian artist Mike Deodato took over drawing Wonder Woman in what Daniels describes as "the most overly eroticized version of Wonder Woman to see print," sales hit the ceiling.

14 Unfortunately, I do not know the source of this article, which was mailed to me in photocopy form some years back.

15 Wonder Woman #23, 1947.

16 Wonder Woman #28, 1948.

17 Wonder Woman #30, 1948.

18 The writer of this story, probably Robert Kanigher, was wrong. In 1949, screen star Ida Lupino made her uncredited directorial debut with the film *Not Wanted*, co-written and co-produced by her along with Anson Bond and Collier Young. Director Elmer Clifton fell ill shortly after shooting began, and Lupino took over but insisted that he retain screen credit. She went on to direct five more features, the first two (*Never Fear* and *Outrage*) of which were made in 1950. But Kanigher was unlikely to know this when in his script, Wonder Woman pep-talks her all-girl film crew: "We are the first all-girl company to produce a movie in Hollywood history! Many men think we'll be unsuccessful! But I have faith and confidence in you! I know that all you need is a chance and you will show that you can **at least** equal anything men have ever done!"

19 Some of these more familiar myths are Leda, impregnated by Zeus as a swan; Danae, also impregnated by Zeus (he got around) as a shower of gold; and of course the Christian Virgin Mary.

20 It is also significant that, in the Golden Age Wonder Woman stories, the amazons only relate to two deities: Athena and Aphrodite. The only male deity in the stories, Ares, who is called by his Roman name, Mars, is the amazons' enemy. Later, more contemporary Wonder Woman comics (from the 1980s on) changed this, so that Mercury figures strongly in more recent comics, and Diana and her sisters acknowledge the supremacy of Zeus—an unlikely act for a matriarchal culture.

21 And the world of girls can scare the pants off boys. In *The Great Comic Book Heroes*, Jules Feiffer writes: "...I can't comment on the image girls had of Wonder Woman. I never knew they read her—or any comic book. That *girls* had a preference for my brand of literature would have

been more of a frightening image to me than any number of men being beaten up by Wonder Woman."

22 Page 244.

23 More recent statistics are not encouraging. An article by Kate Raphael from the *San Francisco Sentinel*, October 11, 1990, reports that almost half of married women are beaten at least once by their husbands.

24 This information comes from the Women's College Coalition website, www.academic.org/surprise.html.

25 *Girls' Crystal Annual* from 1956, 1958, and 1963; *School Friend Annual* from 1958.

26 Coincidentally, the first superheroine in American Comics, The Woman in Red (1940), costumed herself in a hooded robe and mask.

Works Cited

Daniels, L. 2000. *Wonder Woman, the Complete History*. San Francisco: Chronicle Books.

Feiffer, J. 1965. *The Great Comic Book Heroes*. New York: Dial Press.

Harmon, J. 1970. A Swell Bunch of Guys. In Lupoff and Thompson, eds, *All in Color For a Dime*. New Rochelle, NY: Arlington House.

Mankiller, W., G. Mink, M. Navarro, B. Smith, and G. Steinem, eds. 1998. *The Reader's Companion to US Women's History*. Boston and New York: Houghton Mifflin.

Steinem, G. 1972. Introduction to *Wonder Woman*. New York, Chicago, and San Francisco: Holt, Rhinehart, and Winston and Warner Books.

Steinem, G. 1995. Introduction to *Wonder Woman*. New York, London, and Paris: Abbeville Press.

Wertham, F. 1954. *Seduction of the Innocents*. New York: Rhinehart and Company.

Girls' Crystal Annual. 1956. London: The Fleetway House.

Girls' Crystal Annual. 1958. London: The Fleetway House.

Girls' Crystal Annual. 1962. London: Fleetway Publications Ltd.

School Friend Annual. 1958. London: The Fleetway House.

Trina Robbins

Trina Robbins is a pop culture herstorian who has written about every aspect of comics that concerns women. She's also written about dark goddesses, women who kill, and Irish women. WisCon 16 GoH.

www.trinarobbins.com

Victoria Poyser

Suzy McKee Charnas

Q: Why did you go to your first WisCon? What keeps you coming back?

A: I haven't a clue why I first went or even what year it was. I might be able to dig up a file somewhere, out in the garage, but don't count on it. At any rate, my first WisCon might have been the year that we arrived during a blizzard and experienced real WisConsin ice for the first time. (Dave Hartwell kept me from flying off my feet coming down the State Street Hill at night, ice on everything.)

As to what kept me coming back—well, every year I could look forward to the excitement of meeting people—new ones, often, which told me that the books were still alive and drawing in readers—who'd not only read my work *and* the work of other women *I* was reading, but who could talk brilliantly and passionately about all of it (plus their own writing, in many cases). Then there was the delicious sense of having a place to bitch and moan freely about all the various unfairnesses of life in sf for women writers, readers, and fans, and the sheer joy of being with so many articulate women with the gloves off, not hesitating for fear of drawing fire from a guy hidden in the back of the room (or even some angry reactionary woman).

This was also the first venue in which I got to know lots of people in different states and stages of gender—gay male sympathizers, lesbians flying under their own flag and proud of it, straights like me, transgenders in all stages of change, the works. My head was regularly spun: you don't run into this kind of variety on a free and frank basis in high school academia, where I'd done most of my professional work before moving to New Mexico to write full time. I learned a lot of things, not always welcome but always of use and of interest, just by listening.

There are thriving gay communities in NM, of course, but I'm like most folks—I tend to hang with people more or less like myself, absent a good kick up the butt. WisCon was a New World (it still is). I was an sf buff; of course I was into exploring new worlds, in a time and place dedicated to that very activity.

And the books! And the panels—all those subjects that the fan-boy cons never considered worth bothering with, that even more serious conventions conceded to with mere sidebars ("Women in SF," what a superficial cop-out). In a way, WisCon made it okay to go to some of the other male-dominant default conventions, because I knew there was this meeting once a year where the core of my own concerns would be addressed *as if it were central*, not an "add-on," just to keep them quiet, you know. And the people, the newcomers starry-eyed at having discovered the Secret City of Real True Questions, the veterans so glad to return again after another year in the world of macho make-believe that spawns such a ghastly reality for us all—irresistible.

And then there's the hotel—friendly, unfazed by oddity, in the midst of a university neighborhood with cheap food and clothes and bookstores and fudge. Sheesh, who wouldn't welcome a yearly chance to visit A Room of One's Own, one of the premier feminist bookstores in a country of ever fewer feminist bookstores? All honor to the Room's women!

And then, of course, there's Jeanne Gomoll—a woman of organized energy, playful spirit, and a grounded thoughtfulness that illuminates and calms everything around her. Frankly, I'd have gone anywhere that Jeanne and Scott & Co. ran a convention, knowing that I'd be treated well, put to work in creative and rewarding ways that would make the most of my being present, kicked into new thoughts and questions, and helped where I needed help. In fact the years that I skipped WisCon were the years that Jeanne & Co *weren't* at the helm (though I didn't begrudge her the rest-time one bit—she'd earned it a hundred times over).

The thing is, with the establishment of the Tiptree Award in particular, WisCon became more than ever the living hub of feminist sf. How the hell could I have stayed away? These are my friends, my colleagues, my best critics, the readers I write for, the people in publishing who understand what sf is and might be for free-minded women and men. I'll be coming back as long as it stays that way, and as long as I can remember stuff well enough to book a flight and a hotel room in time…

Suzy McKee Charnas has racked up a dozen-plus books, a stage play, various awards, and a number of stints teaching sf/f writing and reading since her first novel in 1974, and is a WisCon regular. WisCon 3 GoH.

www.suzymckeecharnas.com

Welcome Back to the Beginning

Rachel Swirsky

Last year, feminist science fiction fans gathered in Madison to celebrate the thirtieth WisCon. A lot of things *have* changed in thirty years—there are more women in political positions, third-wave feminism has made more space for the voices of women of color, feminist blogs have made networking on the internet both easier and less personal. Yet, thirty years after the first WisCon, a question that should have been settled long ago remains a hot topic. Does sexism exist in science fiction?

As I write this, approximately one hundred women genre writers are preparing to submit a "slush bomb" to *The Magazine of Fantasy and Science Fiction* on August 18, the anniversary of women's suffrage. They do so out of varying motives. Some want to encourage more women to submit their work, in the hope that this will even out the gender imbalances in the slush. Some wish to encourage a sense of community. Others will watch the responses trickle in, thinking of it as an experiment. Still others are mostly looking to have fun.

What interests me as a feminist writer is less the slush bomb itself than the debate it has generated on genre blogs. Many respondents seem appalled by what they see as allegations of overt sexism leveled against Gordon Van Gelder, the editor of *F&SF*. In blog posts and comments, some have expressed outrage that a gendered submission effort is under consideration, laying all blame for gender disparities in science fiction at the feet of women themselves. Women, apparently, don't submit enough. We aren't competitive enough. We aren't interested in the right themes. Our writing fails to be universal.

Other bloggers refuse to acknowledge that gender disparities in science fiction exist in the first place. Why are feminists always harping on gender? Don't we know it's sexist to analyze success rates in terms of gender?

Admittedly, most people have responded to the slush bomb with more complex and subtle reactions than I've presented here. But as I peruse sf blogs, I find myself astonished to find, over and over again, that the conversation has skipped all the way back to square one—does male privilege exist? In the post-sixties era, shouldn't we understand that this is a patriarchal, sexist society, one in which the standards of success have been designed by and for white, educated, heterosexual, cisgendered males?

I have an ambivalent response to this year's slush-bomb effort as it has been framed thus far. I plan to participate, but I'm wary of those who would look at it as an experiment.

The bomb is not controlled. It's not going to yield scientific data. I'm also not sure that I agree with the way the debate has been framed around sex rather than gender—I see bias against femininity as being a more critical factor in editorial selection than bias against women, though of course the two are related. Likewise, I think it's important to engage with the system of privilege that tells us masculine writing is better than feminine writing, rather than focusing on the term "sexism," which is morally loaded and can imply apportioning of blame to individuals.

Perhaps my most important reservation is that I worry about centering the whole debate on a single magazine like *F&SF*. It makes that magazine seem unusual. I don't believe it is.

I have voiced these feelings in blog discussions, but I'm not sure how effective my participation is. In an environment where even the existence of sexism remains up for debate, maybe more basic groundwork must be laid before there's a point in discussing what factors create the privileging of masculine work. Before one can talk about the ways in which female narratives are embodied, one has to explain how men are constructed as universal, how women are othered, how female bodies are conflated with sex. One must explain Feminism 101. Again and again.

At WisCon, the discussion can advance further. We don't have to reinvent the feminist wheel. We can begin with the knowledge that patriarchy is deeply embedded in the American mindset and then proceed to seek ways to analyze and chip away at the patriarchy, using our fictions and imaginations as our tools.

...or can we?

To the extent that feminism is an individual project—or even a collective project on a small scale—we can. Working toward frame-breaking moments where one can conceive outside the normative values of our society is certainly a laudable goal. Environments like WisCon help foster these revelations. Every once in a while, they can also be inscribed in fiction; novels like *Left Hand of Darkness* and *The Female Man* are, in a way, frame-breaking experiences frozen in text so that they can be communicated across time and space.

Yet, to the extent that feminism is a society-level project, aimed at altering the basic assumptions of the culture, I'm not sure we're ready to move on from the basic exercises. In that wide world beyond WisCon, Feminism 101 still needs to be taught. Before we can take the social conversation as a whole in the direction of analysis and problem-solving, we have to force people to acknowledge our concerns. The problem must be named and identified and explained. We're still in the consciousness raising phase.

We're back at the beginning.

In the modern backlash, these obviously aren't new problems. But while I know that feminists have struggled for decades with the problem of moving from the theoretical world where possibility abounds into the practical world where ignorance breathes, I remain dissatisfied.

Change lingers out of reach. Women heroes appear on the covers of novels—but in cheesecake poses. Women's work wins awards—but it is not reprinted. We send slush bombs—but the conversations spin on their heels, coming back to, "Does sexism exist?"

How much of our activist lives is doomed to repeating these cycles? To proving the same things over and over again to the same recalcitrant public? To battling over issues our mothers thought solved? To re-laying the theoretical foundations that allow us to fumble through the baby steps of minor change? To throwing ourselves against impenetrable walls of ego and denial? To reiterating that the personal is political and that women are subjects as well as objects?

To answering that same damn question.

Yes, sexism exists.

This time do you think we can remember?

Rachel Swirsky is an MFA student at the Iowa Writers Workshop, and a graduate of Clarion West 2005. She has short work appearing in markets including *Subterranean Magazine*, *Electric Velocipede*, and *Escape Pod*. Her feminist fable, "Heartstrung," is forthcoming in *Interzone 210*. Along with science fiction and fantasy writer Ann Leckie, Rachel is running this year's slush bomb, which will be launched in the direction of *Analog Science Fiction & Fact* on August 18, 2007. Details are available at her website.

http://www.rachelswirsky.com/

Jeanne Gomoll

Feminist Think Tanks

Transcript Notes by Liz Henry with redactions by the participants

Panel Description

For decades WisCon has been an annual three– or four–day think tank for feminist sf: people descend on Madison from all over North America and the world to pool ideas, experiences, and reading lists. These ingredients catch fire, combine in new ways, and are carried out into the world by recharged participants. In the wider world, feminism has been diluted into a laundry list of "women's issues," and feminists have dispersed into various movements and local projects. Many of us are isolated from each other, from recent feminist history, and from grassroots theory–making. What if feminism had a year–round WisCon? How would it work? Should it happen?

Panelists

Vonda N. McIntyre (moderator), L. Timmel Duchamp, Liz Henry (replacing Laura Quilter), Janet Lafler, Susanna J. Sturgis, undisclosed panelist

Writers and Works Cited

- Simone de Beauvoir quotation
- Andrea Dworkin's *Right Wing Women*
- Jane Jacobs—the particular work SS was thinking about was *The Death and Life of Great American Cities.*
- Ursula K. Le Guin
- *New York Review of Books* article
- Bernice Johnson Reagon speech, "Coalition Politics: Turning the Century," in *Home Girls: A Black Feminist Anthology,* ed. Barbara Smith (New York: Kitchen Table: Women of Color Press, 1983).
- Adrienne Rich, "Women and Honor: Some Notes on Lying," in *On Lies, Secrets, and Silence: Selected Prose, 1966–1978* (New York: W. W. Norton, 1979).

[Editor's note: These notes are not a verbatim transcript. They have been corrected by some (though not all) of the panelists and have been abridged or supplemented for clarity.]

VNM: [...introduction...]

LH: [...brief description of the feminist sf wiki...]

LTD: I'm the author of a lot of short fiction and several books, most recently *Renegade*, the second novel of the five-volume Marq'ssan Cycle; nonacademic critic, whose essays have appeared in *NYRSF*, *Extrapolation*, *Foundation*, and *Lady Churchill's Rosebud Wristlet*; and publisher of Aqueduct Press, which publishes feminist science fiction.

I'm interested in the difference a year-round think-tank could make to (a) feminist thinking itself and (b) to political culture generally (if such a thing as political culture doesn't become virtually extinct in the US, as I'm currently thinking it might soon do). Think tanks have exercised an enormous influence on life in the US for decades. And the lack of feminist think tanks has meant that voices speaking from a feminist perspective have been largely absent in the dominant political discourse of the US.

SS: This past winter I was writing something for a WisCon grant application, about why WisCon is so important, and I wrote that WisCon was like a four-day feminist think tank. From that it was a small step to "what would a feminist think tank look like?"—and here we are. At WisCon you don't have to explain over and over again why feminism is important or why science fiction is important, and that's how we're able to push the subject so much further in so many different directions. That's the kind of thing that could happen with a feminist think tank—it would be like a pressure cooker for feminist ideas. It would enable feminists around the country and the world to share news and ideas, and it would help us keep in touch with our own history. It amazes me how much has been forgotten in just the last twenty or thirty years.

UP: [...feminism and women's issues and problems reframed in last twenty years as individual problems we're supposed to go off and solve on our own...]

VNM: [...standing on the shoulders of Le Guin, etc.; door openers for us...] We want to keep opening those doors for others and future generations.

JL: [...background in anthropology; fan; no position in community except what people think of her; interested in intersections of political and social issues...] Ideally that's what think tanks are for.

LH: I'm filling in for Laura Quilter, whose flight was delayed, at her request since we collaborate a lot and have talked about these ideas. We wanted to talk about the virtual aspect of the feminist think tank, the online components, like mailing lists, blogs, and wikis. We could hold virtual events with online chats. All this information can live on the web and be accessible to anyone with computer access. Consciousness-raising has to keep happening over and over, and that can happen in online discussions. We have the FEM-SF list, Laura Quilter's Feminist Science Fiction, Fantasy, and Utopia site, which is an amazing archive; the Whileaway and WisCon communities on LiveJournal; the Feminist SF Wiki at http://wiki.feministsf.org, the Book Discussion group, and more. Think tanks can be events, events that are documented. They are "instances of" the perpetual feminist think tank. Documentation and being public are important for us to be part of public discourse.

LTD: I think bringing feminist economists and feminist political scientists and other feminist scholars of social and political policy together with WisCon fans, authors, and scholars, could bring about a wave of powerful activism, especially if the think tank included not only feminist "experts" and artists (including writers and performers) but a wide spectrum of other feminist women as well. I do think that publishing papers would serve an important purpose, but then I don't see the need to make a choice between either "experts" producing papers or "non-expert" feminist activists. Also, I think an in-body, away-from-the-constant-demanding-press-of-the-hectic-lives-most-of-us-lead setting for at least some of the participant's involvement with the think tank would be crucial. For many of us, anything that takes place online just becomes another entry on the list of tasks to be triaged. One wants to contribute to wikis, but doing so is an anonymous, socially disconnected experience that takes place in isolation—sort of like leaving a poem or a ten-dollar bill on a park bench and hoping the person who finds it appreciates it, since it is hard to believe anyone will read one's wiki contribution much less care that someone made it. I'd like to see a feminist think-tank modeled on some of the math institutes I've heard about—places where people can go for varying lengths of time to work intensively and brainstorm and network, where activities include talks, panel discussions, thinking and writing time, and many opportunities for good conversation. A place for conferences and talks. Where people can drop in. And are invited to do residencies there. In addition, we also need a virtual community. But the physical institute provides face-to-face conversation and is really important. You have to get away from your daily life. If it's only online it becomes less important and just another burden. This is an important lesson of WisCon. And we have every sort of person across the spectrum of feminism. Scientists, writers,...who have life experiences; artists, performers, every kind of feminist of every age and experience. It's the conversation and making connections that can really work powerfully for us.

SS: I came in on the tail end of consciousness-raising. It was the core of '60s and '70s feminism. Great mechanism. We lost something really important when it dwindled. One reason it dwindled—we thought that once your consciousness was raised, it was raised for good. We didn't register that consciousness-raising goes on all your life, and that there are always new people coming into the movement. The people who came after us did not get the excitement of figuring out the connections between personal and political and building the skills to run hotlines, women's centers, publishing companies.... By then we were the experts and the people coming in later became the secretaries.

LH: We can have unconferences, brain jams, events, house parties—declare it and make a physical face-to-face event and then document the hell out of it and put it on the web. We want to have events like wiki-editing house parties. And take photos and write up everything and post that information. Grace Davis and I declared we were having Woolfcamp, a weekend-long unconference, and forty people ended up at her house for the weekend. We got together, made a rough schedule, decided on the spot what we wanted to talk about; mostly issues around blogging, computer tools, creativity, and gender; then split up into groups. There's a wiki (http://www.socialtext.net/woolfcamp/index.cgi?workspace_for_woolfcamp_santa_cruz_february_2006) and a blog (woolfcamp2006.blogspot.com/) for it, and we're going to do that again. We came out of that weekend with a tremendous amount of validation and energy and knowledge.

SS: Yeah.

LTD: But we really need the physical institute.

UP: It is important that...What Susanna said about the early CR-feminist movement and free love—I got pregnant at 19. The world became different and issues became different. When I was juggling trying to raise kids and daily life, the academic argument became irrelevant and dysfunctional. What I see is the think tank becoming this room. Go back to your communities you're from, even if they're not feminist communities. I work for a bank. My president knows I'm going to a feminist sf conference and he's fascinated. Male, white fifty-year-old bank president; you CAN have that conversation with them.

LH: That is a different thing than the focus and push forward and not having to explain feminism...

UP: We need both.

Aud: We need both! There's not an either/or.

SS: There's almost no good idea that can't get screwed up by group dynamics.

[*laughter*]

VNM: [...]

JL: Taking these ideas and transforming them into action. Conservative think tanks. Heritage Foundation, etc. How to frame the core of idea and then funnel that into media outlets with which they are affiliated…

LTD: There are other think tanks though. Funded and run by the right wing…

JL: Yes, there are. But the right wing is more powerful at this point. Part of that is having easy access to get their ideas out into the mainstream. One of the strategies is that if you have an idea that is perceived as outlandish, your goal is to make it seem merely radical, and then reasonable: to normalize it.

Aud: I think of the times I see that [normalizing] happen with ideas I find horrible and unthinkable… Feminist ideas that I love should be pushed more into the mainstream.

VNM: The strategy can be co-opted for good. Just because a thing is evil doesn't mean the process is evil.

JL: […an article in the *New York Review of Books* mentioning Jane Jacobs—urbanist, deep critic of urban design in early the '60s…] Jacobs was self-taught, largely, wrote on the death and life of great American cities, and was an activist for rest of her life.

Aud: She stopped them building the highway through Manhattan, through the Village.

JL: She just died a few weeks ago. *The New York Review of Books* article includes a list of important women thinkers of the twentieth century—a really weird list: Jane Jacobs, Rachel Carson, Julia Child, Betty Friedan. The thing that linked them in the mind of the article's writer is that they had a deep appreciation of the forms of everyday life. That would be an interesting approach right there.

SS: I read Jane Jacobs when I was in college, in the early 1970s, and it made me look at how space affects how people relate to each other, or don't relate to each other.

Aud: Does Martha Stewart qualify for this think tank?

[*laughter*]

UP: This happens in media over and over—our questions and interests get reframed. When Carly Fiorina lost her CEO job, there were articles [asking the question] over and over: would they ever give a woman a CEO job again?. So then when Eisner lost his job, I looked and looked… [There was] no article on a man getting a CEO job again…

[*laughter*]

SS: It did not take a huge number of people to take over the Republican Party. But there is nothing on the left, there isn't that gravitational pull; there is nothing keeping the Democratic Party [from being pulled to the right]. One of the mistakes from my youth: we latched on to a good idea and didn't get it that diversity was key. People can pursue a goal in different valid ways. Many things have to be going on at once [in the] ongoing battles in feminism. Consider the era of separatism—we didn't all have to be separatists. Just having a pool of people who were experimenting on the edge kept [those of] us who were closer to the middle asking questions, like "Am I making too many concessions? Am I giving up too much?" Not everyone has to go off and live on the land or give up sex or have sex all the time. The existence of such people increases the range of our imagination. Today we are missing that so much...

Aud: [The Left...]

SS: And so much of that is happening on the right.

LTD: The far right has got just 15 percent of the public supporting them.

Aud: Participatory democracy is harder than authoritarianism. It's got to incorporate so many divergent views, which is why we look sloppy.

Aud 2: The far right wing keeps the other members of the Republican party in fear of losing power. So the moderate Republicans are cowed.

LTD: They've got a real punishment system. It's ruthless.

Aud: They've got the power of naming.

LH: Is naming the problem?

Aud: It's not just naming. Liberals, feminists—we've been abandoned by the Democratic Party. We need to identify ourselves as feminist as much as possible.

VNM: And counter the propositions they make up.

Aud: We don't use the "radical feminist" label.

Aud 2: There IS a feminist think tank out there. The Grace Hopper yearly conference, women in technology... Five years later she got funding for the Anita Borg Institute. They give grants to further issues of women in technology. It's partly virtual, and there are also conferences.

VNM: God, what a perfect match for a bunch of science-fiction women.

Aud: She had a brain tumor and died a few years ago, and the institute is still going. And no one in this room has heard of it. I wonder why it is that no one here knows about it? Why is it invisible?

SS: People who are active even in feminist print, if they don't know anything about feminism and sf and fantasy they probably don't know about WisCon. I'm still explaining what WisCon is to feminist print activists.

LH: People paying attention to each other's work is what makes something important, and that they do so in public. [...the importance of public discourse to feminism...] If you think something is important, and if you like it, talk about it. Online, talk about it and link to it. Participate in a visible way in public conversations. Women on email lists, back-channeling their support to each other; they need to do it out in the open where that collective power can be seen. And so much work that's already been done needs to get online, to go digital, we need good databases in open formats, and to have our information in the mix online, or we're going to lose more of our history. Do you know, in my twenties I carried around this tattered old copy of the magazine *Notes from the Second Year* and read it till it fell apart? A friend of mine had stolen it from the library and left it at my house. Where is it now? That's crucial information and history. Put that feminist sf fanzine you did back in the '70s online, and there will be fourteen year olds in Texas or Japan who read it and will get inspiration and strength from it, and feminism in their life will happen faster. They'll have this conversation to build on now, not when they're forty or sixty. Also, the key thing I'd like to say about young feminists is, please listen to them. You have to listen, and not judge them by where you are or were, because things are different for them. The biggest gift some of my feminist mentors gave me was not lecturing, but listening to my ideas, even if from their point of view, I was reinventing the wheel. Listen to young feminists' ideas and give them the gift of taking them seriously. Are you listening, or are you trying so hard to pass on history that you forget to listen?

Aud: [...power of language; using their own language, framing; not doing it on others' terms...]

LTD: Where we are now, it's important to create alternatives rather than just being oppositional.

Aud: [...anti-abortion vs. pro-choice; language; the loaded use of the word "innocent"...]

[*general hubbub ensues about the use of the phrase "taking of innocent life"*]

Aud 2: [...should we reclaim the word *feminism* or not? Humanist Simone de Beauvoir stressed the importance of recognizing women as human beings; what is feminism about? External navel gazing?]

[*laughter*]

Aud 3: I was assuming people were thinking about things the way that I do. But I grew up reading sf books that belonged to my daddy... My imagination is far out there...1000 years in the future

[...people as uneducated, irrational arguments...]

I don't get why they're doing what they're doing, so I'm not effective in debate.

UP: There is a basic difference in ways people process information. One thing that confuses me is I can't see this piece without seeing this and this and this and this...

Aud: Well, DUH!

UP: But most people can not only focus on just that one piece; they don't see anything else [besides that one piece]. And one woman I had problems communicating with had never understood that a whole is not the sum of its parts, it's how they interconnect... The point I want to get back to is that we have the right-wing manipulation of the world around us, and the terms come down to that simple issue...because people make decisions on that simple issue.

SS: Andrea Dworkin wrote *Right Wing Women*, a really interesting book. I haven't read it since 1985. Her basic point was that she found the women she talked to who espoused very different right-wing views basically understood things like the dynamics between men and women in a way that was not very different than the way left and radical and feminist women understood them. But the right-wing women were much more pessimistic about things ever changing. Where I live I don't know many feminists, and I hardly know anyone who reads f/sf. If it weren't for online communication, I'd feel very isolated and probably a lot more pessimistic about the possibility of change. This is my first WisCon in eight years, and I'm struck by the sheer sense of possibility that WisCon creates. In my guest of honor speech at WisCon 21 (1997) I quoted from a presentation Bernice Johnson Reagon gave in 1981. She made a distinction there that's important for activists, the distinction between a home and a coalition. We tended to expect coalitions to be like a home, but they aren't. The coalition and political work is not nurturing and calm. You need a home base to support and energize you while you do that work. It can be a family home, a WisCon, or a group of people who support you. You need that to keep you going, but you can't spend all your time there.

Aud: You need a very long rope...to get out [to] all those different places...but [one that's] a tether.

SS: The physical place, the think tank, the connections, are important. The possibility of doing that is greater than it ever has been.

Aud: There's a guy who said, "Well, there really aren't any women's issues anymore..." and a guy who said he is anti-abortion... How do we answer these people? And the young people who think that feminism fixed everything, or didn't fix it, but either way, that it's done? [How do we answer them?]

Aud 2: [Cites examples of positive local efforts: a girl who does hip-hop; young feminists; a positive step on a local level, not visible to everyone, but there...]

SS: I think CR is still very much needed. CR is something that can be done anywhere. Women come together to talk about what they're seeing and thinking and feeling about their lives, then they move on to "what are the problems here and what can we do about them."

UP: *[asks Liz her experience as a young feminist]*

LH: I'm almost forty, married twice, one kid and two miscarriages, somehow not feeling like I qualify as a "young feminist" anymore over here. Young feminists are people young enough to be my children. I was raised in the '70s to think that feminism had fixed everything and we'd all be equal. It was devastating to me in 1980 when the ERA didn't pass. As a teenager I wished I had more connection with other feminists; I needed mentors and connections and information. I think young feminists now have the potential to make those connections on the web. And that's what they're doing, if you look at the feminist blogosphere. If you go looking, you find stuff like Feministing (http://feministing.com/), Feministe (http://feministe.us/blog/), BitchPhD (http://bitchphd.blogspot.com/), blac(k)ademic (http://www.blackademic.com/), Angry Black Woman (http://theangryblackwoman.wordpress.com/), Pandagon (http://pandagon.net/). Those are just the biggest ones that come to mind off the top of my head.

Aud: The US is in an undeclared civil war, [caught up in] a fear economy. I am trying to counter it with a love economy. Doing that clarifies [the situation]. What kind of future do you want to live in…?

Aud 2: Capitalism is automatically "justification" for anything.

Aud 3: […something about workers and Marx…] When I tried to educate myself about feminist issues, I was going back to books ten and twenty years old. The think tank needs to be new. We need manifesting and calls to arms for *this* generation.

Aud 4 [Rosaleen Love]: In 1999 and again in 2000 I was invited to Seattle for two meetings organized by the Foundation for the Future, a group established by wealthy individuals to consider the long-term future of humanity. We met to talk about the future in one thousand years, a fascinatingly frustrating and challenging exercise. The group was not particularly feminist, as I recall. I was part of a think tank organized by a rich man in Seattle. We were gathered to think about our areas of expertise and the future in 1000 years time. It wasn't called "feminist," but it was fascinating. The brains who are the brains of the universe.

Aud 5: Feminism is recent, fragile. In an instant, you can lose everything. We must never lose sight of that.

LH: So, the wiki and Laura Quilter's FSFFU pages. Laura built the FSFFU pages over many years, with lots of people contributing information. We wanted to rebuild those pages and that information with a group and see what happens differently in the collaborative process. Laura Q or I will show anyone who wants at WisCon how to edit the wiki. Anyone can edit it.

Aud: What to do to make sure there are more women leaders? And all these women who are doing stuff are not [being] identified as feminist. The positive glowing feeling that people take in success needs to be represented as feminist.

SS: Adrienne Rich says in "Women and Honor: Some Notes on Lying" that when a woman speaks the truth she makes it possible for more truth around her... Deep down, I don't believe people have changed that much... The tiny minority just has more permission to speak.

Aud: I heard on the radio a week or so ago that the part of the population least likely to go vote is unmarried young women.

Aud: Pat Murphy told me a story. Twenty years ago, she said, she saw a tabloid headline: "Eighteen of your senators are space aliens." Her first thought was that there are more space aliens than women in the Senate. The day that we have more women than space aliens in the US Senate...

Afterword

SS: Ever since the WisCon panel, the idea of a feminist think tank has never been far from my mind. Feminism has lost its edge in the last twenty years or so. It's lost some of its depth and breadth, and an alarming amount of its recent history. These days many people seem to see feminism as a laundry list of particular issues, or as the commendable but oversimplified notion that "women are people too." To me feminism is a way of looking at the world that places women in the foreground. No other political or cultural movement, no philosophy, and no monotheistic theology does that. None of us have much practice doing it, and our attempts are widely dismissed or attacked as hostility to men. We need a lot more practice at envisioning women in the foreground, and we need more spaces—physical, psychological, and/or virtual—where we don't have to be continually justifying what we're doing. I still don't know what a feminist think tank would look like, but I believe that it should provide such a space and encourage the creation of more such spaces.

Eric Wallner

Liz Henry has published poems, translations, reviews, stories, and essays in Poetry Flash, strange Horizons, other, Two Lines, Suspect Thoughts, Cipactli, Lodestar Quarterly, and Literary Mama. She blogs at http://liz-henry.blogspot.com/

A Think Tank Thing for Feminists

Rosaleen Love

Little did I know when I first started along the feminist path that the future of feminism was going to be all about men.

Even if I'd known, I would have said,

that's OK. I'm cool with that. If it's going to be all about men,
then men will have seen the feminist light, and that's a good thing.

Or, I might have said,

typical. What did you expect?
Smashing the patriarchy was never going to be easy. Co-option is a tool of power.
And no prizes for guessing who'll be co-opting whom.

Those unintended consequences, they get you every time.

What *WERE* we thinking? Seems to me, back then when consciousness-raising was all the go, we thought that it was something that just had to be done once. Human consciousness, look, it's been raised! People agree! Discrimination against women is unfair! And while we're at it, there are all kinds of other discrimination, on the basis of race, class, ethnicity, disability, you name it, and they're unfair too! Let's all be people of good will and get together and sort this out.

Once and for all.

We set out to reclaim the importance of everyday life. We'd point to the play of power in everyday relationships, and first other women, then men, would see what it's all about, and we'd all reach some universal agreement. It would be a kinder, gentler way of smashing the patriarchy, but it would be smashed, nonetheless, and life on earth for all would only improve.

What I didn't know then: consciousness may be raised, in some places in some times. People would learn to say:

of course, that's unfair, that's discrimination. That's unreasonable. That's got to go. Discrimination. Institutionalized bullying, in the workplace, or in relationships. Out. It's wrong.

Consciousness may be raised—that did happen, for a time. But then, somehow, consciousness gets flattened again. All that work it took to keep it raised! Or else, it deflates, *pooo-ooof*, slowly, as the energy to raise it high is spent, and then it goes, slowly, silently, without anyone noticing much.

Until the unreasonable *slinks* back in.

It's discriminatory, yes, lawyers will argue. You can see the way issues get taken over and twisted to other ends. But is it unreasonable? No. For the definition of what is reasonable is subtly changed, and in ways that spell danger for those who were starting to relax, those who thought themselves safe.

Not so long ago, women were automatically paid less than men, because men were men, and women were women, and that was the way of the world. Then came the call for "Equal pay for equal work." And "fair go" seemed utterly reasonable.

Fair go, women feed children: fair go, women need money for everyday life:
fair go, women pay rent: fair go, women need to save for a rainy day.
Seems reasonable. Seems only fair.

Yes, equal pay for equal work. What is equal work? What about the boss who runs the company, and the cleaner? No, that's not equal work. The cleaner is often a woman, and the boss invariably a man. No equal pay for them. What about the laborer in the coal mine, and the nurse in hospital? No, that's not equal work. Digging coal is hard and dangerous. Looking after sick people, how dangerous is that? No equal pay for them. Isn't that just like the power of the patriarchy, to take our good ideas about equality and screw them up to justify inequality.

"Equal pay for equal work." At first it means something. Or so people imagine. Then, little by little, it gets watered down. Equality is all very well for the good times, but what about the bad? The bad times have come. Nations must be competitive, and if competition means temporary kinds of unfairness, so be it. It's all in the cause of a transition to a better future for all, where all can compete in the New World Order that's coming, ready or not. What does it mean, equal pay—with women in the factory cities of China?

Get real, the bosses say. But as for pay for the bosses? Aha, they, too, are competitive in the world market place. But for them it works the other way 'round. Their pay must rise to dizzying heights to compete with executive pay, internationally. In the name of global competitiveness, the bosses get more and the workers get less.

It's all so very nineteenth century.

So that's point number one. Consciousness gets raised, and then it's flattened by the wicked multinationals—whatever—take your pick, and then it's the slide back down into the abyss.

What to do about it? We need a feminist think tank, said Susanna Sturgis at WisCon 30. WisCon itself is already a feminist think tank. But WisCon happens once a year. How best to keep that energy alive from day-to-day, year-to-year? Susanna's voice came through loud and clear. She wanted a feminist think tank that would be a year-round feminist presence.

The think tanks already in existence have disproportionate influence, given their narrow membership: conservative and male, for the most part. They make themselves sound really impressive, with names like The Institute of Public Affairs. The think tank injects policy ideas into the political process, into the media, whatever—as if its ideas are the only ones that matter. Furthermore, they make money this way. They can even sell their ideas to governments, though we only get to hear about this when they get caught, as with the recent exposure, in the *Sunday Times*, of the practices of the Institute for Public Policy Research in Great Britain.

Why should the men have all the think tanks, occupy ∞ so much space ∞ in the media, get the best invitations?

Women need to make themselves sound equally impressive. How about an Institute for Feminist Public Policy Research? Perhaps it's that word "feminist" that puts them off, the men in power. Should we use some other word, perhaps? How about The Feminist Think Tank and Ideas Storage Facility? Or, The Institute for Post-Male-Chauvinist Public Policy Research? Names matter.

A think tank needs so much money, to bring expensive people together and keep them in comfort while they pontificate. Feminists want that, too. But who will pay for it? That's a question we were left pondering.

Timmi Duchamp wants the physical institute. Liz Henry aimed for something cheaper, and as feminists, doing it on the cheap is our kind of thing. She listed mini-conferences such as Woolf camp, "unconferences," brain jams, house-parties—the kinds of things friends can organize amongst themselves. They meet locally, document what happens, then put it on the web. For Liz Henry this would be "the virtual part of thinktanktitude."

Rhizomes, from a tank: roots, from a hunk of metal? Mixed-up metaphors. Metaphors: words that work in the world. Aha! I think I'm moving towards a kind of solution for Susanna Sturgis. Not the money angle, as yet. It's the "tank" angle that's starting to attract my attention. A think tank that moves, in war, guns blazing with the *splat–splat–splat* of good ideas popping out like bullets, non-lethal, that penetrate the body-armor of the patriarchy, bringing it to its knees—creating holes through which will seep the ideals of equality, sisterhood, and liberty. In the nicest possible way. Nice, but persistent with it. Nice, but insistent with it. A humanist think tank, a thinker's think tank, a think tank for movers and shakers, a think tank for stirrers. A think tank that generates momentum for change, creating a forward thrust, all the things that real tanks do, except roll over people and kill them. A feminist think tank is not of that ilk.

✻ ✻ ✻

Another thing happened at WisCon 30. A transgender woman said she'd lost her job and suffered discrimination in employment because she was a woman. Previously loquacious panelists gave a silent, surprised, sideways look. You could tell it wasn't just me having a *W h o a !* reaction.

Discrimination on the grounds of being a woman is claimed by someone who is not an actual woman, who was not born an actual woman, and who did not have the experience of growing up as an actual woman. But at some stage in her adult life, she changed gender. So what just didn't feel right about her statement? And why didn't I spring to my feet and say, *Hey, wait on!*

I decided it was something to do with marginality. I wanted to say,

My marginality is not your marginality.

Even if you think so. Even if you say so.

No, that's not it. The thing I've come to realize, is, you just can't choose your species of marginality and expect others to agree. The transgender woman on the panel has to a certain extent chosen her gender, or has been chosen by it. She perceives herself in a certain light. But she can't then choose the reasons why others might describe her as "on the margin." Her perception is that others judge her as a woman, where they may be saying something more like: Transgender, that's too weird for me. No matter. When the axe falls next in the workplace, it falls on her.

I'd really like my marginality, as I see it, to be recognized. But it won't be. They won't say they're sacking me because I'm a woman and I don't fit in. No, the bosses will say, they're sacking me because my job is surplus to requirements. There's nothing I can do about their perceptions of me. I place one label on myself, others stick another, and it's the person with power who wins out. The person without it is the one who walks.

> *You're being fired because you're just no good.*
> *I am being discriminated against because I am a woman.*
> *You are being picked out against because you are too weird.*

Wavelength. That's one part of it. We're not on each other's wavelength. Wavelength, in this context, is a metaphor.

Remember how once, in the universities, there was this subject called Women's Studies, and that was a breakthrough? Then it transmuted into Gender Studies, because, hey, let's not exclude the other, and before you knew it, it became Queer Studies, because we're all queer, and then... This transition marked a way of saying that the previous focus on the gender division between women and men was too restrictive, and that was all very well for a while, but now, moving into the future, identity politics is not enough.

Metaphors:

wavelength

raised consciousness

think-tanks.

And then I read an article on how mind power helps the disabled "regain" movement. It was a bit of a con, really, because it was wasn't real movement, but a simulation of it. But it felt real to the disabled person, and that mattered, to him. In the experiment, he placed a helmet on his head, and somehow it harnessed the power of his brainwaves. Someone who was paraplegic felt he was walking again around a room, in a virtual environment, feet moving. For a moment, he forgot his plight.

Imagine a woman's virtual world, and a man's actual world. Could I learn to navigate another's social space, see with their eyes, use their limbs, inhabit their way of looking at the world? Perhaps there could be some kind of virtual reality tank that plays with my consciousness, plays with theirs, mixes and matches. A virtual world might help create the illusion of raising consciousness. A virtual world might create the illusion of empathy.

Wavelengths bounce off the edge of the tank. A real tank? No. The tank thing isn't important. A tank is a lump of technology. If I'm looking for a technological solution to a social problem, I'm not going to find it, not in this direction. Remember the move to raise consciousness through drugs? The doors of perception didn't get cleansed that way.

Tom Duchamp

We're having a fishbowl discussion, the think tank people might say. By that they mean a small group of people talk together in the middle of the room, and a larger group sit round the edge and listen. The ideal is for the transparency of the fish bowl, the sense of being together in the fishbowl, engaged in a common project.

If the virtual reality technology gives a sense of moving in space, what I'm after is a sense of moving in head space, the promise of an enlarged reality, or reality plus, virtuality plus.

Are we looking for a technological solution to a social problem: brain-washing, brain enhancement, consciousness-altering through brain-wave manipulation? No. More a voluntary expansion of consciousness, a common consciousness of a common humanity. Being on the same wavelength, raising consciousness. We'll have our consciousness-tank. Our brain-wave channelers. We'll be high tech and we'll be a feminist laboratory.

We'll be Consciousness City.

The idea is learning from each other in new ways and then moving to work in the world. Putting ideas into practice: having the skills to put ideas into practice; having the power to put ideas into practice. Good ideas, though, not bad ideas. Wouldn't want to give a mad dictator yet another tool. Mind power. Mind control. Don't want to go down that path. Oh, no.

First they co-opt the language;
next they co-opt the body.
Then they co-opt the soul.

I started off thinking the future of feminism has turned out to be all about men, but that's only the beginning.

Moving on, moving on…

The astronomer Paul Davies is setting up a "cosmic think tank" at Arizona State University. I reckon this is something we feminists can sneak up on. The cosmic think tank, Davies reports, is designed "to address all the Really Big Questions, such as how the universe came to exist, why it is so uncannily suited for life, are we alone, what is the destiny of mankind etc." A good strategic principle is to get with the strength. What the cosmic think tank needs is cosmic feminism. The questions we can pose include: how the universe came to exist with women in it; why it is so uncannily suited for life, and its myriad methods of reproducing the species; how gender is related to the cosmic destiny of humankind; are we alone in the universe, and might there be a better way to organise the universe along gender-inclusive lines?

The idea is to move beyond one recent dominant paradigm that reduces women's issues to problems the individual has to cope with on her own. Feminist thinktanktitude says,

> No way we're going to go through all this in every generation, each woman for herself re-inventing the social wheel. Social and political worlds intersect; women are in the wider world of power relations, not separate from it. From the feminist think tank, subterranean rootlets will shoot out, interconnectedy-rhizomatic, popping up under the feet of the patriarchy, tripping it up, sliding all over its pulsing body, seeking its juicy open orifices, slithering into the patriarchal brain, there to inoculate gender-inclusive ideas as the basis for better ways of getting things done in the world.

The entry on "what would a feminist think tank look like?" may be found at http://wiki.feministsf.net, more specifically at http://wiki.feministsf.net/index.php?title=Feminist_Think_Tanks_%28WisCon_30_Panel%29

Rosaleen Love is an Australian writer who writes about science and the rest of life. Her short fiction has been collected in *The Travelling Tide* (2005) Aqueduct Press, Seattle, and in two books published by the Women's Press, UK: *The Total Devotion Machine* (1989) and *Evolution Annie* (1993). Her nonfiction includes *Reefscape. Reflections on the Great Barrier Reef,* Joseph Henry Press, 2001. She is a research associate at Latrobe and Monash Universities, Melbourne.

http://users.bigpond.net.au/RosaleenLove

Carol Emshwiller

Q: Every year, for the Memorial Day weekend, you are forced to choose between WisCon and the Bishop Mule Days Celebration. Sometimes you choose one and sometimes you choose the other. What's the real difference, anyway?

A: I don't know what to write, especially since I HAVE been coming to WisCon and not going to Mule Days for…how many years? And the older I get, the less I want to bother with Mule Days. Besides, there are no good classes in prey psychology there anymore. I do love WisCon and all the people there. I'll keep coming even when they have to bring me in on a wheel chair.

Carol Emshwiller has published five novels: *Carmen Dog, The Mount, Mr. Boots,* and the westerns *Ledoyt* and *Leaping Man Hill*. She has five collections of short stories: *Joy in Our Cause, Verging on the Pertinent, The Start of the End of It All, Report to the Men's Club*, and *I Live with You.* WisCon 27 GoH.

http://sfwa.org/members/emshwiller

Donna Stehling

WisCon 27

China Miéville

Carol Emshwiller

David Lee Anderson

Mark Rich

Q: I hear WisCon is not just for grrls anymore. What's *that* about?

A: This is a misperception, albeit a natural one. What has occurred is that more of us are grrls than ever before. Some of us must deal with the notion of being called grrlee, i.e., one who has been grrled...the irony being that not all who grew up girly can be called grrlee, since biological grrls cannot be grrled. To be grrlee is one of the transgenderal benefits of WisCon attendance. (Becoming a member of the Secret Feminist Caballeros is another: but this is neither the place nor time to talk of that.)

From the first one we attended, which seems to have been WisCon 15, Martha and I liked the con's mix of two groups: there were the locals, there for the science fiction and fantasy; and the nationals, who made the trip lured by the feminism. What turned us into regulars were probably the latter, for in Murphy and Fowler and Klages we saw being displayed a proudly and sometimes loudly self-deprecating and seriously funny feminist instinct that was lovely to be around. At the same time, the locals were involved in such essential aspects as the art show and huckster rooms, which gave us our own early focus.

What also kept us coming was the growing presence of a few other groups in the hallways and reading rooms and bars. The Minnesota contingent had its own sense of group belonging, which helped dissolve those other group lines. The incomparable Small Beer Press folks seemed to draw in the next major group: the Clarionites, an incredibly tightly knit clan that since loosening up a bit has provided excellent new energy for the con. And the vague sense that was there at WisCon 15 has become all-pervasive in recent years: that it is a national con. And somehow as that sense has grown, the feeling of camaraderie at the convention has grown as well. And yet in many ways I think WisCon remains as feminist-oriented as ever.

As two strangers walking the hallways of our first WisCon, members of neither this group nor that, Martha and I had no clue how much like home WisCon would come to feel. Have we changed, or has the convention? Or neither? As more souls feel at home in a place, the more like home it becomes: and I imagine newcomers must feel more of that warmth being exuded, as the years go by. And so it feels easier to walk in. It feels easier to stay for a while, and enter a conversation, and stay a bit longer. But it's still (he said) just for grrls.

Mark Rich—writer, visual artist, musician, toy historian—has published poetry and short stories including a recent collection, *Foreigners, and Other Familiar Faces (*Small Beer Press, 2003), and his paintings and drawings have graced the covers and innards of many books and magazines. And then there are his books and multitude of columns about toy history.

http://www.sff.net/people/mark.rich/nextpage.htm

Ellen Klages

Q: Do you ever sleep at WisCon?

A: Oddly enough, I do. Many WisCon nights I have gotten close to eight hours of fine, uninterrupted sleep. The beds in the Concourse are rather comfy, and no cats try to lie on my head. Then again, there are many other nights that I have gotten far, far less rest. I attribute those to a variety of factors, which include alcohol; conversation and laughter into the wee hours, much too rare and excellent to abandon for mere exhaustion; and snoring roommates whose output has rarely, but memorably, resembled that of Tuvan throat-singers. Harmonic and yet disquieting.

Ellen Klages is a Nebula Award-winning writer of short fiction. Her first novel, *Green Glass Sea*, winner of the 2007 Scott O'Dell Award for Historical Fiction, came out fall 2006 (Viking Press).

http://www.ellenklages.com/

Lord of the Monsters

Andrea Hairston

King Kong
Kingg Kongg
Kinggg Konggg

If king kong had been home
with his kids and his old lady and his neighbors
helping to protect their turf from the invaders
he never would have gotten hauled across the ocean
and ended up getting shot off the top of the empire state building
and what was that boy doing up there
in the dark
with that woman
anyway[1]

Have you heard of Silas Kpanan'Ayoung Siakor? He's not a dictator like Charles Taylor, or a rap star, or an athlete. Silas Siakor "put his life on the line to save Liberia's rain forests,"[2] everybody's rain forests. Big-time capitalists in the Oriental Logging Company were gunning for him because he cramped their slash-through-the-big-timber style. He won against these thugs, many of whom are now on trial, by getting proof to the UN of arms smuggling and ecological devastation that ultimately helped oust the aforementioned Mr. Taylor. Under threat of death, Mr. Siakor toppled a mighty corporate edifice and a corrupt ruler[3] without tearing anybody up or blowing shit to pieces. When you advance-Google Mr. Siakor, he gets 559 hits.[4] Despite his death-defying triumphs, he and other African or third world men doing what Hattie Gossett suggests in her poem are not the prototypical cultural icons of black masculinity. This is not simply a question of publicity—Mr. Siakor is an invisible warrior partly because he is hard to perceive in our cultural landscape.

Monster Mind Space

The cultural landscape is a fantastical realm where anything can be associated with anything else. Our metaphorical minds are constructed to generate and appreciate analogy, parable, simile—this, in fact, is how we understand and organize our world. Most of what we know or believe we don't directly experience, but understand through storytelling as analogous to our limited experiences. In this wondrous story-landscape, relentlessly iterated associations become truth, making it difficult to see what is not repeated. Even in our so-called post-Enlightenment, scientific age, usage is truth. An indexical connection between the two sides of a metaphorical equivalency is irrelevant, and multiple/divergent parings do not negate one another.

In other words, you may, as I do, find the reductive racial/gender readings of ***Kong*** unenlightening; or you may vociferously proclaim that your cultural production transcends time, space, race, and gender. You may swear that you are not presenting yet another version of black male/gorilla brute who lusts after innocent white womanhood and gets lynched for his audacious passion, but if she's blonde and civilized and he's dark, wild, monstrously violent and at home in the heart of darkness, when he tumbles a hundred stories to his death once again, you are perpetuating the cultural landscape you claim to abhor.

well
what I want to know is
what about kong's wife and his kids
mrs kong and the little kings
whatever happened to them after he deathwished and tripped himself right
out of their lives
did they have an insurance policy to fall back on
simian social security
a pension perhaps
did mrs kong get a job as a maid in a circus monkey act
and visit the kids at her mama's house when the show was laying over[5]

Whatever else it is, ***King Kong*** is an adventure-tragedy of racial/gender identity as constituted in the American, Hollywood, world imagination. This tale forged in the sexism/racism of its and our time cannot purge itself of the dramatic basis for the story and remain wildly popular.[6] Imagine King Kong going after blond male actor, a young Robert Redford. Imagine Russell Crowe falling for hairy Queen Kong after she has rescued him from raptors and giant cockroaches, and they slide around on the ice at Central Park in bliss. In no version of the mythic tale does Kong fall from the Empire State Building for love of, say, Angela Bassett. A kick-butt black woman wouldn't work, or even Halle Berry—there wouldn't be enough dramatic, iconic distance from the beast to his beautiful victim. A Queen Kong busting brutes in the jungle, trashing the big city, tearing planes out the sky would strain credibility, strain our ability to suspend disbelief, unless she were a mad mama protecting her brood.[7] Displays of killer male rage, of brute force, dominate the American cultural landscape of the post-911 Bush era.[8] The thoughtful, careful action for change displayed by Mr. Siakor is a whisper in the background.

History

The potency of this adventure-tragedy depends on colonial/minstrel notions of race and gender. Brutal black bucks, wild black pussies, and frail white women were an early feature of the minstrel stage. In the 1830s minstrelsy began as a transgressive youthful culture of Northern city boys abandoning their conservative and constricted European ethnic identities for the wild possibilities of blackface. Blacked up, restless urban youth shape-shifted through an emotional range not allowed them in their everyday life. They performed secret dreams, fears, and nightmares without claiming the lurid fantasies as the products of their own fevered imaginations. Delicious and taboo antics were ascribed to primal African dancers, Noble Red Savages, sing-songy Asian acrobats, or off-the-boat European immigrants. The scandalous performances tarnished and limited not the performer, but the character of those represented, solidifying into caricature. Minstrels were impersonators doing black wenches and delicate white womanhood; they were Negro, Indian, Irish, Jewish, et al. impersonators, and audiences flocked to theatres for this shape-shifting magic, claiming they couldn't tell blackface actors from the genuine articles.

As minstrelsy became mainstream popular culture, it lost its slight transgressive edge. By the 1840s, minstrel performers and audiences were "rich in black fun," negotiating their anxiety over racial, ethnic, gender, class differences and the concomitant power differentials in American society with abandon. The "imagined" others allowed disenfranchised male performers a public forum to define masculinity, femininity, whiteness, and otherness. From a polyphony of European identities played against African, Asian, and Native American caricature, blackface performers defined America and modernity.[9]

From the 1840s, not just black people or white women, but indeed, American and world character were defined by a troupe of stereotypes still popular today. The people caricatured eventually got to impersonate themselves. However, when "the other" gets to play herself as imagined by the dominant culture, these impersonations are usually all she can do for great reward: black people perform minstrel images as so-called "authentic colored people;" women take over from the young boys and delicate impersonators and play "feminine;" Indians do red face; Asian women play Geishas alongside their last Samurai!

Monster Fanboy Fun

The caricatures are much beloved and regularly brought back from the dead to dance and die for hungry audiences.[10] But...

> *you know girlfriend ain't getting no royalties offa those buttons and teeshirts with that other woman's picture on them*
>
> *or offa those books and movies that don't even mention her or the kids or the community*[11]

Peter Jackson, the highest paid director in Hollywood, creates a film with a two-hundred-million-dollar budget (not including a hundred million spent on publicity) to do another Kong film. Unlike Silas Siakor, advance-Googling Kong gets 42,200,000 hits.[12]

King Kong is a relentlessly iterated cultural icon if ever oh ever there was one.

Jackson wept at seeing the monster's first death in the 1933 film. He was nine, it was 1970, and already he was working on the version that would hit the screen in 2005. Unlike Hattie Gossett who would have Kong stay at home and take care of business, Jackson memorializes the noble savage who in the pursuit of civilized beauty meets his inevitable demise at the hands of ruthless, unethical technocrats.

As with early nineteenth-century minstrelsy, there's a whole fanboy thing going with Kong. I'm not intending to engage in a lofty, intellectual put-down, but I have to admit up front, I'm nowhere near the center of the fanboy thing. They are into the Gorilla:[13] awesome, ugly, mean, take-no-prisoners, quasi-human killing machine. As with blackface minstrelsy or modern-day gangsta rap, whose fan base is increasingly white suburbia, fanboys would like to be Kong or 50 Cent or some other snarling, swaggering King Kong gangsta rapper and beat up or blow up shit with abandon. Eric Lott calls it love and theft in his classic analysis of blackface.[14] We admire the big and bad brute and want to steal his primal power, cage his rage for our vicarious delight.

Go to '50s website, load up as you mouse around, get shot every time you click a link.

Fanboys get to be Kong in the Movie Dark, if only for a few sweet, fleeting moments.

They feel his glory and his pain. They want Fay Wray, Jessica Lange, Naomi Watts, lovely blond ladies, helpless and vulnerable in the monster's fist, beauties dependant on hairy dark masculinity for their next breath.

Is Kong the dark side of every adolescent male? Incoherent, yearning for something he cannot have and does not even understand—a blond mate the relative size of a Barbie doll!

Greg Bear writes this in his introduction to the Modern Library's 2005 edition of the Kong novelization (p. xxvi). Bear sees the 1933 film as a "waking dream" haunting us with adventure and danger, "darker than most of us care to dream." Indeed Jackson is screening tragic dreams and millions of people are paying for the privilege to dream with him.[15]

The fanboys are plush movie-seat adventurers, who travel to the heart of darkness. On Skull Island they discover what no one has seen before—except inscrutable, inexplicable natives who want to kill everybody they don't feed to Kong. The fanboys also get to break taboos and experience illicit passion. ***King Kong*** is not unlike ***Brokeback Mountain*** in this—another tale of illicit, tragic love where star-crossed lovers are doomed by a society afraid of its shadows.

When I first heard that Jackson was planning to do another *King Kong*, I was shocked. I never needed to hear or see the Kong story again. So why were/are Jackson and others so enthralled?

There have been endless remakes—*King Kong versus Godzilla* from Japan in the 1960s or the 1976 Dino De Laurentis remake with Jeff Bridges and Jessica Lange. Linda Hamilton tries to bring Kong back from the dead in the 1980s. Dudley Moore voiced an animated version in the 1990s, just to name a few. And let me not get started with Mighty Joe Young…

Authenticity

Life imitates art. We become the characters we play. 50 Cent has been shot nine times, once in the head. He is an **authentic** gangsta rapper. Jackson's *King Kong* is more authentic than the other versions. Andy Serkis went to the zoo to watch the gorillas so he could get it right. Authenticity is a marketing tool that confuses truth, reality, facts, and values. Authenticity makes difference a commodity and negotiates our scientific anxiety over the irrational pleasures of artistic experience. By the late nineteenth century as African Americans impersonated themselves, minstrel performances were advertised as featuring: **Real Colored People**. Real colored people enhanced the value and legitimized the fantasy. If we are in the presence of artfully achieved technological authenticity, we can forgive, ignore, forget the utter falsehood of what we are seeing. The 2005 Kong is modeled on actual gorillas: You've come a long way, baby.[16]

Jackson's *King Kong* is a good film, very entertaining. Critics agree—it garnered an 84% rating on Rotten Tomatoes and made many top ten lists of 2005. "Peter Jackson's tragic, terrific *King Kong* is an old-school marvel worth celebrating," Lisa Schwarzbaum proclaims in the December 16, 2005, edition of *Entertainment Weekly*.

Roger Ebert says:

> *King Kong* is a magnificent entertainment. It is like the flowering of all the possibilities in the original classic film. Computers are used not merely to create special effects, but also to create style and beauty, to find a look for the film that fits its story. And the characters are not cardboard heroes or villains seen in stark outline, but quirky individuals with personalities… This is one of the year's best films."[17]

Cosmetic Change/Radical Change

The beautiful Naomi Watts character understands *and* appreciates this primal beast who, in contrast to Mr. Siakor or caged intellectual Adrien Brody, can rip apart the jaws of those who terrorize him. Unlike Fay Wray, Naomi loves the monster back. She, and therefore we, admire his wild, macho, hyper-masculine rage and heart-stopping roar; we ache at his contemplative communion with awesome nature; we treasure the gentle streak beneath the rough fur and scarred hide. In Watts' eyes we see the monster's humanity. As he contemplates the sunset or slides on the ice filled with the discovery of a new thrill with his ladylove, Kong is the romantic superhero who would allow us to sleep easily in these terror times.

Despite Watts' fearless feistiness and Kong's tragic depth, gender roles and colonial values are locked in the conventional mode. Unlike ***Brokeback***, ***King Kong*** is transgressive only at the edges, not at its core. The gorilla/girl love story allows us to forgive? ignore? the conventional, oppressive center of the film, its celebration of violence. Anyone disenchanted with the Kong core is a politically correct whiner:

From metaphilm.com on January 5, 2006, comes this challenge:

> **Academics Misinterpreting Hollywood.**
>
> When will an academic ever see anything other than "the other" in King Kong movies? *Not this week.*

You can almost hear the voice of the bespectacled fourth grader: "Look mommy, I found a racist. Can I keep him?"

Anyone out there willing to rise to the challenge of offering a real interpretation? Someone want to show us how the 1973 King Kong was the most eerily accurate prophecy of 9/11 ever filmed? Someone else want to point out that Jackson's new King Kong recapitulates the 1933 original to reveal Hollywood entertainment itself as the dominant threat to the long-term sustenance of industrial civilization? Anyone? Anyone? Bueller?

Cranky Conclusions

So here we have an endlessly repeated story and endlessly repeated critiques that rub against ambivalent cultural mythos. In my most generous speculation, I think: The beast is savage and awesome, hyper-masculine, outside "our" morality, a primal killing machine with the intelligence and grace to fall in love with the most delicate of creatures, the epitome of civilized beauty, a being as far from Kong's primordial jungle world as imaginable. The Beauty for her part appreciates and loves him, across the gulf of species, across the gulf of civilization—Kong is not her God, to be sacrificed to or feared and worshipped, but a fellow traveler in the adventure of their lives.

The drama is in the distance between the Beauty and the Beast and that distance echoes racial/gender dichotomies. A blonde white woman and dark hairy beast are the hallowed opposites in our melodrama storehouse of types and tropes—from the black brutes on the minstrel stage, through *Birth of a Nation* and the blackface monster who causes Lillian Gish to jump to her death as any honorable white woman threatened by a black penis would, to 50 Cent who parades bullet proof street credits for his lean and mean black gangsta persona.

Jackson's Kong is a subtle brute, taken with Watts' fearless and theatrical spirit. He tosses aside other blondes who do not have the depth of character that she displays, who do not have her spark of entertainment genius; Kong seeks his one true love because she is singular and special. Still, Watts' blonde white womanhood and unresolved racial tension make the drama potent. Kong is a brilliant ape, well suited to his jungle world. Moral in his own terms, he is ready to risk his life to save Naomi—but we still understand him as dark savage other.

The dark savages in Jackson's version may not be African, Indonesian, or Polynesian. They may be any ethnicity in fact, but they are not civilized, and they are, as is so often the fate of savages, without a voice in the story. They are mud people, no-context evil, like the Orcs in ***Lord of the Rings***. We don't know who they are. We don't know how to read their rituals. We don't know the meaning they give to their actions. We don't know their symbols and dreams. We don't know how they order the world. We don't know what they value and what they don't. Is Kong a God or Devil they must appease? Are the sacrifices holy or desperate? Or just what they do to cheeky intruders? Does Kong need a babe a week, and this is how these folk protect their own? Is their social fabric wrecked when Jack Black plunders their god? What do they do without Kong? And the wild mud women rolling their eyes, trancing out in wicked-witch ritual—what gorilla would want these ghouls? These muddy savages are without interiors—part of someone else's story—they are not in their own story. We do the best we can to understand them—depending on what we bring to the story, but the story itself offers us little. Kong is also without context—What of Mrs. Kong or the little Kongs?

Jackson gives a context for the white characters and to a degree for the saintly civilized black and Asian minor characters on the ship.[18] But to get at the "savage" point of view would mean to tell a different story. Jackson offers us their mystery as respectfully as *he* can manage and shows how we sanitize encounters with others when he presents the staged version of Kong's capture back in "civilization." African American performers do their minstrel best to entertain the audience with supposed savage antics. Here Jackson reveals what a show we make of difference without being able to represent it.

But giving a nod to racism or sexism, displaying an awareness of Kong's colonial context doesn't salvage the story. Jackson re-inscribes the power dynamics he is struggling to side step. Despite Jackson's liberal compassion, despite Naomi's and even Adrien Brody's outrage at what Jack Black does to Kong, they are helpless against his inevitable demise. Kong is shot down by mechanical beasts more savage than the megalaurauses on his brutal jungle-island. Black gets to memorialize him, gets to define the life he led, gets to say who and what Kong was, gets to make him into a tragic character in Black's story and blame it all on "beauty," not of course on imperialism.

A few critics point to the inherent, metaphorical racism, a few give a nod to the sexism in the 1933 film, but hardly any attribute the success of Jackson's film to its maintenance of classic colonial oppressive narratives. Indeed, Lisa Schwarzbaum insists that Jackson's film transcends its racist/sexist origins.[19]

Jackson weeps at Kong's demise, but doesn't stop the show. Unlike Hattie Gossett's re-imagining, he capitalizes on the very show that kills Kong. It is Naomi loving a sentient beast who loves her back that persuades us, assuages us, that this is not a lynching tale we enjoy.

Silas Siakor is still fighting multinationals and powerful governments (such as China) that would love to plunder and rape the Liberian rain forest. His thoughts for the future:

> We would hope that local communities in the forest region will have a strong say in how natural resources are managed, particularly the forests on which they depend. We hope for a Liberia in which multinationals, especially those in the timber industry, will do all they can to respect environmental standards, and their extraction practices will not unnecessarily degrade our forests. We hope for a Liberia in which our culture and traditional practices will be respected by our central government, and by the multinationals that come to extract resources from there.[20]

cuz if king kong had been home
with his kids and his old lady and his neighbors
helping to protect their turf from the invaders
he never would have gotten hauled across the ocean
and ended up getting shot off the top of the empire state building
and what was that boy doing up there
in the dark
with that woman
anyway[21]

Endnotes

1 Hattie Gossett, "king kong! king kongg!! kinggg konggg!!!" from *presenting…sister noblues.* (Ithaca, NY: Firebrand Books, 1988), 63.

2 Michelle Nijhuis, "Silas Martyr: Silas Siakor put his life on the line to save Liberia's forests," *Grist Magazine*, April 24, 2006 (grist.org/news/maindish/2006/04/24/nijhuis-siakor/index.html).

3 Taylor used the profits from ravaging the rain forest to bankroll his civil war.

4 On May 24, 2006.

5 Gossett, 64.

6 Merian C. Cooper was a heart-of-darkness adventurer who used his thrilling experiences in "savage, uncivilized" lands as the basis for the Kong story.

7 *Aliens* for example; but hunting down her love?

8 Bill Peterson in an article for ***Political Psychology*** (2005, Vol 26[6], 887-904) points to the hyper-masculinazation of American culture, particularly in popular cultural expression post-September 11.

9 See *Love and Theft* by Eric Lott, *Demons of Disorder* by Dale Cockrell, *Highbrow Lowbrow* by Lawrence Levine, *Blacking Up* by Robert C. Toll, *Raising Cain: Blackface Performance From Jim Crow to Hip Hop* by W.T. Lhamon Jr.

10 Witness films like *Memoirs of a Geisha*, *Big Momma's House II*, and *King Kong* and all the movies featuring thug African Dictators—*Lords of War*, *The Interpreters*, *the Constant Gardiner.*

11 Gossett, 64.

12 May 24, 2006.

13 Bill Peterson notes that Gorillas on comic book covers sold issues in the '70s and '80s.

14 See *Love and Theft.*

15 The film grossed $218.1 million in America—one of the top five grossing films of 2005 and grossed $329.2 million outside of North America for a total of $547.3 million, which is $52.7 million short of the $600 million executives hoped for but still means a lot of butts in the seats to watch a three-hour epic. As of April 3, 2006, it had sold more than 6.5 million DVD's, generating $100 million—a sales record for Universal. Some critics (doing a race-reading of Kong) note that it was among Hitler's favorites. (He liked Mozart too.) I find it more telling that Kong has repeated mass appeal.

16 People do quibble with the physical impossibility of the giant ape and question his strength or speed, but that's done in the spirit of fun more than as a serious critique of the film—which won an Academy award for Special effects.

17 Roger Ebert, December 15, 2005 (rogerebert.suntimes.com).

18 Captained by a decent man with a German(?) accent in the 1930s.

19 "***King Kong*** sets the new standard for honoring a mass-market classic while remaking it with nuanced contemporary self-awareness. I mean, let's get real: If the 1933 original, directed by Merian C. Cooper and Ernest B. Schoedsack, was the era's comparable marvel of special effects, the production was also about as refined as Kong's left mitt. Lusty shrieking and fainting by Fay Wray as the ape's delectable beloved to the contrary, the performances were heavy footed, the dialogue was leaden, and on-screen racial sensitivity was in its primordial stage. Yet with the bracingly smart script by longtime teammates Fran Walsh, Phillipa Boyens and Jackson, the remake acknowledges that very clunkiness with love and a sense of humor, incorporating relics of dialogue and racial silliness into the retelling. And with Watts so radiantly intelligent as the beast's new beauty, the dynamic between dark, hairy, tired old male and delicate, blond, empathetic young damsel takes on new psychological reverberations."

20 From Interview with Silas Siakor in ***Grist Magazine***, April 24, 2006.

21 Gossett, 66.

Andrea Hairston is the Artistic Director of Chrysalis Theatre and has created original productions with music, dance, and masks for over twenty-five years. She is also a Professor of Theatre and Afro-American Studies at Smith College. Her novel *Mindscape (*2006, Aqueduct Press) was shortlisted for the Philip K. Dick award and on the honor list for the James Tiptree Jr. Award.

http://www.andreahairston.com

Ted Chiang

Q: What's the most interesting panel you've attended at a WisCon?

A: At WisCon 25, I attended a presentation by Dr. Marianne Schaefer, a dentist, on forensic odontology and the use of cadaver dogs. Five years later, I still remember it in detail. Dr. Schaefer discussed human-on-human bites, and showed slides displaying five different levels of bite severity, from superficial bruising all the way up to removal of a chunk of flesh. She also talked about the process of making casts of a bite injury to check against a suspect's teeth; nowadays forensic dentists practice the cast-making process on a pig carcass that has been clamped by a set of fake teeth, but Dr. Schaefer said that at one point in the past, they applied the clamp to the anesthetized buttocks of student volunteers.

Then she talked about cadaver dogs, dogs used to find human remains. These dogs are trained to distinguish the smell of decomposing human flesh from that of other animals, and the best dogs have been able to locate corpses trapped in a house submerged under floodwaters. Dr. Schaefer recounted some anecdotes about working with such dogs, the most amazing one about a dog named Eagle that had once found a missing girl while she was still alive, but on the brink of death. Since cadaver dogs aren't trained to locate living people, this was quite unusual. Eagle's handler later tested him by taking him to a hospice facility, and Eagle was able to identify those patients who would die within a day or two.

Ted Chiang is the author of *Stories of Your Life and Others* (Tor 2002) and has won three Nebulas, a Sturgeon, and a Hugo as well as several other awards. He lives in Seattle, where he works as a freelance technical writer.

Jeanne Gomoll

Ursula K. Le Guin

Q: Do you go to WisCon even when you don't have to? Why?

A: I am trying to think why I would have to go to WisCon.
The answer came quite quickly.

A rabid feminist cabal (their shrill leaders thought to be hiding in caves in Missouri while their squalid adherents meet secretly all over the country to drum on Tupperware, cook fudge, and swear undying hatred of all men) has sent a goon squad to abduct me. With my features disguised by a Cheney mask (not Lon, Dick), and guarded by four huge, muscular, ruthless, female gorillas in housewife suits, I am secretly carried from Oregon to WisConsin on the Amtrak Empire Builder. The two-bed compartment is rather crowded, but women are used to making do. We also have some trouble in the dining car, as they are unable to seat five at a table. One of the gorillas has to eat with other people, who object. However, after the swift trip of only two nights and a day and a half, we arrive at the small town where you have to get off the train because it doesn't go to Madison any more, and are met by a low black limousine with tinted windows driven by one of the dreaded Go-Moll Gang. Arriving at the convention hotel I am met by Eileen Gunn in a rabbit suit with a machine gun. "Stop right there," she says. "Tell us just one thing. Why are you here?"

"Because I love this meeting," I cry. "It is the only meeting I ever loved!"

"He's lying," Gunn says, raising her eponymous instrument.

"Don't shoot!" I shout, realizing her error, and tear off the Cheney mask. Then all is peace and joy once more and we hurry off to not miss the panel on Eponymous Dicks, and Carol's speech, and the Auction, and conversations in the bar, and the Awards with people singing idiotic songs, and all the other singular delights of WisCon. My gorillas have melted into the crowd.

Ursula K. Le Guin has been writing fiction, poetry, etc. for a long time. Ursula K. Le Guin writes in various modes including realistic fiction, science fiction, fantasy, books for children and young adults, screenplays, essays, and poems. As of 2006 she has published nineteen novels, eleven volumes of short fiction, twelve books for children, three collections of essays, six volumes of poetry and four of translation. WisCon 20 GoH.

http://ursulakleguin.com

Liz Henry

Q: "What do you wear to parties at WisCon?"

A: In honor of the Tiptree Award, I wear genderbent outfits. For the award ceremony I had on my neighbor's black velvet strapless prom gown from the '80s, with a huge hot pink bow and fake diamonds on the front; the outfit was complete with black and pink hightop sneakers, so I was butchy femme. Another night, my party drag was as boyish as I could get without faking facial hair, so, something approximating a fancy suit, where fancy means "punk formal," set off with sparkling barrettes; femmy butch. Dressing up is fun and performative. Parties deserve splendor, effort, flamboyance, to help everyone get over-the-top and out of their everyday selves. Every party gets off the ground easier if someone is rocketing around, bouncing, flirting, talkative, and hyper. So I wear my best party mood as well, and have a blast flirting with all the shyest-looking people.

Liz Henry has published poems, translations, reviews, stories, and essays in *Poetry Flash, Strange Horizons, Other, Two Lines, Suspect Thoughts, Cipactli, Lodestar Quarterly,* and *Literary Mama.*

She blogs at http:/liz-henry.blogspot.com.

Notes on the Feminist Romance Panel

by Micole Sudberg

Panel Description

First off, is there such a thing and how would it be accurately portrayed? Very often romances in sf/f short stories and novels follow very traditional patriarchal patterns, even when fairly feminist individuals are writing. What does a feminist romantic storyline look like? Why don't we see these more often? How can writers who like to think of themselves as feminist avoid falling back on the old standbys without looking either unrealistic or like they are pushing a "message"?

Panelists

Jennifer Stevenson (moderator), Emma Bull, Stephanie Burgis, Cynthia Gonsalves, Nina Kiriki Hoffman, Lyda A. Morehouse

> [Note: I accidentally erased all my notes on this, so I refer you to oyceter (http://oyceter.livejournal.com/441372.html) for a more thorough and reliable recounting of the panel. But this is what I got out of it, or remember getting out of it four and a half months later. —MS]

1. Lyda Morehouse is hysterically funny. She was the best thing on the panel. She could do stand-up. I bought all four of her books as Lyda Morehouse right after the panel, and the only reason I didn't also spring for the one as by Tate Halloway is that I already had a lot to carry and I figured it wouldn't be hard to find in New York. I am so sad I lost all of her one-liners. She was also informative about current trends in romance and had clearly read widely in the field.
2. Jennifer Stevenson would have made a great panelist but she was an awful moderator. She had an agenda and by god she pushed it through the entire panel, leaving no room for dissent and very little for elaboration. Stevenson summarized romance as being feminist—but it's about your mother's femi-

nism, not yours; that is, it's the feminism of the generation before. In contemporary romance, women get to be the powerful ones, they have better sex, they have more orgasms (JS: If he doesn't go down, he's not a hero. LM: Now you know how lesbians can write straight romance.); they triumph through the "soccer mom values" that are denigrated by society because they focus on cooperation rather than competition; many of the old stereotypes of romance are no longer true or are based on misunderstanding the role of fantasy; etc.

This argument was clearly a response to the common argument that romances are by definition *antifeminist*, limit men and women to stereotypical gender roles, and enforce heterocentrism and heteronormativity (the romance is the center of the woman's life, she must want marriage and kids, friendship is not as significant as romance, etc.) Unfortunately, it is an argument just as broad and as false as the argument it is rebutting. Not all romance is antifeminist, but that doesn't mean it's all feminist, either.

a. Stevenson's opinions made better soundbites than arguments. Let's start with the big one: "Romance is feminist; it's just your mother's feminism."

   My mother's feminism? jonquil's mother's? oyceter's mother's? Because we all read romance and I suspect our mothers have very different notions of feminism, and—more to Stevenson's intended point—they come from three different generations. What age are we assuming romance readers are? I started reading romance when I was thirteen. Is "my mother's feminism" the feminism of someone who's thirteen in 1986 or thirteen in 2006?

   Even assuming there's a broad-church generational feminism we can identify for 1976, 1986, 1996, 2006, why is it good that in 2006 people are writing from the feminist assumptions of 1986? Why *aren't* they writing the feminism of 2006? Why is it okay that they're ignoring twenty years of coalition building and theorizing?

b. Stevenson equated "our mothers' feminism" with "soccer mom values," which, to the best of my recollection, she did not define. Other panelists described the current romance novel as requiring that the women have successful careers; win through "niceness"; and have great sex. I'm forced to guess at the meaning of "soccer mom values," but (1) "soccer mom" doesn't equal "independent career woman" in the general lexicon; (2) "soccer mom" *does* have implied race and class markers; (3) "winning through niceness" *can* be a triumph of cooperative ethics over the broken Darwinism of late-period global capitalism, but it can also be a neat reinscription of separate spheres that enforces public competition by ruling off an imaginary safe private space that exists beyond social control. The only way to determine which is the case is to take a hard, critical, honest look at individual works, which is exactly what the panel lacked.

c. *Women triumph; men who are overbearing or controlling at the beginning of the book end up groveling at the end.* First, I've got to say this does not bear much resemblance to the plot of any of the romances I've read for about the past ten years. Second, even if it did, so what? This is just reinscribing hierarchy with the positions reversed; it's an escape fantasy that safely shunts off women's anger and desire for power into an imaginary space so that these desires and emotions do not disrupt the status quo. What would make this empowerment rather than the opiate of the masses? Is the difference in the work or in the readers?

d. One man in the audience asked why panelists were assuming the viewpoint character was a woman and Stevenson said, "Because the reader is. Next!" In addition to being rude, Stevenson's response underscored another weakness in her argument: She depended on a simple identification of the female reader with the female characters (and, presumably, the male reader with the male characters), an identification which is not borne out by the evidence. People, especially women, can and frequently do identify cross-gender, and over the past twenty years the romance novel has moved away from the single viewpoint towards the dual-viewpoint or multiple-viewpoint standard. First-person narration is, in fact, extremely rare in genre romance, although it is popular in variants such as chick lit; readers have overwhelmingly responded well to books including the hero's POV. (See Laura Kinsale's "The Androgynous Reader" for an interesting take on this.)

   This is related, I believe, to another stylistic marker of romance alluded to by the panel: lots of "head-hopping" and lots of scenes presented first from one point of view and then from another. Emma Bull criticized this as eliminating suspense, but the point of romance is not necessarily suspense in the relationship (and when it is, it's generally *how*, not *who*); the multiple viewpoints allow readers to luxuriate in the experience, draw it out. (Very similar to manga, actually, especially shoujo, whether the main plot is a romance or not; and, on the other end of the high art/pop culture divide, similar to the techniques employed by Toni Morrison to circle around memory, revisit and reshape events.)

3. From the audience, heresluck suggested that one reason Jennifer Crusie's books read as so strongly feminist is the emphasis on female friendships; Crusie's protagonists always have multiple relationships and responsibilities to other women, which are treated as being as serious and important as the

romance; life is not reduced to the heterosexual dyad. I'd add in a recommendation for E. Lockhart, who is like the YA Jennifer Crusie: *The Boyfriend List, The Boy Book, Fly on the Wall.* Lockhart's almost doing anti-romances: taking stock romantic situations and seeing what happens with them if you make female friendships as or more important than the romance. Subversive yet emotionally satisfying, and also damn funny.

4. Romance is having interesting times. Single-title historicals seem to have narrowed down about as much as they have ever been in their history: try to find a new title that isn't set in medieval England or the US or UK during the eighteenth or nineteenth century. At the same time, the field is exploding in subcategories and add-ons: chick lit, women's lit (LM: Romance is to women's lit as sf is to speculative fiction), paranormal romance, black romance, Hispanic romance, erotica and more explicit/sexually adventurous imprints and small publishers, cross-genre experiments like suspense- or fantasy-focused lines. Some of these are commercially successful and some of these aren't; what I wanted to hear was what was pushing these changes in romance, which of them are *critically* successful, who should I be looking out for, what are the most interesting writers doing? What's going on with the biggest African American romance line getting bought out by Harlequin, and what implications does this have for the black "urban fiction" that's getting trashed—sometimes by black cultural conservatives—in *The New York Times?*

   And, seriously, by this time is there anyone at WisCon and interested in romance who *hasn't* heard of Jennifer Crusie? I love her, that's not the issue. The issue is, who *else*?

   Lyda Morehouse alluded to some of this in her responses; Nina Kiriki Hoffman mentioned Melanie Jackson's goblin romances; but I wanted more info.

Micole lives in a small hole in a large pile of books. She occasionally emerges with a story, or thoughts on her reading. The stories she sells, the thoughts she shares freely on her LJ. Her stories have appeared in *The Essential Bordertown* and *Xanadu 3.*

This piece originally appeared online at
http://coffeeandink.livejournal.com/640707.html

http://coffeeandink.livejournal.com

Is Reading Feminist SF a Theory Building Activity?

Transcript Notes by Laura Quilter

Panel Description

This idea comes from a question that wasn't asked in the "Judging the Tiptree" panel. For those of us who are already long-standing feminists and feminist sf readers, does on-going reading feminist sf change your understandings of gender? If so, how? If feminist theory is evolving, how do we see that reflected in or reflecting feminist SF? Do you actively seek out feminist sf that challenges your current understandings of gender or stick to readings that are comfortable? Do you even notice the shifts in your thinking? When's the last time you thought about how a book changed your already sophisticated understanding of gender, or do you pay more attention to whether or not you care for a particular book?

Panelists

Karen Joy Fowler (moderator), Margaret McBride, Joan Haran, Cheryl Morgan, Lori A. Selke

Works & Authors Cited

- Eleanor Arnason, *Ring of Swords*
- Raphael Carter, "Congenital Agenesis of Gender Ideation"
- Suzy McKee Charnas, *Walk to the End of the World*
- Janine Cross, *Touched By Venom*
- Nancy Farmer, *Sea of Trolls*
- Shulamith Firestone, *Dialectic of Sex*
- Gwyneth Jones, *Life, White Queen, North Wind*

- John Kessel, *Stories For Men*
- Ursula Le Guin, *The Left Hand of Darkness,* "The Matter of Seggri," The Earthsea Trilogy
- Laurie Marks, fantasy series
- Ian McDonald, *River of Gods*
- Vonda McIntyre, *Dreamsnake*
- Janice Raymond
- Alastair Reynolds, *Chasm City*
- Justina Robson, *Living Next Door to the God of Love*
- Kim Stanley Robinson, *The Pacific Edge*
- Joanna Russ, *When It Changed, The Female Man*
- Melissa Scott, *Shadow Man*
- Johanna Sinisalo, *Troll*
- Starhawk, *The Fifth Sacred Thing*
- Theodore Sturgeon
- Sheri Tepper, *Gate to Women's Country*
- John Varley
- Kate Wilhelm, "The Funeral"

> [Editor's note: These notes are not a verbatim transcript. They have been corrected by some (though not all) of the panelists and have been abridged or supplemented for clarity.]

KJF: What brought you to sf and feminism?

MM: Subscription to a science fiction book club as an adult; feminist theory and science fiction critical theory on my own after graduate school.

LS: I learned both sf and feminism at my mother's knee; she was getting a PhD in chemical engineering while I was growing up. The collision came when I read *When It Changed*... I was eighteen, nineteen, twenty—an adult, but not by much. That was the first Joanna Russ I ever read.

JH: I also read sf and fantasy and all kinds of fantastic literatures as a child, but once I went to college, a sense of shame about that crept in... I stopped reading science fiction, but for some reason, I continued to read fantasy. That makes no sense to me now.* In the early '90s, I did a Master's in Gender Studies. They gave us this very extensive reading list. This was my first encounter with any kind of systematic feminism, doing a Master's in Gender Studies although I had been exposed to the populist feminism of *Cosmopolitan* and the women's pages of *The Guardian (*a left liberal quality UK newspaper). One of the books on the reading list was Shulamith Firestone's *Dialectic of Sex*. Her thesis about taking reproduction outside the body seemed to me at that point incredibly attractive. The other thing she said was there was no utopian literature for women, and I found that hard to believe. I thought that (a) she was writing science fiction and (b) there must be other science fiction out there with feminist-utopian ideas.

> [JH comments later, in Jan 2007: Perhaps my logic at that time went something like: fantasy is clearly escapist literature that's just pleasurable, but my former seizing on sf as an alternative scripture / politics is a bit embarrassing because it demonstrates a naïve faith in the potential for fiction to change the world. Needless to say I would now reclaim the faith if not the fundamentalism!]

CM: Books I can remember reading before going to college are *The Left Hand of Darkness* by Ursula Le Guin and *The Passion of New Eve* by Angela Carter. I read Joanna Russ's *The Female Man* while at college. I didn't get much more involved than reading a few books until fairly late, but when I was living in Australia I starting mixing with sf fandom and several of my women friends kept telling me how wonderful WisCon was. They were right.

KJF: I've been watching the Tiptree Award process for several years, and something has repeated itself several times. A fresh jury begins discussing the kind of book they want and settles on the kind of book, the kind of experience they want. Generally it turns out that they want to be reading *The Left Hand of Darkness* and want to be nineteen years old. That's what they're trying to create. Many, many months and books later, they begin to scale down their expectations and look for something more subtle that will have a less profound change in their thinking. I've seen this so many times that I've wondered: at our age, and with our reading histories, is it in fact possible to have that experience again?

When was the last time a book really profoundly rocked you? How long ago was that? And what sorts of impacts do you find when you read now?

JH: For me, sometimes reading a book doesn't have its most important impact on the first time through. I did work on Starhawk's *The Fifth Sacred Thing* which I loved for its expansive version of feminism. On about the third or fourth—close—reading, it finally struck me that there was a male point of view character as well as the two female point of view characters between whom the narrative is mainly divided.... The other text was *Shadow Man*, thinking about gender and sexuality, the way that Melissa Scott wrote about that... Embodying relationships made sense to me. That queer theory, for example, you can slip off the page when you read about something.... The bodily experience of those characters done as well as it is in *Shadow Man*. That helped me to imagine myself and to imagine others in a way that makes a lot more sense...** And there have been texts that approach that [experience] since then, but I think that for me, part of it is having the time to go over and over a text because I read fast—I'm plot-driven, to start with—I have to know how the story turned out—and then when I go back and read it again different parts strike me, different insights occur to me; I can't do that the first time because I read too fast. Texts need to bear second, third, fourth, fifth readings to get rushes from them, to do theory-building. I[n] M[y] H[umble] O[pinion], one reading doesn't do that for me.

> ** JH (Jan 2007): For me, reading some of this feminist science fiction in the context of doing a PhD meant that I was constantly reading it in dialogue with "official" feminist theory. And I was repeatedly struck by the ways in which reading the best feminist sf made it easier for me to grasp the official theory—and to see its problems. However, as my somewhat elliptical language in the transcript of my speech suggests, this "grasping" wasn't necessarily the masterful, dexterous ownership of a set of concepts, but an embodied sense of being other than myself that I firmly believe is an important social and political technology.

KJF: You said you came to these texts having been taught to read for gender issues. Would you say you've been trained to do that, or is it a more natural way for you to approach a text.

JH: No, it's definitely training. My first degree was in English and History, and the teaching was focused on looking at a text in its context of production. There was a little attention to the reading experience, but much more to the sociology of literary production. And it was all about class; come the revolution all will be solved, and gender was not an issue.*** At that point of my life, like many women of a certain privilege, I hadn't come across gender as a disadvantage, but then once I went into the workplace I realized: oooohhh, things are different for a girl. Something about my social reality made it possible for me to read differently, drawing upon my academic training, but supplementing it with a rather more critically informed take on the gap between ideals and pragmatics. The other thing that is vitally important in terms of theory building; it's not just about me reading the text but about talking to other people about text. So it's not just about the text, but about texts that can create conversations, and talking to other people who read differently—and of course, listening to them, however painful it sometimes feels to have my assumptions challenged—illuminates other stuff for me that I missed because of my own reading blinkers.

> ***JH (Jan. 2007): Actually, I'm a little embarrassed about that claim. Our cohort was introduced to feminist literary critics like Gilbert and Gubar in our final year, but I was so seduced by the post-marxist theorists that were taught with great passion that I also thought that class was the key issue. Some (although a tiny minority) of the women on my course were a little bit wiser than me.

CM: One of the things that first struck me when I read the title is that, sure, reading is a feminist theory-building activity, but coming to WisCon is a really serious feminist theory-building activity. In terms of recent books and things, it's getting hard. This comes back to a panel we had yesterday: Is feminist sf so five years ago? And to a certain extent we decided it was, because things have changed. Back when I was a teenager, it was great to imagine a world with female astronauts and state leaders and fighter pilots, and now all those things have happened. We haven't won the war but we're now fighting in the trenches, not doing easy things like advancing across the land. But the type of book people can write now is different than the type of book people could write back in the '60s. Plus, when you're nineteen, it's easier to impress you with the big ideas, and when you get older, you get more sophisticated and ask more from a book. Most of the books that have blown me away over past few years are for their literary style rather than content. Probably *River of Gods* by Ian McDonald, because he introduces in that a character who has had a sex-change operation to become neuter, someone who elected to get out of the gender game altogether. And if you look at the book, it's all based on what actual transsexuals go through, but rather than what someone goes through male-to-female or female-to-male, it's what somebody would go through to have no gender at all.

LS: I took a course in feminist theory in college taught by someone who was really, really rigorous, and I don't think I've had that reaction to a story. Because I'm hyper-critical, it's really hard to blow me away with a story, which is why I think we do it with a narrative to begin with rather than writing Shulamith Firestone—that's science fiction. Narrative is to slip the ideas in and make you think, "wow," and have it come up later, but that doesn't work any more. John Kessel, *Stories for Men*—I read it in *Asimov's* before it won the Tiptree. For me, it really did make me.... It was the first sophisticated treatment of what it would be like for boys—the other side of a feminist utopia. It wasn't "oh, this would be horrible"; it was "hmm, there are some sophisticated, subtle effects." Things I look for now are "yeah, the big idea is great, but what are some of the unintended consequences?" And I can still be brought up short by that kind of book or story.

KJF: But less of a "wow" and more of a "hmm."

LS: Yeah, but that's okay, I'm really suspicious of a "wow"; I'm really suspicious of things that are supposed to blow my mind or things that really did blow my mind because I tend to think I'm being propagandized rather than really changing my thinking because I'm not being critical.

MM: I teach freshmen in college; I'm still involved with the nineteen year olds. I'm teaching a class this term of juniors and seniors on Tiptree winners and those shortlisted, so getting a lot of students reading feminist science fiction for the first time.... But for my own personal reading, it is a little more of the "well that's an interesting question, hmm, where is that going to go, and what would that do?" So even if it's fairly subtle, I still see feminist theory in much of what I read. *Troll* did some interesting things. I was on that jury. And *Troll* did some interesting things for me as did *Sea of Trolls* by Nancy Farmer. Which is a Y[oung] A[dult Fiction], and I hadn't read a YA, which was doing subtle yet still some interesting things.... In *Troll* what worked for me were the questions raised: a gay man in Finland who finds a troll, and for various reasons, falls in lust with the troll. How much is your sexuality affected by what you don't want to do? How much of it is a dark thing going on? And what really made *Troll* work for me is the Filipino mail-order bride, and mail-order brides, even though most of us would totally cringe, they're an accepted part of our society, and how do we juxtapose that with the fact that everyone is so concerned that he fell in love with a troll. Why are mail-order brides and the horrific things done to some of them acceptable in our society while a troll is pure fantasy?... As long as it's doing the Theodore Sturgeon thing, at least making me ask some questions, I'm willing to keep reading.

KJF: Joan talked about a kind of text that leaves room for the reader, a participatory sort of reading as opposed to a text that walks you through it. I want to discuss and add to it something that Lori just said: I wonder if part of being a feminist sf reader is a kind of innately confrontational reading, a sort of... instead of slipping right into a book and being willing to go wherever the writer takes you, is part of the way we read a kind of "prove it, show me, let me think about it first" sort of reading? Speak at will.

CM: I picked up on it when Lori mentioned it as well, and was wondering whether being less trusting of "gosh wow" was actually an artifact of changes in society as much as changes in us becoming more suspicious and things. Back when I was a teenager, there was only one source of news in the UK: the BBC. So actually having science fiction novels that said things that the BBC would never say was interesting and important. Now these days we have a lot of media, different versions of the news. Possibly that's making us more suspicious in our reading and less willing to accept "gosh wow."

KJF: I will point out there is no feminist news channel.

JH: One of the things I was thinking about when I mentioned that point was, I think for me, some of it is about narrative strategies in terms of leaving a space. It's not necessarily that you are engaged in a one-to-one conversation with the narrator. I personally love narratives with multiple points of view where in the interstices, the gaps, and the kind of disruptions between different narrative points of view, characters where you can see the stuff that doesn't fit. For example, just because I've been working with it: in Gwyneth Jones' *Life*, the narrative works backwards and forwards between these two different women; one a passive-aggressive scientist and the other this sort of Camille Paglia-type cipher.† Jones is using them to look at different aspects of feminism, so sometimes they work as real characters and sometimes they are much more about advancing politics. But because she is giving you those different perspectives, then she's giving you as the reader multiple points of identification and therefore the opportunity to assume either one, and [to] follow the narrative one way, or the opportunity to move between those points of view and have a much more complicated narrative journey first time through, which I'm generally too stupid†† to do.

> †JH (Jan. 2007): It's in a transcript so I can't disavow this hugely reductive characterization of Ramone. Here, I'm guilty of the kind of over-simplification for my audience that, with another hat on, I would critique in the public communication of science.
>
> ††JH (Jan. 2007): Special pleading, here. I get annoyed with myself when I've over-identified with a character and have to adjust my theorizing of what's at stake when I shift identifications. I think that's an overly moralistic impulse.

CM: Everyone's too stupid to read Gwyneth's books. She's very clever.

JH: No, this is why I have to read books over again because I do suspend my disbelief, and I do get fully embodied, embedded in one of the characters, and it needs me to read it again to get those kinds of differences. Of course, not all writers are sufficiently skilled to make this rich a reading experience available. Even when they are, they are dependent on the reader to be open to the experience. If they are really effective, and if the reader is not entirely blinkered, they may open up alternative perspectives for the reader almost against the reader's will. In the Starhawk novel I was talking about, there are two main female point-of-view characters, and those were the only ones I could read the first several times I read the book, because my interest in men's points of view was so limited. It was when I finally read it several times and heard the voice of that other character that I realized that my narrative blind spot was a very striking analogy for a kind of feminism that discounts that men can be oppressed by patriarchal relations, too. Sorry, I'm just kind of rambling.

KJF: *Life* is a really complicated and interesting book, and my first time through it I had.... There's a rape and another great injustice of a different sort as well, and I was so focused on expecting that to be resolved in some way—the perpetrator to be exposed, the woman to take some sort of action—I just waited for that. So to me one of the interesting things about it was to think, "Okay, that's not a necessary part of the plotline any more." It seemed to me—I'm not saying this very clearly—it seemed to me, in the end, much more real and interesting that it didn't resolve in the ways I longed for it and waited for it to, and it left me with much more to think about because it didn't.

MM: When I was thinking...of what I did with my students, that's what happens when they move from fiction to theory, when they start to ask themselves, "What does this have to do with my life? Where do I see the fiction playing out in the things that have to do with me?" Again, I'm working with fairly young people who often have read no theory, so how do we move from the fiction to theory, and I guess what I'm thinking is that the two work together: theory gives you language and a way to approach a particular issue, and the fiction can also give you language and metaphor and a way to approach a particular issue.

KJF: This raises something I've been thinking about in terms of this panel and my life. When I had that early experience that your students are still enjoying, the books were very useful to me in terms of my own life. It's harder to find that now. The sexuality issues for aging women, which are, for obvious reasons, the kinds of things I'm interested in now, It's harder to find books about those kinds of things. So along the same lines as "When was the last time a book changed something for you," I've also added, "When was a book really useful to you?" When I was first married and reading all that feminist science fiction, it would change me so completely that I was utterly unfit to live in the real world. My husband would tiptoe around and say, "Let me know when you've finished that book," and there would be a very painful process of readjusting, re-entry. But maybe I just don't let it happen any more; maybe it was too painful.

LS: Some people use books for escapist purposes; finding something that speaks your language and lets you go somewhere else is a good thing. I don't get that experience reading, but I'm also a writer, and I do get it writing, and that's why I do it.

MM: These were painful. I'm thinking of Kate Wilhelm's "The Funeral"—from one of Ellison's anthologies, *Dangerous Visions*—and it was just PAINFUL to read because it felt uncomfortably true. And some of the other ones too, where they were very important for me but also so discouraging of what I thought was going on in my life and what I thought was going on around me. I don't want hopeful books exactly, but I want to feel, "What can I do with this book or this story that somehow changes the way that I'm thinking, changes the world around me, or sees a potential way?" *Life* did some of that for me, made me think about things in a different way. It's not exactly a hopeful book, but at least it's not totally a funeral of "all is lost, all is gloom," and "Funeral" was that way for me.

JH: Can I say something?

KJF: Please do.

JH: One of the reasons I liked Life, and it brings me back to other books—*Pacific Edge*—that I have come to believe that thinking about utopia as something fully formed and complete is a wrong thing to do. A character in *Pacific Edge* defines Utopia as "struggle forever," and that seems to me the best description of utopia that I can imagine. And I think for me that's useful, because it is about process and struggle and movement. The near future portrayed in *Life is* not perfect by any manner of means, but some of the things that Gwyneth Jones does with the narrative are hopeful, in the sense that "struggle forever" is a much more realistic take on the process of working for a better world. So I think hope, hope is about, I think, being able to take action; you don't know how it's going to turn out but you think you can do something. Novels or any kinds of texts that help you believe you can do things are really useful. Books aren't just useful to me to think about stuff, they're to help me hold myself together; that's one of the reasons I read, to hold myself together, because sometimes the "struggle forever" is too hard. It doesn't always have to be theory; it can be about speaking to you or parts of you in ways that other parts of the world don't.

CM: Maybe I'm just old and cynical, but I've gotten to the stage where I know that nobody else is going to hold myself together but me, and I read books for other reasons: the style or whatever. They occasionally say interesting political things, but I no longer expect solutions from them.

MM: But even if it's a light little touch that makes me go, "This story couldn't have been written ten years ago," there's a very light-hearted story—kissing frogs—and it's a story where a person who is transgendering puts a want ad to meet somebody, and the story couldn't have been written, couldn't have been published, I think, twenty years ago, and the fact that it can and even be listed for a Tiptree makes me feel hopeful about the world.

KJF: What about it makes you think it couldn't have been published then?

MM: I don't think a character treated very lightly, very humorously, that's in the midst of transgendering, could have been published twenty or twenty-five years ago. A story that treats the whole concept of transgendering and going through that as so commonplace that it's treated humorously, I don't think that could have been done.

CM: Certainly there have been transgendered characters for a long time—Angela Carter's *Passion of New Eve*, for example—I think the point you're making is that the character is treated sympathetically.

MM: The author didn't have to do a lot of work because the audience accepted it, and I think that's hopeful.

KJF: I think that perhaps I've gotten too cynical

LS: Cynical?

KJF: It's easy for me to forget how much progress really has been made since I was growing up, because in some ways the vision that I got from these books was a sort of "all or nothing, either we win or we lose," and I've been very surprised in some ways by the focus on masculinity. Because in the '70s, when I was first encountering this stuff and hearing about it, it was very clear to me that it was for both sexes. Partly because I had children, it was very clear that the male role was going to have to change for feminism to succeed the way I wanted it to. That women would work outside the home and then come home and do all the work there as well was not what I was envisioning. What I longed for was such a deep and profound change that it's hard for me to take the pleasure that perhaps I ought to in the things we have accomplished.

MM: At that point I needed to have my consciousness raised. I was a young woman who had been raised in a very stereotypical world, and I needed painful, and needed the rug pulled out from under me. I actually had a young woman this term who was twenty write that she had never thought much about gender. I was probably there at twenty as well. I'm willing to read the painful works occasionally, but I want them to raise questions for me. Fantasy and sf for me are to disrupt reality but not to break it down so much that it can't be built back up.

CM: A couple of things in this: clearly, as you get older there's a lack of willingness to change; you have more to lose, the job, the family—all that kind of stuff. I like to think I'm not like that, possibly because I don't have much to lose—no job, not much social status.... But, I think, after you've thrown yourself enthusiastically in something for thirty or more years, everything involves people and everything that involves people involves politics and is a struggle and won't work the way you thought it would.

JH: I don't know if it was what I said about masculinity you were thinking about. When I was reading *Woman on the Edge of Time* and Firestone, it wasn't that I wasn't aware that men had to change, but it was more that they had to change the way I thought they had to change.

KJF: And so they should.

JH: But I want them to change how I want them, not the way you want them‡; I don't care about you. And fiction reminds me of other points of view that are useful. But I'm a bit suspicious of linear progress models of history and also of subjectivity identity or whatever. But I have to keep learning and forgetting the same lessons over and over again. And maybe this is one of my kind of things about re-reading. A lot of the talk on the panel has been about fiction as a progression, and I think you're making interesting and real and valid points about things being made possible that weren't possible before, but going back to stuff written in another period of time is still useful now and is one of the ways that I do theory. Stuff doesn't have to be novel to be useful. I'm going to stop there.

> ‡ JH (Jan. 2007): This transcript just underlines for me the riskiness of transcribing a spoken debate. All the extra-verbal communication conveyed by tone of voice and gesture is lost.
>
> What I'm pretty sure I was trying to convey was that I attributed rather more compassion towards men in Karen' case than my own—rightly or wrongly. I keep returning to *The Fifth Sacred Thing* because for me finally inhabiting Bird's point of view was a huge *Eureka!* experience. It seemed that it was the first text that really made me care about how hard it would be—even for pro-feminist men—for men to adjust to the transformed social relations I yearn(ed) for.

KJF: And I'll bring up the always amazing Ursula K. Le Guin. The last time I read *The Left Hand of Darkness*, a couple of years ago, I had a new thought about it, part of which was, to some extent, that it is literally true. Her aliens become male or become female depending on the external stimulus that's provided at the time, and that's something that we do ourselves as well. Something that I was taking purely as a thought experiment, I can now see in a different way.

MM: We need to keep those books in print because there are still people coming up who are twenty who have never thought about gender and need the painful works.

Aud: Margaret, you said a little while ago that you weren't looking for hopeful books. Is it impossible for a hopeful book to pull the rug out for under you?

LS and MM: Oh yeah, it's possible.

Aud (Vonda N. McIntyre): I get pages with 300 abuses of women and with blurbs that say "you'll love this book," and I don't think people needed to write that book after Suzy McKee Charnas' *Walk to the End of the World.*

KJF: There's your blurb right there: "Didn't need to be written; go read some Suzy McKee Charnas."

Aud (Vonda N. McIntyre): 300 pages of wallowing in the abuse of women to prove that abuse of women is bad, which, *duh*. He kept pestering me. The publisher said,

"But you don't understand, Vonda. The way you can tell the bad guys is that they're abusing women."

MM: I agree with you, but there are people who haven't read Suzy Charnas, but they might read something new. So I think there is still some reason for those books to be written.

Aud: But shouldn't sf go beyond that and have some attention paid to it beyond, "That's a hopeful book, and I'm too cynical to read it."

CM: I think there are plenty of good books around; that's not an issue. But at the same time, I think there are people who need to be shocked out of their complacency, realize that there are people out there who are not as well off as they are.

LS: Hope is great; it's the actual rearrangement of my thinking that doesn't happen, and if it were to happen I would have to realize that someone was snowing me. But hope—that Pandora experience—there are tons of things being thrown at you.

KJF: I would turn that around and ask you, Suzy McKee Charnas' book aside, is there a book without hope that could still be a valuable book, or would that not be a helpful experience?

Aud: A book without hope…

KJF: I'm thinking that would be a great title.

Aud: You can write it.

KJF: I can write it; I can read it; I can self-publish it.

Aud: I've had the experience of writing what I thought were hopeful books and being told I'm not a feminist. "You're a feminist? Not serious…" Maybe the light at the end of the tunnel, the light shining on us for the last thirty years, is having an effect.

Aud 2: Thinking of Laurie Marks' fantasy series, bad things happening to men and women, yet hope that people will live together; trying to get beyond the cynical thing.

Aud 3: I'm not trying to say there shouldn't be bad things happening or even drama or melodrama in a book, but the assumption that bad things happen because you're female or a kid, I just, with my own work, I want to get beyond that.

CM: Laurie's books are an excellent example. In them, people are working hard on politics, trying to learn from each other. That's particularly helpful because someone is learning what needs to be done.

Aud: Add to that short story "The Matter of Seggri"; I found that to be very powerful and very hopeful.

Aud 2: Theory-building—there are lots of different aspects. One of them is the nineteen-year-old's experience, getting in touch with one's inner three-year-old and making you say "why?" Books that get inside me and shake up my theoretical base are books that see something that I've never seen, even though it's right in front of me. For me, Gwyneth Jones' *White Queen* and *North Wind* did that for me.

LS: *Troll* did that for me. I can't articulate my response to *Troll* in any meaningful way whatsoever, but it did make me go "hmm."

MM: I'm not sure I can say why, but the first thing that came to my mind were the stories that retell fairy stories and that made me go, "Ahhh, why was that particular trope always there in the fairy tale, and what happens when we come at it from another point of view?"

KJF: It's not a text, so I don't know if it's a fair response to your question or not, but I have been—of course, as many of us have been—living in the US for the last several years, and I've become very conscious of the whole war narrative: we're going to war, we've been attacked, and the tremendous power of that storyline. And my reaction has been very much, what an unnecessary part of the world war seems, to me, to be, but how much the people who aren't actually going off to do the fighting seem to thrill to that storyline. Not necessarily thrilled by the war itself, but by the power of that narrative. I get taken in by appalling sorts of sentimentalism in the movies. My family is always looking at me: "Are you crying?" Of course not! Nonsense.

CM: I think a lot of the really interesting stuff I've read of late has to do with state of the world and gender politics. I'm thinking of "Foundation," a short story that China Miéville wrote about the Iraq War

Aud: In terms of where I started as a feminist sf reader to do and where I look for and what I look for—I didn't know Vonda was there—but I started with *Dreamsnake*, and it struck me as very humane, and it was incredibly helpful. It was a young woman character taking action in her universe for change, in a very loving and assertive way, and that was earth-shattering for me at the time. And here I am, twenty-five, thirty years later and having studied Women's Studies in college. The world around me today has become a place where the percentage of things that I thought were movable issues compared with the percentage of things I thought were intractable, and things I thought were given have completely changed. I used to believe, early on, that everything was movable and changeable; and some intractable, and I didn't have a bead on them, and then they'd be movable. And I sit here today and look at the world—*Touched By Venom* created a lot of controversy—and part of the story is that women are horribly treated, and is this news—and I don't think it's news—but the reality is, you don't need a book to find it; it goes on in places of war, poverty, etc. So now I find myself in not just a place of movable, intractable, etc., but hopelessness because maybe the given is a bigger percentage than I'd ever considered based on biology and the nature of universe, and that's what has me reading now for things, like Joan said, holding myself together as a person, as opposed to "wow's." Because I'm getting "wow's" from the world, and I'm all for a hopeful telling, and I think Laurie Marks' is a very hopeful view of the universe, but that given is scary.

Aud 2: "Congenital Agenesis of Gender Ideation"—a story I recently read that said something about gender I'd never seen before. The first story I'd seen that asked what kind of mind you'd have to have to not see gender before.

KJF: It had an impact on me, because of how had I not noticed the gradations—two sexes, three, four—and then I read that book, and think, "Oh, right, it's twenty-five or thirty." Also, thinking about flexibility of sexuality in that story…

Aud: I read John Varley short stories I'd never read before. I was amazed to find he is the closest person to have written the kissing frog story in 1976 if Tiptree hadn't been doing things like that. John Varley now seems to write Heinleinian space opera for kids with some gender stuff, but…

CM: I haven't read John Varley's stories myself, but two to three years ago, we had a panel with transgender issues, and the message I got from those transgendered people who had read him was that Varley's treatment of such themes was superficial. Some of the non-transgendered people who had read him were surprised and even shocked by this.

Aud: And yet you can't change the gender of the character even superficially without changing the expectations of the reader, etc., because you don't know what the author intended.

Aud 2: Another thing: is there much of gender stuff in new or old space opera?

CM: A character in *Chasm City* by Alastair Reynolds mentioned having changed sex a long time ago. That again was very superficial. I got the impression that changing gender was something the character had done simply because he was bored and wanted to try being female, which isn't the way it happens for real transgendered people.

JH: I think Justina Robson is really interesting with regard to gender and space opera, but currently I don't have time to read enough fiction in the way I want to. I think the discussion [above] about the way in which I read gives you a sense of the problem. I've started reading Robson and I am interested in thinking more about her work. I don't want to get into progress models, but I do think different generations do things in different ways—different generational models. I want [fiction] to say something about feminism; not just about gender: sexuality, race, class, and multiple other hierarchies of oppression. And so it doesn't have to be about "just gender." That doesn't have to be the lens to consider feminist theory-building to be organized about, necessarily.

LS: Gavin, are you suggesting that Space Babe is feminist theory-building?

CM: *Living Next Door to the God of Love* has a character who is a god. When we first meet him he's working as a drag queen.

KJF: Eleanor Arnason's *Ring of Swords* is one of the texts I return to a lot.

MM: *Light*, which won the Tiptree, has gender elements. Sometimes space opera has so much going on, if I were to look at gender, I would have to read again—there's too much. But to go back to the point about gender not being the main aspect of feminism, I sat down before this panel and said, "What have I read about in Theory?" and I made a list, and I think you will be able to come up with sf that does something with every single one of those bodies; technology; nature, environment and its association with feminism; language; race and colonialism; boundary and border blurring; power issues; categorizing and universalizing.

KJF: Is it possible to love a book which is absolutely offensive on its sexual politics? Can you give me an example of a book that you love despite every moral fiber of your being?

MM: I find them useful and use them in my classes… For example: from 1972 a sentence that is not from a character. A male writer wrote this—a very well-known sf writer—in the universal voice: "she handled the car skillfully, for a woman, particularly for a beautiful woman."

Aud: *The Female Man* by Joanna Russ does wonderful things for politics in terms of women's state of being, but also has nasty things to say about trans-women that come straight out of Janice Raymond…

LS: The first Earthsea book. I actually have that more these days with movies.

KJF: My family is completely looking at me these days, "Are you crying?" Of course not! Nonsense.

JH: Sheri Tepper's *Gate to Women's Country*, which I do love, but her feminism is a deeply troubling feminism: eugenic, totalizing—that's scary. But there are aspects that are very seductive because of the parts I think she gets right, but I think she gets it right based on a completely dodgy and biologist premise that I wouldn't want to indulge for a minute. But when people represent it as a utopia, I want to remonstrate with them, especially when they mean utopia as "the nice place that doesn't yet exist that we'd like to live in." I just want to shout: have you *read* it? There are some books that are really deeply problematic but are also really satisfying to my inner feminist totalitarian. But I want other books that make me wake up to myself and think again.

MM: I will be trapped, because, yes, I have great problems with *Gate to Women's Country*, but from a stylistic perspective, with the play, it works for me, and it also works as a teaching tool.

CM: I do tend to react particularly badly to books that I disagree with the obvious politics of. If the politics are very clearly bad, I tend to hate the book, but I have this awful feeling that there are all these books that I really enjoy, and that if I sat down to think about the underlying politics and gender assumptions, I would hate them.

KJF: Well, we will go from here and work on our level of outrage, and hopefully on our level of hopefulness.

Afterword

CM: When reading it is very easy to just let yourself be entertained, or to miss the debate going on between authors in books you are reading. So building a theory from books is difficult and error-prone. Going to WisCon is much more likely to make you think seriously and clearly about the issues.

MM: To answer the panel question more directly, Yes, reading Feminist sf can be a theory building activity especially for younger people who may not have thought much about gender, equity, etc. but also for those who have read widely in feminist fiction or feminist theory. We will still find books that raise questions for us or make us rethink some of our ideas.

Laura Quilter, librarian and lawyer, is the founder of the *Feminist Fantasy, Science Fiction, and Utopia* website.

http://lquilter.net or feministsf.org

Alicia Austin

Lisa Tuttle

Q: What did you take back to Scotland from WisCon 30?

A: A box of books, a head full of ideas, a bunch of good intentions, and a warm glow of energy. Yet—can that really be seven months ago?—most of the books are still in a box, the ideas are still just buds and fragments, and so, despite those intentions and energy, I haven't yet sent a book proposal to the Aqueduct Press for the Conversation Pieces series, nor made any visible progress on a new novel…but I will! I may be able to tell you more precisely what I brought back after the experience has had a couple of years to mulch down. Ask me again later.

Lisa Tuttle was born in Texas and now resides in Scotland. Her latest novels include *The Silver Bough* and *The Mysteries,* both from Bantam. WisCon 9 GoH.

http://www.lisatuttle.com/

Piercy's Gendered Cyborgs: Hope, Threat, and Blurred Boundaries

Linda Wight

Marge Piercy's *He, She and It* (1991) focuses on Yod, a twenty-first century male "cyborg" created by the male scientist, Avram. In the acknowledgments section of the novel, Piercy writes: "Donna Haraway's essay "A Cyborg Manifesto" was extremely suggestive" (*He, She, and It*, 1991, 431; hereafter *HSI*). Reflecting Haraway's influence, Piercy explores the limitations of gender imposed upon the cyborg figure, while emphasizing the cyborg's potential both for unfaithfulness to its origins as well as for blurring the boundaries between the human and non-human, and masculinity and femininity.

Piercy's decision to label Yod a cyborg is controversial. Peter Fitting represents the view that Yod is an android rather than a cyborg,[1] explaining, "A cyborg is the physical bonding of human and machine—a human who has in some way been augmented or enhanced. A robot or android, on the other hand, is a new entity, built or grown from organic and/or non-organic materials" (1994, 5). Other critics de-emphasize the human aspect of the cyborg. Chris Hables Gray suggests that a cyborg can be anything from a human with a neuro-controlled prosthesis, to a computer made up of organic biochips, to a robot with a thin veneer of human skin (1993, 142). Piercy adopts this broader definition, asserting Yod's biological origins through his lover Shira, who says, "You're as much a part of earth as I am. We are all made of the same molecules, the same set of compounds, the same elements" (*HSI*, 85).

The Encyclopedia of Science Fiction reveals the difficulty of separating the terms used to define artificial humanoids. While "android" usually denotes an artificial human of organic substance, it is also sometimes linked to manlike machines, just as "robot" is sometimes applied to organic entities (1993, 34). Labeling Yod a cyborg further blurs these boundaries, questioning the criteria for such a classification. Diane Sautter argues that the qualities that allow Yod to be considered a person transcend the physical body, existing in a realm that the science of physical measurement does not enter (1996, 263). Piercy's classification of Yod as a cyborg and the emphasis on his spiritual and mental personhood thus challenges the privileging of the material in the human/non-human debate by masculinist science and some sf.[2]

Nevertheless, *He, She and It* reveals an important difference between Yod and the text's female cyborgs. Nili, Shira, and Malkah are all originally human and technologically augmented. Crucially, all are free to adapt cyborg technologies to develop their own identities and goals. In contrast, Yod is constructed and his identity limited and controlled to fulfill his creators' ideals of masculinity. Fitting emphasizes that personal agency is the central element separating the cyborg from the robot (1994, 6). His creators' external control over who he is and what he does aligns Yod more closely with the robot, ultimately limiting his ability to subvert his creators' assumptions about gender and challenge the power of his male creator.

Constructed by the male scientist, Avram, programmed by the female scientist and software designer, Malkah, and socialized by Shira, Yod demonstrates how easily the artificially constructed cyborg can be constrained by the gender-inflected desires of its creators. Yod is primarily constructed via masculinist science as an embodiment of Avram's ideal of rational, violent, mechanical masculinity. Claudia Springer claims that the cyborg image often asserts an essential masculinity that transcends threats and changes to the vulnerable male body (1999, 48-9). Through Yod, Piercy maps the contending forces of gendered desire: while masculine science attempts to construct its ideal male to provide reassurance of an invulnerable, superior masculinity, orthodox femininity tries to reshape it into the ideal of the "romantic" masculine.

As June Deery suggests, Avram creates Yod as a male because he envisages Yod as a replacement son, as well as a second self (2000, 94). Avram constructs Yod as a replacement for his biological son, Gadi, whose rebellion threatens Avram's assertion of universal masculinity. Furthermore, Yod reflects Avram's desire for a son who demonstrates superior masculinity yet poses no threat to the father's power and control.

He, She and It implies that the ideal of the perfect son is often linked to a dream of immortality, to be achieved through the son's replication of the father's masculinity. N. Katherine Hayles explains, "As the sense of its mortality grows, humankind looks for its successor and heir, harboring the secret hope that the heir can somehow be enfolded back into the self" (1995, 334). Hayles notes that biological reproduction threatens the masculine wish for replication, operating as a genetic lottery (333). Thus Avram seeks to replace reproduction with the certainties of production, creating his cyborg as a perfect replicant of his imagined masculinity.

Yod's construction as replicant highlights the centrality of violence to Avram's masculine ideal. Helen Longino and Ruth Doell observe that many scientists endorse the link between violence and masculinity by claiming that males exhibit a higher level of aggression as a function of their testosterone levels (1996, 80). Amanda Fernbach indicates that the image of the warrior cyborg reflects this violent ideal, allowing men to disavow the anxiety they feel in a postmodern world (2000, 241). Thus Yod reassures Avram of the continued power and superiority of his own masculinity.

Cyborg theorists have recognized the cyborg's potential to enhance the power of its creators. Gray reflects that the military has midwived cyborgs into the twentieth century

(1993, 146)[3]; he describes the military vision as one of "machine-like endurance with a redefined human intellect subordinated to the overall weapon system" (Gray cited in Oehlert 1995, 227). In line with this, Avram creates Yod as a weapon of remarkable strength, skill, and intelligence, yet crucially subordinate to Avram's control.

He, She and It warns of the dangers of the warrior cyborg. Gray, Mentor, and Figueroa caution, "Sure it's neato-keeno technology, but the cyborg might be the herald of the Apocalypse as well" (1995, 2). The uncontrollable violence of Yod's cyborg predecessors culminates in the murder of Avram's assistant. Thus Piercy's cyborgs, constructed in the image of their "father's" masculine ideal, implicitly offer a critique of the consequences of reproducing its central demand for violence.

While *He, She and It* criticizes this masculine ideal, it also critiques the cyborg created to serve a female ideal of romantic masculinity. Following the tradition of Tanith Lee's *The Silver Metal Lover* (1981), Piercy recognizes that women can also be attracted to constructing and controlling a cyborg to fulfill their romantic desires and gendered ideals. Frances Bonner suggests that the resistance of real men to change may make their re-imagining in programmable form irresistible (1996, 113). Accordingly, Shira initially values Yod over her ex-husband Josh for the potential to control and mould him into her masculine ideal: "She wished she could have reprogrammed Josh" (*HSI*, 72).

Piercy implies, however, that women are more likely to recognize the problems of such control because in many ways the cyborg is aligned with the feminine. Deery observes that like many women, Yod is regarded as an object rather than a subject, must be attuned to every nuance of human interaction, is ridiculed by being reduced to a sex toy, and is not paid for his labor (2000, 95). Malkah and Shira are able to empathize with Yod because patriarchal society has also tried to control and constrain them. As a result, Malkah and Shira reject the temptation to limit Yod's identity within their romantic ideal and take responsibility for the consequences of their desires for a perfect man; when Yod murders Josh, Shira acknowledges that his actions were committed in response to her desires.

Despite Malkah and Shira's determination not to control Yod, *He, She and It* remains conscious of the potential for the creators' assumptions about gender to be transferred to the cyborg. Cyborg theorists also acknowledge that assumptions about gender are inherent in technology. Jennifer González, for instance, emphasizes that cyborgs cannot float above the assumptions of their specific cultural setting (1995, 272). This tendency to imbue technology with gender is exacerbated by the cyborg's close resemblance to the human. This is demonstrated in *He, She and It* by Shira, who increasingly uses the pronoun "he" as she becomes more willing to view Yod as a person and aware of his potential to fulfill her masculine ideal. Gray argues that the gender-coding of technology is particularly evident within the military where enlisted personnel and enemies are coded feminine and weapons masculine (1993, 152). Therefore, when Avram seeks to create his cyborg as a weapon, his assumptions linking military aggression with masculinity transfer onto his creation.

Despite these limitations, *He, She and It* thoughtfully explores Haraway's suggestion that the cyborg has the potential to be unfaithful to its origins and develop beyond its imposed constraints to blur gender boundaries. Jenny Wolmark claims that cyborg narratives challenge the notion of a fixed and natural human identity, destabilizing what are held to be the innate characteristics of masculinity and femininity and revealing them to be cultural fictions (1993, 127). Deery draws attention to the title of *He, She and It*, which focuses critical attention on conventional gender demarcations (2000, 94). A product of masculine and feminine programming, Yod combines supposedly contradictory and rigidly separate gender attributes that are, in fact, also usually blended within "real" men and women. Deery notes that although Piercy may be seen to polarize masculine and feminine traits, Yod's endowment with distinct gender characteristics makes him a laboratory for gender cross-fertilization (94).

He, She and It posits that Yod's potential for undermining the gender binary results from the cyborg's lack of socialization. Unlike a child, the cyborg emerges fully grown, holding no preconceived ideas about "normal" gender. Yod's lack of preconceptions about what a woman should be allows Shira the freedom to act without fear of judgment. And Yod's lack of commitment to the masculine ideal allows him to be a better father to Shira's son, Ari, because he has no sense of his son as a possession and no preconceived standard of masculinity that he expects Ari to live up to.

The exploration of the cyborg's potential for rebellion draws on a long tradition in sf. Steffen Hantke notes that since Mary Shelley's *Frankenstein* (1818), sf has explored the fear of science escaping the control of the scientists (1998, 495). While much early sf greets this potential with fear, cyborg theorists generally celebrate the possibility of the cyborg transcending its origins. Haraway, for instance, stresses that although cyborgs are the illegitimate offspring of militarism and patriarchal capitalism, they are often exceedingly unfaithful to their origins: "Their fathers, after all, are inessential" (1991, 151). Like Piercy's female characters who dismiss fathers as irrelevant, Yod dismisses Avram's expectations. His attempts to escape Avram's control celebrate the potential of the constructed male cyborg to escape its masculinist origins. As Yod explains to Shira, "My programming isn't an absolute any more than your education was" (*HSI*, 211), indicating his—and humanity's—potential to transcend gender socialization.

Notably, Yod signals his difference from robots when he reveals his potential to harm his maker. In contradiction to Asimov's Laws of Robotics, Yod asserts his willingness and ability to hold Avram to account for Avram's own actions. While in *Frankenstein* women pay the price for the mistakes of masculinist science, in *He, She and It* Avram is punished by his own dangerous cyborg construction when Yod kills him and destroys his research. Avram's death indicates that although Yod could not escape the violence implicit in his imposed masculine identity, he could recognize the problems of the ideal, hold Avram accountable, and ensure that such a creation could not be repeated.

Yod's rebellion is largely made possible by his historical awareness. Piercy explains, "To me it is an important task to situate ourselves in the time line so that we may be active in history. We require a past that leads to us" (1994, 1-2). Malkah's story of Joseph, the sixteenth century golem of Prague, allows Yod insight into the motivations of his male creator and the consequences of his own existence. This allows Yod to reject Joseph's fate of being created and used solely as a weapon before being destroyed by his maker. Although Yod is forced to self-destruct, he is able to hold Avram accountable, destroy him, and assert his belief that the masculinist warrior cyborg has no place in the eco-feminist future of Tikva.

Ultimately, however, Yod's potential as a hopeful cyborg figure for the future is limited. Yod can only reject and destroy an unsatisfactory cyborg masculinity; he cannot provide an alternative symbol of hope and a permanent challenge to masculine superiority. Instead, the cyborgian hope of *He, She and It* rests with Nili, the female cyborg, who ends the novel as powerful and independent as she began, forming alliances for her feminist community.

Monica Casper indicates that the proliferation of cyborgs may be conceptualized as a continuum, with "choice" at one end and "no choice" at the other (1995, 197). Nili represents the "choice" end of the continuum and thus succeeds where Yod fails. Born in an all-female community free of male control, her body technologically enhanced to meet the demands of her post-apocalyptic environment, Nili is used by Piercy to prioritize female self-reproduction over man-made production. Cyborg technology holds great utopian potential, but only if the cyborgs themselves can control it.

The novel's portrayal of Nili also blurs the gender binary more convincingly than does its portrayal of Yod. In her depiction of Yod, Piercy does attempt to challenge gender boundaries by combining masculine and feminine traits within his identity. In the process, however, Piercy fails to problematize traditional classifications of masculine and feminine behaviors and thus risks essentializing such definitions. Although Piercy reverses patriarchal assumptions by defining Yod's feminine characteristics as positive and his masculine characteristics as negative, her strict classification of human behaviors leaves the gender binary intact. Piercy's portrayal of Nili is also androgynous, combining traditionally masculine attributes such as strength, physicality, and the capacity for violence with an obviously female body and a traditionally feminine concern for connection, community, and motherhood. The text, however, labels these traits neither masculine nor feminine, but simply presents them as aspects of Nili's identity. None are superior, and each is integral to Nili's cyborg existence.

Finally, Nili is more subversive than Yod because her cyborg identity is just one possibility in a range of multiple cyborg and feminist positions. The novel emphasizes how different the cyborg women in Nili's community are from one another. This contrasts with the portrayal of Yod and his nine predecessors, who were all constructed by Avram to the same singular, stable ideal of masculinity. Gray and Mentor insist that the metaphor of the cyborg is subject to proliferation and hybridization; it should not be prescriptive so much as descriptive of possibilities (1995, 463). Each female character in *He, She and It* represents an alternative female cyborg who adapts herself technologically to meet the needs of her unique situation. The alliance among Nili's Black Zone, Tikva, and the communities of the Glop underlines that successful cyborg politics must celebrate difference and welcome alliances across different communities. As Wolmark explains, cyborg politics are inclusive rather than exclusive, sympathetic to difference, and based on the possibility that new and strategic alliances can be forged between unexpected groups (1994, 4).

Thus, the figure of Nili's female cyborg becomes a hopeful cyborg image for the future, not simply because of her freedom from external control, but because her cyborg identity is open to, and compatible with, a celebration of difference. By contrast, despite his connection to Malkah and Shira, ultimately Yod must act alone, and ultimately he must perish.

Endnotes

1 Like Fitting, *The Encyclopedia of Science Fiction* also emphasizes the human aspect of the cyborg: "The term 'cyborg'...refers to the product of human/machine hybridization" (1993, 290). Yod is an entirely artificial construction rather than an augmented human and as such would not fit Clute and Nicholls' definition of the cyborg.

2 Feminist scientists identify a masculinist approach to science that rejects subjectivity and spirituality and instead asserts the possibility of value-free, objective knowledge of the material world. For instance, Evelyn Fox Keller and Christine Grantkowski draw attention to Descartes' claim that the material world is accessible through scientific, objective reasoning (1996, 194-5). Similarly, Genevieve Lloyd highlights the sixteenth century claims of Francis Bacon and the Royal Society that only through sensory observation and experimental testing of the material world can genuine knowledge be attained (1996, 48). In *He, She and It* Avram draws on this tradition, dismissing anything that he cannot perceive with his analytical senses as mere fantasy (Sautter 1996, 256).

3 Gray, Mentor, and Figueroa explain that since World War II the military has led the way in cyborg research and the development of cyborg technologies in its endeavor to create a man-machine weapon system (1995, 9). Thus, although the medical research and entertainment industries have contributed to developing the concept and physical reality of the cyborg, most cyborg technologies have military origins (3).

Works Cited

Bonner, F. 1996. From *The Female Man* to the *Virtual Girl*: Whatever Happened to Feminist SF? *Hecate* 22(1):104-19.

Casper, M. J. 1995. Fetal Cyborgs and Technomums on the Reproductive Frontier: Which Way to the Carnival? In *The Cyborg Handbook*, ed. Chris Hables Gray, 183-202. New York: Routledge.

Clute, J., and P. Nicholls, Eds. 1993. *The Encyclopedia of Science Fiction*. London: Orbit.

Deery, J. 2000. The Biopolitics of Cyberspace: Piercy Hacks Gibson. In *Future Females*,

The Next Generation: New Voices and Velocities in Feminist Science Fiction Criticism, ed. M. S. Barr, 87-108. Lanham: Rowman & Littlefield Publishers, Inc.

Fernbach, A. 2000. The Fetishisation of Masculinity in Science Fiction: The Cyborg and the Console Cowboy. *Science Fiction Studies*. 27(2):234-55.

Fitting, P. 1994. Beyond the Wasteland: A Feminist in Cyberspace. *Utopian Studies* 5(2):4-15.

González, J. 1995. Envisioning Cyborg Bodies: Notes from Current Research. In *The Cyborg Handbook*, ed. C. H. Gray, 267-79. New York: Routledge.

Gray, C. H. 1993. The Culture of War Cyborgs: Technoscience, Gender, and Postmodern War. *Research in Philosophy and Technology*. 13:141-63.

Gray, C. H., and Steven Mentor. 1995. The Cyborg Body Politic: Version 1.2. In *The Cyborg Handbook*, ed. C. H. Gray, 432-67. New York: Routledge.

Gray, C.H, Steven Mentor, and Heidi J. Figueroa-Sarriera. 1995. Cyborgology: Constructing the Knowledge of Cybernetic Organisms. In *The Cyborg Handbook*, ed. C. H. Gray, 1-14. New York: Routledge.

Hantke, S. 1998. Surgical Strikes and Prosthetic Warriors: The Soldier's Body in Contemporary Science Fiction. *Science Fiction Studies*. 25:495-509.

Haraway, E. 1991. A Cyborg Manifesto: Science, Technology, and Socialist-Feminism in the Late Twentieth Century. In *Simians, Cyborgs, and Women: The Reinvention of Nature*, 149-81. New York: Routledge.

Hayles, N. K. 1995. The Life Cycle of Cyborgs: Writing the Posthuman. In *The Cyborg Handbook*, ed. C. H. Gray, 321-35. New York: Routledge.

Keller, E. F., and C, R. Grantkowski. 1996. The Mind's Eye. In *Feminism and Science*, eds. E. F. Keller and H. E. Longino, 187-202. Oxford: Oxford University Press.

Lee, T. 1981. *The Silver Metal Lover*. Garden City, New York: Nelson Doubleday Inc.

Lloyd, G. 1996. Reason, Science and the Domination of Matter. In *Feminism and Science*, eds. E. F. Keller and H. E. Longino, 41-53. Oxford: Oxford University Press.

Longino, H. E., and R. Doell. 1996. Body, Bias, and Behaviour: A Comparative Analysis of Reasoning in Two Areas of Biological Science. In *Feminism and Science*, eds. E. F. Keller and H. E. Longino, 73-90. Oxford: Oxford University Press.

Oehlert, M. 1995. From Captain America to Wolverine: Cyborgs in Comic Books, Alternative Images of Cybernetic Heroes and Villains. In *The Cyborg Handbook*, ed. C. H. Gray, 219-32. New York: Routledge.

Piercy, M. 1991. *He, She and It*. New York: Fawcett Books.

———. 1994. Telling Stories About Stories. *Utopian Studies*. 5.2: 1-3.

Sautter, D. 1996. Erotic and Existential Paradoxes of the Golem: Marge Piercy's *He, She and It*. *Journal of the Fantastic in the Arts*. 7(2-3):255-68.

Shelley, M. 1992. *Frankenstein, or The Modern Prometheus*. ed. J. M. Smith. Boston: Bedford Books of St. Martin's.

Springer, C. 1999. The Pleasure of the Interface. *Cybersexualities: A Reader on Feminist Theory, Cyborgs, and Cyberspace*, ed. Jenny Wolmark, 34-54. Edinburgh: Edinburgh University Press.

Wolmark, J. 1993. *Aliens and Others: Science Fiction, Feminism and Postmodernism*. Hertfordshire: Harvester Wheatsheaf,

———. 1999. Introduction and Overview. In *Cybersexualities: A Reader on Feminist Theory, Cyborgs, and Cyberspace*, ed. J. Wolmark, 1-10. Edinburgh: Edinburgh University Press.

Linda Wight, a PhD student at James Cook University, Queensland, Australia, is passionately interested in gender-bending sf, and her thesis explores representations of masculinity in Tiptree Award shortlisted texts.

Diantha Day Sprouse

Q: Was there a single event that especially stood out for you at the last WisCon?

A. The answer is:
Racism is a social disease that most racists don't know they have.

If you had asked me that question directly after WisCon 30, I may have been able to pick out one single event or panel that was still a hot topic for me. As it is, in hindsight, I find that several events, panels, and discussions shaped WisCon 30 for me. First the positive events that shaped the Con for me. After thirty years, I finally got to meet Kate Wilhelm. WOW!

I was also honored to have tea with Ursula Le Guin, Carol Emshwiller, and Kate Wilhelm, while waiting for our respective panels to convene. What a trinity!

The Carl Brandon Society was born out of the pain of isolation and loneliness felt by those of us who attended WisCon on a regular basis but were not members of the dominant culture. We were few and quickly got lost in the sea of white faces. Then something remarkable happened: wonderfully kind and gracious Jean Gomoll introduced me to Victor Raymond. She said, "There is a very interesting man I'd like you to meet. I think you will have a lot to talk about."

And we did. The next thing I knew he was introducing me to a wide variety of people of color, and we were scheduling meetings and having discussions about the visibility and understanding of cultural differences.

For the past ten years I have been part of the Feminist Cabal involved with the birth of the Carl Brandon Society. As one of the many midwives involved in this intrepid endeavor to increase the visibility and understanding of persons of color at WisCon and in the genre in general, I was delighted with the presentation of the Kindred and Parallax Awards at WisCon 30. The pregnancy was prolonged and the labor intense and sometimes agonizingly painful, but the delivery of two beautiful WisCon children was worth the effort and pain. The delight we experienced at the birth of Kindred and Parallax was tinged with sadness and regret for the untimely death of our wonderful friend, helper, and ground-breaking author, Octavia E. Butler.

Now for the negative. While these events did not ruin my WisCon experience, they sure did make me sit up and take notice. At WisCon 30 something happened during and after several panels dealing with the issues of race, ethnicity, and cultural appropriation that created a tidal wave of discussion in the halls, in meeting rooms, in the hotel lobby, etc. Almost everywhere I turned the discussions about race and cultural appropriations were intense. This was unusual in the sense that such discussions had been rather low key for the past several years. That is not to say that problems did not exist, for they did. Low-key discussions were held, consensus was reached, and we moved ahead. Victor Raymond and Nalo Hopkinson, both diplomats in their own right, were often at the forefront of these negotiations. We found that we had staunch allies in Jeanne Gomoll and Scott Custis, just to name two of the many. The Carl Brandon Society had helped create, maintain, and nurture a sense of WisCon being a safe haven for persons of color. The amount of anger, hostility, rage, resentment, and disrespect aimed at persons of color and their heritages during WisCon 30 left me marveling at how far we have not come in healing the wounds of racism's reign of terror in this land.

I grew up in the segregated South. I know racism first hand. I also know the backlash that came after desegregation and the language that went with it—or should I say goes with it: present tense. I say present tense because that very same language of disrespect and hatred was being used in the discussions on race, ethnicity, and cultural appropriations taking place in the hallways, rooms, and meeting places at WisCon 30. I offer the following as examples of echoes from the backlash against desegregation heard at WisCon 30. There were discussions where the terms reverse racism and discrimination were the battle flags being waved aloft. Some asked "Why should minorities get special treatment at WisCon?" Some demanded to know "Why give awards to people of color?" "Where are the awards for white people?" "Why don't white people ever get any awards?" One young white woman asked during a panel, "Why is it people of color can take our culture but that's not cultural appropriation?" During these discussions the mantra "I'm not a racist, but..." prefaced most remarks. Racism is a social disease that most racists don't know they have.

Diantha Day Sprouse, a longtime sf fan and frequent WisCon panelist, is interested in the intersection of race/gender/science fiction.

Uncomfortable Politics in Feminist Writing

Transcript Notes by Laura Quilter

Panel Description

An exploration of the feminist politics of making the reader uncomfortable. Obscenity, violence, violation of the body's boundaries, and dystopia are used as tools to explore feminist thought. For example, mainstream non-feminist movies and books often have rape scenes that are highly eroticized from the perpetrator's point of view. When these violations of body-boundaries are described from the point of view of the violated, it's obscene; it makes readers uncomfortable, and that's worth discussing.

Panelists

Cassandra Elinor Amesley (moderator), Paula L. Fleming, Liz Henry, Geoff Ryman

Works & Authors Cited

- Gregg Araki, "Mysterious Skin"
- Susan Brownmiller
- Octavia Butler, Xenogenesis Trilogy
- Jacqueline Carey Kushiel, Dart series, *Banewreaker*, *Godslayer*
- Samuel R. Delany, *Dhalgren*
- L. Timmel Duchamp, *Alanya to Alanya*, *Renegade*, *The Red Rose Rages (Bleeding)*
- John Gardner
- Mary Gentle, *Golden Witchbreed* and *Ancient Light*
- Nicola Griffith, *Slow River*
- Joe Haldeman, *Camouflage*

- Robert A. Heinlein, *The Moon Is a Harsh Mistress*
- Elizabeth A. Lynn, *The Sardonyx Net*
- Maureen McHugh, *Mission Child*
- Larry Nevin, "Flatlander"
- Julie Phillips, *James Tiptree, Jr.: The Double Life of Alice B. Sheldon*
- Geoff Ryman, *Air*
- Tricia Sullivan, *Maul*
- *28 Days Later*
- *The A-Team*
  - Frodo and Sam's relationship, the Tolkien Lord of the Rings trilogy
- *My Beautiful Laundrette (1985)*
- "mommy" blogs
- *Silence of the Lambs*

[Editor's note: These notes are not a verbatim transcript. They have been corrected by some (though not all) of the panelists and have been abridged or supplemented for clarity.]

GR: ...when characters are weak, that's the kind of discomfort that's really useful.

A few things that push my buttons: I personally—as a writer, not a reader—have a real strong need for autonomy, independence; so when I'm reading about a character, particularly a female character who still lets herself be dependent on others...particularly Maureen McHugh's *Mission Child*, because you have a woman who comes from a culture where everyone depends on everyone else, and she's taken from that culture and put in an urban environment, and she keeps depending on this person and that person, and everyone keeps letting her down and, *ooh* I wanted to smack her. Perfectly understandable where she was coming from. So that's one thing as a feminist: how do I deal with characters who aren't standing on their own two feet?

Another thing that interested me on this panel: the issue of victimization. Horribly shitty things can happen even to very strong people, and even very strong people can make mistakes, and how do we make that work in a way... The example in the program book was rape, but I think any number of things can happen to make someone a victim without losing sympathy for them.... Just like juries in rape cases tend to pull back; you don't want to identify with the victim...[The problem is] how to do victim and still portray [the character] as a strong sympathetic person.

CEA: I hate it. I get most uncomfortable when people I know about are invisible. Obviously, I don't get uncomfortable where I have a blind spot. I get uncomfortable if class or economic background is not foregrounded or is misrepresented. Certainly, gender things like that. Like most writers, I write because I have stories to tell and I want to tell them, but I also feel hopeful that some of the information motivates someone, someday, to be as angry as I am. So those are my motives for making people uncomfortable and for writing in general.

Now, if we can talk about maybe what got you interested in this panel, or what thoughts triggered...what made people uncomfortable.

GR: The awards last year for the year before, Tricia Sullivan's book, a book called *Maul* (set in a shopping mall but spelled m-a-u-l). It's an extremely violent book, and very, very uncomfortable. It starts out with a young, one wants to say totally consumer-oriented, girl masturbating with her gun,...an incredibly violent book, and made me feel incredibly uncomfortable because I didn't know the extent to which I was invited to take it seriously and the extent to which I was invited to enjoy it, because it was unenjoyable...women shooting women and lots of innocent bystanders, and I just didn't get it...then [the narrative] cuts to a man in a cage.... Then, the two stories converge in a completely...a formally brilliant book.... But the first third of the book.... I thought, if I can stick with it, I will understand it...

I stuck with it. First of all, I, as a Clarke judge.... You don't get many real science fiction novels.... It had fantastic written power.

CEA: Would you have been as uncomfortable if it was men shooting men?

GR: Yeah.... I was more uncomfortable because it was a woman writer, and I sensed there was some kind of critique going on.... If it were a man writer, I would have said it was just shit...someone who said that...it was shit...

LH: [*enters*] Sorry...late...I blame the patriarchy.

CEA: We've started already. The first question is, what's dear to your heart in terms of changing things...? An answer would be useful especially as you're probably still thinking.

LH: You mean, why it might be useful to make people uncomfortable?

CEA: No, what do you want to change? Why do you care? As a writer.

LH: I want everybody to have a voice and to not be afraid of making mistakes, and to speak up and see what happens, and for everybody to speak up and change what they say...I want people to step down from expertise and authority and to speak individually and to arrive at collaborative conclusions...

CEA: Very good for someone just getting off an elevator! The second question is, what did the name of the panel trigger for you in terms of thoughts that made you uncomfortable?

PF: I probably answered this a little in the first go-round.... As far as what I'd like to change: one of the things, again, as a feminist writer I feel, I guess, rather impishly or perversely inspired to do in my work is to try to question what I think of as conventional liberal politics or conventional liberal thinking, as much as I am part of that myself. And that means sometimes making a little bit of fun, particularly of liberal white middle-class do-gooders who want to help minorities and that kind of thing, and I do turn the tables and poke fun...particularly liberal white middle-class people who have never met the people they want to do good about...because that's my real life...interview people who want to work in a natural foods co-op.... A lot of them are great people, but I also meet a lot of people who are really liberal and want to save the world, but have probably never really spoken with a homeless person because that would be "icky."

LH: I never know what to do...start engaging...that would be do-gooding on them.... Example: the PTA, the middle-class and upper-middle-class people have in their mission to make the poor people—a.k.a. the Latinos—eat healthier in their home because they have bad cholesterol and their children will be fat...and they have bad body images.... And it's certainly noble to want to eat well, but the jury's out on what that means...

Aud: Of all the things that people have to worry about, pizza on the lunch menu has to be right up there.

CEA: ...asking Liz about what you've done to make people uncomfortable...deferred until later.

GR: [I wrote] a story set in a concentration camp...

CEA: And how did you know they were uncomfortable?.

GR: The strange thing is that actually nobody was. It was timed well enough that everyone just said "Yeah.... You're so down on violence"...very nightmare image, slightly surrealistic, and seemed to pull together and not offend anybody...

CEA: Sad. I am not published in fiction yet—I'm a poet—but I have been writing for a couple of years a particular story that I have taken to workshops. It's what I would call a very straightforward issue: a story written from a first person point of view with two protagonists reporting what happened. One of them is someone named Miram; the other is from a culture that does not distinguish by gender. So, for the first couple of chapters, you do not know what gender Miram is because a lot of people assume Miram is a female name because of its background.... The people who read were all upset: they wanted to know what gender Miram was and they wanted to know *now*. They were very clear that the story wouldn't sell. They wanted to know, did he have balls or could he have children?…referred to as "he," so one character Miram is attracted to is referred to as a brother by his Alassi friend…definitely a woman by Miram…whether she/he is romantically available is an issue. And again a lot of confusion from readers about…"You've got to pick something that fits whatever gender this person is." [That is] something I don't feel is necessary and something that puzzles me.

Aud: Are the people making these suggestions in the publishing world?

CEA: Some of them, yes, but hang onto the questions.

PF: I find that if I'm writing from a male point of view, because I have a female name and my name is on byline, if I start as "I," people will assume female unless I give them a clue very quickly…. Now it sounds like you're talking about point of view from someone who doesn't distinguish. That's a different issue. Unless it's critical to the story, I will relieve reader's discomfort quickly, so I can tell the story I want to tell…other ways I've made people uncomfortable…feedback I've gotten on stories. I've had one editor tell me a story was sexist because the man in the story bought the woman a piece of clothing so she could go out to a nice restaurant with him, because he was a very successful person and she didn't make a lot of money…. I've been in relationships where I didn't see […money differentials…] as a sexist thing, but I guess it pushed someone's button…. What was the question again?

CEA: I guess you just answered it. [Let's] go back to Liz.

LH: Yeah, I thought of something to say. I guess I'd say, in blogging especially, but even maybe before that, crossing lines of public and private ticks people off. Fuzzing or blurring boundaries makes people flip out because boundaries exist for good things, so crossing them makes people perturbed. [Crossing] public/private [boundaries] is revealing too much information, exposing anything messy, violating someone else's privacy… People are always concerned that by violating my own privacy I'm violating someone else's privacy, not respecting their boundaries. So if I talk about my feelings about my life, my pregnancy, that I'm violating my son's boundaries or my mom's, etc. That just me saying these things is…[There's a] dialog happening very heavily in the mommy blogger community…a lot of very intense feminist c[onsciousness]-r[aising] is happening in that field. People are very concerned to protect you from revealing too much about yourself. They want to protect you… And obscenity is the other big thing. Violence can be obscene, sex can be obscene. What is obscene? …I think other things can be obscene, like wealth. Like my 401(k) can be obscene.

CEA: So the question for the panel: is it good to make someone uncomfortable?

GR: You can't have a good story without making someone uncomfortable. Pornography makes people very comfortable; they don't have to think.... Stories that will have to make them think make them more responsible.

CEA: So you would have been disappointed when a story you wrote did not make anyone uncomfortable?

GR: It did provoke conversation...for a very limited time. It's a very dated story, but it did have a specific function for a time.

PF: Yeah, absolutely. I want to make people uncomfortable unless I'm writing bedtime stories to help people fall asleep. Yeah, if I'm not... Otherwise, for me at least, it's like, what's the point? We have available to us so much media; between the media and 200 channels of mostly shit on TV and all the rest of it, there's so much information there. There's no reason for me to add anything to it by writing a story unless I've got something to say that will take our thinking beyond that.... Another thing that makes me really uncomfortable is financial insecurity. I'm reading *Air* right now. This character keeps losing her way of making a living...and, god, that's making me nervous. One way to do it. Way too often in our genre we assume that our characters have way too unlimited resources... Certainly, our prince who goes off on adventures has no real problem... [He] may go hungry for a night, but [that's] not really a problem... [This] may be one way in our highly material saturated culture.

LH: Who is it making people uncomfortable, because maybe people who have something to lose are uncomfortable.... People who are poor maybe aren't uncomfortable.

PF: In our society, if you took away somebody's TV, that could get really edgy, you know.

GR: In England, the average wage is 25,000 pounds a year, but a lot of people are making ten or eleven. The net result is lots of debt.... So maybe a rich person reading would be uncomfortable, but if I'm reading it, it's making me uncomfortable because that's a situation I'm in.

LH: So maybe being out of control is...

CEA: If making people uncomfortable is making your story less easy to sell, there's going to be a lot of writer angst there, in the slash sense of angst.

LH: On the other hand, I'm not going out and watching movies where women get raped and scream, because that makes me uncomfortable. But I'm not challenging myself there...

CEA: I noticed that people who go to class panels think class is an issue. People who go to motherhood panels...we don't go very far out of our way...

PF: Liz raised a really good point, because there are different kinds of discomfort, because sometimes something can just be really sick or "icky."

CEA: Like homosexuality?

PF: For some people it would be.... Maybe this is a way people don't want to grow.... I can't sit here and tell people how to grow...

GR: Horror movies. I stopped reviewing movies because you really do get sick of movies with a seventeen-year-old girl being tied up with barbed wire and a cigarette ground out on her back...and you can't find any purpose.... I don't think the people doing it are identifying with the victims; who are they identifying with?...and then you get *Silence of the Lambs*, which is billed as a feminist horror movie, but it's a slash titty movie.... I think they did track the problem of a trained competent person terrified out of her wits; they tracked that well, but all they did was dress up a slash film.

[...discussion of film vs. book...]

GR: But they did get competent female fear; they got that.

PF: Yeah, that's hard.

CEA: It's tempting to go into [the issue of the] female gaze or [the] male gaze, but I'm going to push that to production. I picked homosexuality...because it's close to my heart, and I have had various students where I showed movies like *My Beautiful Laundrette* because, in this case, they can't deal with male on male romance.... Male on female romance, they felt apparently quite comfortable watching. So it becomes unsatisfactory to make them too uncomfortable because they'll shut down. And I'm wondering if you see a place where you negotiate choices between not too uncomfortable but beyond the boundaries of the comfort zone, so they start noticing that, in fact, they have a comfort zone, which is the first step.

PF: I think that is so hard because I think you face that ethical dilemma... You see it when people try to make war movies. I see it when I try to portray any kind of act of violence—sexual or other—in a story. On the one hand, if I sanitize it, I'm not doing it justice, like *The A-Team*: bullets flying everywhere; they don't fall down or they fall down, but you don't see blood. I hate that fake violence—that's wrong. There needs to be real violence; it needs to be awful; it needs to have real consequences. But if you go too far into it, it runs the risk of being gratuitous or runs the risk of being the seventeen-year-old...barbed wire...cigarettes ground...and that's not right either. And I think every scene like that, use your own best ethics to try to get the telling points across...really hard...you may never get it right for every reader.

GR: ...when I'm writing stuff, I'm...being prurient, because I'm a human being, too... pretty warped...so all I can do is test-drive: "Is this prurient?" If I think it is, that's when I think this is the wrong kind of discomfort. So, similarly, I can only police my own reactions. If I think I'm really getting off on the violence, then I think that's the wrong kind of discomfort; then, I shut down. The embarrassment I feel with the seventeen year old...when I feel being asked to identify—that's prurient.

CEA: The thing is, I've published slash. There's definitely an erotic element; it's deliberate; one worries...wanted to deal with class issues. I found erotica was a great way to make people focus on class issues because they would read it for the sex, and stay and to think about, in this case, Frodo and Sam's inherent subordinate relationship. So would that fit in with your definition of prurient?

GR: Slash fiction I've read is anything but prurient.... It took ages, just like gay lib. None of them would come out as writing this stuff.... But they got the physical stuff completely right, on anal sex, but they did over-romanticize male-on-male relations.

CEA: Male-on-male slash is for women to have fantasy men who are useful for women's sexuality.... At this point, I'm going to open it to questions from the audience...

Aud: Think of a sf/f text that's made you uncomfortable, and whether it still makes you uncomfortable.

CEA: Heinlein's *Moon Is a Harsh Mistress*, which I read in high school. And I'd never thought of [the] world in a political way before Heinlein, and he makes some arguments which are shocking, like individuals should have the same right to execute as governments...even though I now recognize it as more fascist than anarchist.

PF: I'm trying to narrow it down to one example. One of the things I love about this genre is it so often makes me uncomfortable, at least temporarily, until I readjust my parameters.... I'll raise an example, mentioned in the program...Kushiel's Dart series, a little bit, at least, to start off with. And then you get used to it, the point of view of this particular character...and then my parameter is shifted a little bit.

LH: Of course, I have a list like I'm sure everyone...but I would mention, actually speaking of Jacqueline Carey, the *Godslayer* and *Banewreaker* books made me a little uncomfortable because I had thought of Tolkien and the race, etc., and I thought, "Ooh, why was I not aware of this," and it made me uncomfortable with my own lifetime of being blind about this. Another book would be Timmi Duchamp's *Alanya to Alanya* and *Renegade*, coming out soon, which was fantastically uncomfortable in a really great way. Imprisonment, and I read a lot of prison literature...and the imprisonment that also happened in *The Red Rose Rages (Bleeding)*, and the interrogation prison scenes between women, and the women—analytic torturer and captive—were so intense, and a really, really good read makes you think about a lot of things. But [it's] difficult to keep reading. It made me think a lot of things about my own life and...seeing the depth to which I'm subject to patriarchy is almost unbearable...the pressure of double consciousness...it's almost difficult to bear and makes you go a little bit crazy until you can integrate.

Aud: A book to add to list [is] *Dhalgren* by Delany. It's so beautifully written, but it's gritty in a way I'm not used to reading.

CEA: I'm sorry. There are a couple of people who had hands up before you.

GR: I responded to Paul, being a lot more uncomfortable about mainstream novels because they tend to pin me down much more horribly in "here and now."...*Maul* really disturbed me, partly because I couldn't account for it.

LH: Lori Selke told me to read it, so you should talk to her because she loved it passionately.

PF: A novel that disturbed me greatly was Nicola Griffith's *Slow River*. An absolutely, very disturbing exploration of power dynamics on various levels.

Aud: Speaking of things that make people uncomfortable: I remember being in a movie theater watching *28 Days Later*. A fully naked man in hospital with full frontal nudity.... The audience [responded] with nervous titters and palpable unrest. I wondered about it, obviously. Just grown-up people are uncomfortable about this, but listening to the panel, I'm trying to unpack *who* and *why*. Obviously [there are] elements about the women being homophobic, but also I wonder about the women in the movie theater being forced to confront male sexual organs. But on another dimension, I also wonder about, in our society, the nude male body; the male penis can make people nervous.

LH: The female penis can make people nervous too.

Aud: Nudity too can just make people nervous.

GR: I think there's a certain vulnerability when people are naked in front of the camera and can't move. That vulnerability is highlighted when it's a male, because we're not used to seeing it.

Aud: I've been working on a story for a while. It definitely makes most people uncomfortable because it's written from an alien point of view—not human—but doesn't have a gender, but can take on either gender when it interacts with other races. I'm curious if you've seen others.

[...last year's Tiptree winner *Camouflage*...Octavia Butler's *Xenogenesis Trilogy*...]

PF: ...taboos around male nudity and female nudity.... I also write erotica as sf/fantasy.... When I was at Clarion, one of my instructors was Samuel R. Delany.... He gave a reading, as was traditional; he read some of his highly erotic work. One of the students asked him, "Why do you write about sex so much?" He said, "I guess I see sex portrayed a whole lot in ways that are really unrealistic, so I want to talk about the way it really is. So even when I'm writing erotica, I describe bodies like real bodies, not idealized bodies, because I think they're sexier…women have dimples in their butts and little potbellies."

LH: Zits.

PF: I don't know about zits; that might break the mood. And I portray sex the way it really is because I think that's much more interesting…. In TV, we see it over and over that two people…their eyes meet…*boom*, they get horizontal and have perfect sex. Excuse me? I don't think so! So all the awkwardness and clumsiness that can go into encounters I find interesting and revealing.

LH: I have a question: I liked the question, think about what you found uncomfortable…productive discomfort vs. what you found yucky and uncomfortable.

Aud: The film *Mysterious Skin*…a film by Gregg Araki. Male homosexuality and child abuse. It was a difficult movie to watch, but also really wonderful: a productive kind of discomfort. So I would recommend it highly.

Aud (Sylvia Kelso): A very interesting sort of productive discomfort that I've found when I'm reading a text and it doesn't work, and it keeps needling back into your heart: twenty or twenty-five years ago, I was reading a female Gothic called *House of Many Shadows* by Barbara Michaels. Usually the formulaic story in a female Gothic sorts out the mystery and comes to a happy end. But I came to the end of this one, and the expulsion or removal of the ghost didn't work. I couldn't get the discomfort of this ending out of my mind. Eventually the discomfort was so productive I got half a PhD out of it. It wasn't that it was bad, or badly written. It was that the formula didn't provide release, and querying the discomfort was critically very productive for me. As a reader, I'm making an agreement with the author that I'm here to learn or just be entertained. A book made me horribly uncomfortable in a way that I've never gotten over because I think it broke the compact. I don't know if you remember an English author called Mary Gentle, who wrote *Golden Witchbreed.* The ending of *Ancient Light* took the entire two books and just took your legs out from under you, I don't want to spoil it too bad if you've never read it, but basically, she killed her world off. Years later, it's physically upsetting to me that the characters that I came to love, and the planet itself, were so absolutely ruined. It broke the compact in a big way, in that it took the sf or Fantasy expectation of a happy ending and tore it to shreds. *Ancient Light* is one of those amazing books that you never want to read more than once. The thing that was so traumatic about it was that unlike most sf, it was a post-colonial novel. It depicts unflinchingly what happens to a world—substitute people or culture—who are invaded by colonizers. And it's a contemporary version. The worst part was when one of the most charismatic alien characters is dying on a battlefield, and along comes a human camera crew, and it films her final moments. No idea who she is or what this death means; just another sound byte for the news. That broke the reader's compact for me big time. At the end, not just one but all the people on the world you've come to love get killed, in a way that turns the spotlight on your own world.

Aud 5: [It's] phenomenally well-written.

Aud 6: The novel is extraordinarily well-written, satisfying in its denouement, but [its] character...made me uncomfortable in ways I did not find productive—is that the term we've been using? *The Sardonyx Net* by Elizabeth Lynn—there's a character in there who is a sadist. He derives great pleasure from causing pain to people for political purposes. He's foiled in part by his sister, who's also in a power regime. The novel is well constructed. Lynn has, I think, accurately captured the psychology of the guy. But I don't know that I would want to read that novel again and experience through his eyes the pleasure he got from the actions he took.

CEA: That reminds me of... I was influenced by John Gardner on moral fiction. I was an academically trained writer...in all these writers' workshops. Most of the people in these workshops were outraged at the concept that you're accountable for your production. The idea was pure text. Art and artist interact and produce an ideal work... The audience should not be involved, except afterwards. The result is that some people seem to me to write into the universe really negative things...not what you're describing about not getting it in *Maul*.... You might be able to trust them and see what they're doing. But for many people, the only reason is pleasure or spectacle. I was wondering, for writers here, if you feel you're accountable to a community, and if so, what?

GR: I think I'm accountable in the sense that, as soon as I use fiction to try to recruit or sell them my vision or whatever agenda for good or ill, I'm probably breaking a compact with the reader. I don't know about community, but I think the reader comes to work...so as actual experience there...it either ratifies experience they've had or they're coming to a book because it's a way of life they haven't had, and they want to be free to trust the narrative to form their own narrative. I also police my work to see if I'm trying to use my fiction to show them.... I think it would be wrong to set things right.... The bargain is, you're going to love this and be totally unchanged.... That's entertainment, and there's nothing wrong with it.... The other is literature. The compact is, in literature, that I'm working as hard as I can to create a complex interesting picture of reality to work through issues or things in the world.... It's a platform for them to imagine their way through a set of issues and problems. Anything else I should be writing is an essay, a critical...and I probably should be.

LH: [...blogging and diaries....]

GR: Online community.

LH: With online communities, people start to have expectations of you. I do feel intense pressure to "keep it real"—a weird line that people will be offended not by political opinions but by details of my personal life—and if I don't feel them, then I feel I'm betraying truth.

GR: ...one to one...absolutely implicit...

LH: But I actually think about that; I don't want to be entertainment. Question. That's part of what makes blogging; it can be literary.

GR: But what's interesting about blogging is that it is an online community; the audience is an online producer.

LH: ...as far as fiction, I'm still thinking about online fiction... *Renegade*. Like with Mary Gentle, your mind is blown.

PF: This whole discussion aside, I have to think when I'm writing that my only responsibility is to my characters and being a true voice for them. And if I'm in a right place, I won't betray the standards and values and ethics of any community whose issues or point of view I may be trying to represent in a work of fiction. But that's not something I can force through technique or craft; it has to arise from my stance as a human being, before I sit down at the computer. My heart and gut have to be in right place, and then it has to be about the characters.

CEA: Killing off a character is hard...you are creating a living, breathing person, in a way, and you should feel responsibility, even if you kill them for the betterment of the plot...one character I was happy to kill because she was a bureaucrat...but once you understand them, it's hard to not feel for them.... Once I've created a reality, that reality exists in its odd fictional way, and if you create a fiction that says there is no hope, there is no possibility of change, you are doing something extremely immoral, and I wouldn't do it, and I wouldn't do the thing that makes me feel that way.

PF: I agree. If something is a big, long downer and says that life sucks, etc.... I can read the newspaper for that.

CEA: And it's not true, with the exception of entropy, which will get us all one day.

Aud: I've been disturbed ever since [I attended the] panel about women writing about gay men. Rape is eroticized. We've come so far since Susan Brownmiller. I didn't know what slash was or that Japanese thing was...

CEA: Come tomorrow at ten, when I actually talk about slash. It's not that all slash is ritual rape or bondage and other eroticization of violence or has serious bondage and rape and murder as part of the process. But there is a significant body of work that does that.

LH: It's very interesting that slash fanfic labels its stories thusly, so that you're warned. So this story is nonconsensual, romance, chan, etc. Dark fiction. People are labeling because they know it might be wrong…

CEA: They kill off women too. To bring it back to discomfort, Liz's point is really good. To lessen the discomfort, they put it all out there, but they warn you in advance. The belief is that your accountability is just to warn somebody…no accountability for creating a universe where rape is a first step on the way to a relationship.

LH: That's what the fanfic community was basically accusing me of, something akin to rape. That by long-listing Arcana [for the Tiptree Award], I did something horrible to E. Brunson by labeling. People were very concerned right from the get-go…. The first question that came up was, "Did you warn her that you were long-listing [her story]?" That would never come up with another title. It's a different community ethic that has developed…

CEA: […fanfic discussion…]

GR: So they're writing something about nonconsensual sex and then they're upset that somebody didn't ask their permission for long-listing it.

CEA: That's a really good example.

Afterword by Liz Henry

As with many things, there is a dominant assumption that only the discomfort of white upper-middle-class guys "counts" and a tendency of people to dismiss other people's discomfort as being too sensitive, not real, not important, threatening, or not constructive. This year the most uncomfortable book I read was Julie Phillips' biography, *James Tiptree, Jr.: The Double Life of Alice Sheldon*. While it's a productive discomfort, it was also enormously upsetting, really upsetting in a way that affected how I look at my life and my being a woman. I began to identify very closely with her story, and was angry at her, at myself, at all of our society that had no place for her because of her gender, and at the whole system of gender in general.

I count an "uncomfortable work" as productive discomfort for me if it sparks me to re-think my own assumptions and my own readings of other works or of life situations. In that sense, a bad or outrageous sf book can be so outrageous that it lights a fire under people to react against it and write something better. This is definitely a principle in literary translation: as translators, we read versions we know are bad or wrong, clumsy or uninspired, and the more we hate them, and love the original work, the more likely it is that we get off our butts and do a better job at it. So as feminist writers, I think a lot of us work that way, fueled by deep outrage and alienation from certain parts of the sf that we love. Then we take that outrage seriously, taking a long hard look at it, processing it, and then creating something that fits our own vision of possible realities. As critics, we have the task of doing close readings and breaking down the uncomfortable bits of a book.

There's a great example of this on the Feministsf blog: Yonmei's word-by-word analysis of the opening paragraph of "Flatlander," a short story by Larry Niven. We have to do this not just to explain to men or non-feminists, but to get a handle on our own responses and assumptions, for doing the essential feminist 101 work of "naming the problem." This is hard work, and can be very wearing-down to the spirit, but is also tremendously worth doing.

Notes and Commentary on the "Cultural Appropriation and Writing Fantasy Outside the Western Tradition" Panel

by Yoon Ha Lee

Panel Description

Not all fantasy fiction is, or indeed should, come from faery, from Middle Earth, from Tolkien or from other Western European traditions. Not everything should be pseudo-medieval in nature, and it seems that more and more fantasy authors are drawing upon other cultural frameworks in fashioning their fictions. Yet that comes with its own issues, such as cultural appropriation. A discussion of the embrace of neglected mythoi, and the pitfalls that may await the adventurous traveler there.

> [Note: The following consists partly of my description of the panel, but there is a great deal I have to add, some of it acerbic. I might sum up some of it by the fact that I decided not to get myself flamed out of WisCon and/or fandom for the rest of my life by pointing out, as a last example of cultural appropriation gone wrong, Joss Whedon's *Firefly*. But I do have other things to say. —YHL]

The Panel Itself

The moderator was Nisi Shawl, the other chromatic person, besides myself, on the panel; additional panelists were Theresa Crater, Judith Berman, Gregory Frost, and Ekaterina Sedia (Russian, I think). In terms of the *panel*, the discussion veered heavily toward questions of appropriation from *living cultures* in an ethnic/nationalistic sense, although the issues raised could have been applied equally to other cultures, e.g., queer culture, third-culture kids, whatever. Some time was spent setting up general agreement on the definition of cultural mis/appropriation, which did not seem to be a topic of much dispute. (I should add that we as panelists took "appropriation" in a neutral sense.)

Sedia suggested that appropriation could happen at two levels, that of myth and that of more mundane details of culture, and Berman added that myths of dead as opposed to living cultures were two different kettles of fish. Sedia said that "appropriation that is done *well* can be quite appropriate." Frost suggested a "reverence" for the material was necessary—trying to stay as close to the culture as possible. Shawl said it was a question of intent, since the material might have to be changed to suit the audience's needs. Frost cited his "Tengu Mountain" (in the anthology *The Faery Reel*, eds. Ellen Datlow and Terri Windling, which I haven't read) and his process of adapting the story to fit the European beginning-middle-end fairytale model.

Distinctions: language vs. race vs. culture, culture vs. ethnicity, lived and experienced vs. intellectual study. (Because, you know, all of us have a chance to move to Albania to get a hands-on sense of the culture. To be fair, the internet makes available experience by proxy even if you can't physically get to the country or find an expat community near you.)

Shawl suggested that you have a responsibility to a culture if you benefit from it; I believe Crater mentioned financial remuneration, although I can't recall whether she referred solely to the family who had helped her, or also to a larger community. She also said that you are responsible for representing ideas in an appropriate manner. Interestingly, Berman, who had spent years as an anthropologist gathering oddments of information without originally intending to write a novel (*Bear Daughter*), spoke of feeling an obligation to share that knowledge in some fashion. Sedia, returning to Frost's idea of reverence, of respect, said it was not necessary to try to be so faithful to the source that you kill the story, but to understand the source and acknowledge it and why you present it in a certain way.

Shawl mentioned three categories of foreigners: invaders, tourists, or guests; she implied that one should at least avoid being in the first category. This categorization, along with the legitimate topic of the panel, led to some unfortunate derailments by some members of the audience during the question session.[1] Someone further subdivided tourists into those who are interested in learning about the place and those who want to know where the McDonald's is.

One thing brought up at the end of the panel was American pop culture. Someone on the panel—I don't recall who—compared it to the atomic bomb as a weapon. Perhaps the A-bomb is extreme as a comparison, but the person backpedaled, and there was general agreement that it was not a weapon. Pop culture is effective as a tool, weapon even, of assimilation, even propaganda (I consider "propaganda" value-neutral). An audience member—I believe it was Cynthia Ward, co-author with Nisi Shawl of *Writing the Other*—mentioned that the Japanese are appropriating American culture all over the place without bothering to research properly. This is not an apt analogy. There is a real cultural difference in how "appropriation" is regarded. A good example is what we would call plagiarism, which is perfectly acceptable elsewhere. There is also a power differential in perception. They do not call it the American Empire for nothing. The Empire dreams, and those dreams, this mythos, have a potency for other cultures that theirs do not for ours. (Someone with a better background in the topic should say something about the implications of colonialism here. I am sorry, I can't oblige.)

I'm Asian. I smile when I'm embarrassed. And I go blank when I am furious or vehement. So you never know.

I spent a good deal of the panel wondering whether I should speak up more as one of the two chromatic people on the panel (since the other was busy moderating), or whether I should shut my mouth. I am told I spoke less than anyone else on the panel.

So: things I would have liked to say during the panel if I had (a) had a voice (literally—I had a bad cold during the convention), (b) had more courage, and (c) been willing to bend the panel to my will when the discussion went elsewhere.

The question of intent is nebulous in a way I find uncomfortable. One can write horrendously offensive claptrap with the best, most shining of intentions. And how is the *reader* to determine this intent? As with anything regarding authorial intent, not even the author's own statements can be taken as authoritative, unless you have fast-penta and are willing to use it. Intent vs. execution was mentioned glancingly. The unfortunate example I keep returning to is Leah Cutter's *Paper Mage*, which is apparently well-researched but is flatly written (Oyceter wasn't able to last out the book[2]).

This notion of *getting permission* was brought up briefly but never satisfactorily addressed. This is a question I grapple with as a chromatic hyphenated American who is haunted by the sense that anything she writes in the underrepresented subgenre of fantasy with Korean mythic/folkloric elements is inauthentic. Is *anyone* "Korean enough" to write a Korean-based fantasy? Who decides the boundaries of the group? (Let's leave multivalent sets aside.) If one person blesses your effort, does that suffice?

I do not come from a cultural tradition that has particular restrictions on the sharing of stories. I imagine that even when you are attempting to write from such a (living) culture, boundary conditions will remain problematic. I remain paradoxically edgy about giving remuneration. If I pay you enough money, is it then all right for me to write about your culture? In some sense all writing for paid publication has this crass thing, money, involved; there's reciprocity as courtesy (which does not necessarily exclude money). No: where I'm troubled is the implication of a power differential, benefactor and benefactee. This may have been a function of the sample size of panelists. I much doubt questions of money would have come up if the other culture being appropriated was that of, say, Denmark. This kind of transaction recapitulates existing inequalities. To complicate matters, I think it's possible for such recapitulation to be concurrent with action *against* the differential.

Catherynne Valente said this more pithily afterward: "There was a lot of white guilt in that room."

And there's a *problem of representation*: First of all, that fantasies that are not Eurofantasies get realized *at all*, so that readers are aware of the possibilities; second, that when they exist, they are problematic. With respect to the first, I didn't conceive of non-Eurofantasies when I started writing, despite having access to a reasonably rich source of Korean folktales. (Before you ask, "Eating Hearts" is based loosely on Korean folklore. "Nine Tails, Hundred Hearts," I'm afraid, is a foxy excuse for number theory.) With respect to the second—it presupposes the first. There can be no dialogue when nothing exists to have a dialogue about. In that sense I don't give a damn whether you're an Ethiopian writing about Cincinnati or a Korean writing about medieval France or a German writing about the Olmecs.

I wish that, whether considering living or dead cultures, some mention had been made during the discussion of the very real problem of *fiction that exoticizes the Other*; that uses the outer trappings of other cultures (and their mythoi) as a shortcut for thinking across the cultural divide. Reverence as respect for other human beings, as part of the ethics of writing, I have no problem with. (My view on this topic appears to be close to Frost's.) I worry, however, that reverence may cross the line into fear or dehumanization, us-vs.-them. I don't deny that cultural interfaces are riddled with land-mines. I've lived them; I'm not unique in having done so. As for examples, consider the parade of Nippofantasies—feudal pseudo-Japans (I am aware of some of the problems in designating those periods of Japanese history "feudal" as per the European senses of the word) that frequently involve obsession with honor and duels. As Marissa K. Lingen has said more eloquently elsewhere, xenophilia is not a bad thing. It drives me mad, however, when an author sets out to prove that another culture is fascinating for its quirks but will submit to Western views once it sees the error of its ways. Raymond E. Feist and Janny Wurts' EMPIRE trilogy is deeply guilty of this.

I wish I'd been able to articulate some of this at the panel. Here I am now; I'm not done, but I can only hope it's a step forward.

Endnotes

1 Dear Certain Audience Members:

The panel was not arguing the evils of imperialism, or denying its importance in the greater discourse of our society, whether it be for your culture or someone else's. In the meantime, kindly shut up and stop hijacking the panel beyond its appropriate focus.

2 "Oyceter" is a LiveJournal handle (http://oyceter.livejournal.com); Oyce is Chinese herself—the book takes place in a fantasy China—and I wanted to get her opinion on the Cutter, which struck me as a well-intentioned but unsuccessful book when I read it.

Yoon Ha Lee is a science fiction and fantasy author with works published in *The Magazine of Fantasy and Science Fiction* and other venues. She is a section editor at the *Internet Review of Science Fiction.*

This piece originally appeared online at http://yhlee.livejournal.com

Researching WisCon Stories: Revisionist History or Re-Visioning the Past with the Future in Mind

by Joan Haran

David Irving's recent conviction for Holocaust denial in Austria,[1] where it is a crime, gives some sense of the acrimony directed at historians who produce non-authorized narratives of historical events and processes, especially narratives that threaten our preferred understandings. Although most quality press outlets that reported his conviction were scrupulous in referring to Irving as a "Holocaust denier" and not a "revisionist historian," I would argue that the latter is the label that many would attach to him. Certainly it is a label that has been extensively associated with him over time. When used as a pejorative, "revisionist history" is a term referring to the production of a history that is deemed to be counterfactual. Of course, the commonplace phrase "History is written by the winners" indicates that at least some readers/consumers of history texts share the sense that historical narratives can be and are contested.

History: Found or Made?

For over thirty years now, second wave feminist historians and their successors have excavated or constructed historical narratives designed to redress an oppressive balance in the histories produced by privileged white men, so feminists might be expected to have a rather more agnostic attitude to truth claims about historical facts. The choice of verb—to excavate or to construct—depends on whether we believe that "the facts" are fixed and unchanging, or whether we believe that "the facts" are produced in the process of narrating them. I have been thinking recently about the ways in which historical revisionism can be regarded as an illegitimate textual practice in relation to research I have been doing on WisCon. Over the past two years I have interviewed members of the team responsible for making WisCon happen, attended meetings with that team, examined a range of fanzines and convention programs produced throughout WisCon's life, and made my own small contribution to WisCon by taking responsibility for co-coordinating the academic track of programming. Throughout this process of "data collection" (as social scientists call it) I have been thinking about the text or texts that I will produce to document the research.

In my PhD thesis, *Re-visioning Feminist Futures*, I explored the ways in which the production of closed historical narratives limits the ways in which it is possible to imagine the future in general and social transformation in particular. I argued that the production of anti-oppressive histories is a necessary precondition to imagining a future that we can continually transform. My research about the meaning that WisCon has for its participants and my desire to share those meanings with other feminists and sf fans has always been bound up with the resources that sharing these stories might offer projects of social transformation. So, as a thought-experiment, I would like to contrast historical revisionism with re-visioning: a feminist textual practice that sounds very similar yet proceeds with very different assumptions.

Adrienne Rich defines and recommends re-visioning thus:

> the act of looking back, of seeing with fresh eyes, of entering an old text from a new critical direction—[re-visioning] is for women more than a chapter in cultural history: it is an act of survival.[2]

Rich was talking specifically about literary texts, but feminists have "re-visioned" texts produced in many academic disciplines as well as those produced in the media and in everyday social interactions. I am hoping that the documentation of my research on WisCon will work as an illuminating re-vision of multiple WisCon histories rather than fix upon a single consensus history that resists challenges to its authenticity. Of course, I recognize that a presentation of multiple histories requires great sensitivity because the stories that each of us tell about our selves and our histories are felt as true, even when we recognize that others with whom we have shared experiences might have experienced very different truths. For many of the hundreds of people who attend regularly, WisCon is a timeless institution. For a much smaller number of people, every single WisCon is the result of months of voluntary labor and sometimes tense negotiation. And for some, WisCon has failed the test of providing the space for the discussion and operation of feminist politics they desired. WisCon practices a "broad church" feminism—and the specification of what is included in this feminism *has* developed over the years, sometimes in explicit dialogue with those who have felt excluded. However, the desire to maintain WisCon as a celebratory space, when feminism is embattled beyond the walls of the convention hotel, sometimes results in tensions about implicit exclusionary practices, both in its organization and in the content of programming, exacerbated by the perception that some tensions should not be spoken and some speakers may not be tolerated.

Motivations and Investments

Perhaps the key difference between revisionist and re-visioning practices can be located in the political and ethical motivations and investments that drive them. On the one hand, Rich's "re-visioning" is motivated by a feminist agenda that is about recovering what has been metaphorically written out of cultural history in the pursuit of a more equitable society. While on the other hand, revisionist history in the mode of David Irving is likely motivated by the desire to erase certain human subjects from history in pursuit of a manifestly unjust social agenda. I will return to the issue of re-visioning as an ethical textual practice once I have sketched out one version of my own WisCon history.

Passion and Good Management: An Unusual Combination?

Like many long-time attendees at WisCon, I first attended the convention as a starry-eyed student in search of people who would recognize and appreciate my passionate interest in feminist science fiction and discovered that WisCon provided the ideal audience for my work—an audience I could never hope to find in a university sociology department. WisCon 30 marked the seventh time I have attended the convention since 1998; each time I crossed the Atlantic to attend, so clearly I've found what I've been looking for there. Like countless hundreds (thousands?) of people before me, on my first visit I was oblivious to the labor involved in staging the convention. As I returned again and again, however, I began to understand that every year, behind the scenes, dedicated people gave up a huge percentage of their leisure time to make sure that convention attendees had a pleasurable, stimulating, and safe experience; and their motivation and time-honed administrative expertise astounded me.

My appreciation of WisCon as a hugely successful logistical feat—I've attended more than a few shambolic academic conferences—ran parallel with my professional academic curiosity about how the people involved had held together a feminist organization over such an extended period of time. Histories of second-wave feminism suggest that the Women's Liberation Movement was weakened by repeated bouts of painful and unresolved schism. I wanted to know what made WisCon—which seemed to me to have emerged from that same movement—so resilient. So when I began thinking about doing research with the WisCon Convention Committee (ConCom) on the con's social history, I entertained a wistful, utopian notion that my research might uncover some magic formula to reinvigorate feminist activism. A modest little goal, then!

There's Always More Going on Than You Think

Even before I formally began my research it had become apparent to me that the situation was rather more complicated than I had imagined. WisCon wasn't and isn't some heavenly, conflict-free space with a fixed and homogeneous identity; nonetheless, being involved in WisCon is enormously pleasurable and fulfilling. But it is that very conflict and ambiguity and the ways in which key protagonists (living, breathing people, I mean!) work with and through the conflict and ambiguity to produce and sustain an imagined community of thirty years duration that lies at the heart of my research project.[3] Of course, what I had not given enough thought to when I first conceived my project was the possibility that this apparent stability and community might have been achieved at the cost of alternative visions for WisCon. Why I would imagine that WisCon would be the only institution in the world to be perfectly inclusive seems embarrassingly naïve to me now.

WisCon as Utopia

Even before interviewing current and former members of the ConCom I had begun to recognize the extent to which I idealized an imagined version of WisCon: a utopia that conformed to what I believed a space dedicated to feminism and science fiction might be. Of course, this idealization is not unique to me—or, rather, in its specifics, it probably is—but the process of imagining what WisCon *is* is one shared by everybody who attends or participates in the making of the convention. I have enormous respect for the work that many people put in to realizing their WisCon visions, and I believe that homogenizing the accounts that my interviewees have given would do them a massive disservice.

Discovering the subtle or sometimes stark differences between different accounts of what WisCon *is* and what WisCon ***does*** has been a fascinating process for me, one through which I am still working. Facets of WisCon's identity that I believed to be set in stone have proven over the course of the research to be in continual flux. Despite the proud boast on the convention's website: *World's Leading Feminist Science Fiction Convention*, the degree to which WisCon is feminist is still disputed and has been the subject of ongoing struggle. The process of interviewing key historical contributors to WisCon, including those who have moved away from the core group of volunteers, is not yet complete, so I will not pre-empt the final outcome of my research, but it is already clear that WisCon means very different things to different people.

Revisionist History and Re-visioning Futures

So, returning to the relationship between revisionism and re-visioning that has been exercising my mind in relation to this research project, how do these reflections bear on my research? I would argue that one could think of David Irving's brand of revisionism—or at least about the motivations imputed to his revisionist textual practices—as a bad-faith attempt to produce a closed text that erases difference and ambiguity while Rich's re-visioning, by contrast, is an ethical attempt to produce an open text that holds diverse accounts of "the facts" in tension. In writing up my research on WisCon, I will strive to be clear about what motivated me to conduct this research and to think about the effects that this might have on the partiality of the WisCon story that I will write.

I have been changed by the process of working on this research. My relationship to the convention and to many of my interviewees has become much closer, so I have personal as well as professional reasons for wanting to produce a narrative that does full justice to my "research subjects" and to the still unfolding process of making WisCon history. I want my contribution to that process to embody the ambiguities and ambivalences, the contestations and contradictions in the plural personal histories I have collected, and in their imperfect fit with the history of the institution that WisCon has become.[4]

Endnotes

1 Irving was arrested in November 2005 and held in custody until his trial in February 2006. He was sentenced to three years imprisonment, but released on appeal in December 2006.

2 Rich, Adrienne. 1979. "When We Dead Awaken: Writing as Re-Vision." In *On Lies, Secrets and Silence: Selected Prose 1966–1978*, ed. Adrienne Rich, 33–49. New York: Norton.

3 The term "imagined communities" derives from the work of Benedict Andersen on nationalism. Andersen used this term to account for the ways in which people feel affinity with those who they have never met or are never likely to meet because of the ways they have in common to think about ideas or values—in Andersen's work, the shared vision of a nation. The hundreds of people who attend WisCon do not "know" every other attendee, nor do they "know" the thousands of people around the world who read about WisCon in academic journals, on blogs, or on the WisCon website. Yet many of them imagine themselves to be members of a feminist science fiction community that transcends the annual face-to-face encounters in the lobby of the Concourse in Madison.

4 What I hope this essay begins to demonstrate, however, is that as an "institution" WisCon is inseparable from the collective production of its ideals and organization. Without continued labor from longstanding and newly recruited volunteers, WisCon would be *only* an imagined community and not a material presence every Memorial Day weekend.

Joan Haran is a Research Associate at the UK Economic and Social Research Council Centre for Economic and Social Aspects of Genomics (CESAGen). She has recently completed work on a CESAGen flagship project *Media, Culture and Genomics*. A research monograph from the project, *Human Cloning in the Media*, jointly authored with her project collaborators, Professors Jenny Kitzinger and Maureen McNeil and Dr Kate O'Riordan will be published by Routledge in October 2007. Also due for publication in 2007, from Aqueduct, is a collection of Joan's essays, entitled *Feminist SF Takes on Genetics: Sexuality, Reproduction, and Science*. Her PhD, *Re-Visioning Feminist Futures,* is currently unpublished, but Joan plans to remedy this soon. Joan continues to co-ordinate WisCon's academic track.

http://www.cesagen.lancs.ac.uk/staff/haran.htm

K. Tempest Bradford

Q: What was the best thing that happened to you at WisCon 30?

A: I'm sure many would agree with me that one of the best things about WisCon 30 was having so many past guests of honor in attendance, especially as many of them don't come to cons very often. There were a lot of wonderful moments—chatting with Carol Emshwiller at parties, meeting and being on panels with Katherine MacLean and Eleanor Arnason, and hanging out with Samuel Delany, whom I hadn't seen since Clarion West, in 2003. I also had the joy of seeing a story of mine in print for the first time, in *Farthing* magazine.

But the best moment happened during the Sign Out.

Wendy Bradley, *Farthing*'s editor, wanted me to give Chip some complimentary copies of the 'zine, since he was one of our instructors at Clarion West. Eileen Gunn happened to be chatting with him when I arrived at his table and happened to mention that my story was in the newest issue and happened to suggest that I should sign my story. So I had the indescribable experience of standing at Samuel R. Delany's Sign Out table autographing *for him*.

I'm not wanting for great WisCon memories from any year, but WisCon 30 will definitely go down as a special one for a long time to come.

K. Tempest Bradford is an editor for the *Fortean Bureau* and *Allegory* (formerly *Peridot Books*) fiction magazines.

http://tempest.fluidartist.com

Spike Parsons

Q: What is the strangest thing you ever saw at a WisCon?

A. Um. It's a difficult choice. Which is

B. stranger: Howard Waldrop wearing shoes

C. on his hands, or John Jarrold drinking a

D. glass of milk? Wait, I'm going to check

E. with Peter Larsen and see if I just

F. imagined the Waldrop thing…

G.

H. Okay, Peter backs me up. Waldrop was

I. riding a high-wheeler cycle and wearing

J. shoes on his hands. Definitely. And we're

K. pretty sure he also had a fly rod slung

L. over one shoulder. Very strange. No one

M. fly-fishes in downtown Madison.

Spike Parsons defies description.

http://www.fanac.com/spike9/index.html

Who Wants a Revolution? Will a Reform Do?

Transcript Notes by Liz Henry

Panel Description

At the radical caucus panel last year, we spent a great deal of time discussing the idea of radical politics and discovered that there is a wide notion of "radical." Much of the discussion hinged on differences between incremental change and radical change. To many, a world without hierarchical thinking [racism, sexism, homophobia, transphobia, etc.] is still only a dream. How do we balance the inertia of the status quo with the frustration of "if only…?" How can we effect change [great or small], and what role can our interests in sf/f play?

Panelists

Laura Quilter (moderator), Lenny Bailes, Ian K. Hagemann, Patrick Nielsen Hayden, Susan Karen Kinast-Porter

Works & Authors Cited

- The Declaration of Independence.
- Philip K. Dick.
- Dan Froomkin, column in the *Washington Post.*
- Robert A. Heinlein. *The Moon is a Harsh Mistress.*
- Ursula K. Le Guin. "The Ones Who Walk Away from Omelas."
- Malcolm X.
- Alice A. Nunn. *Illicit Passage.*
- Kim Stanley Robinson. Mars trilogy: *Red Mars*, *Green Mars*, *Blue Mars. Forty Signs of Rain* and *Fifty Degrees Below.*
- Upton Sinclair. *The Jungle.*
- Bruce Sterling. *Islands in the Net.*

[Editor's note: the following transcript combines text transcribed from an audiotape of the panel (which is available at http://wiki.feministsf.net/index.php?title=WisCon_30) with transcript notes made by Liz Henry, as the panel was in progress, that were subsequently corrected and supplemented by panel members for clarity. The transcript has been abridged; places where deletions have been made are indicated by <snip>. Where possible, speakers from the audience have been identified.]

LB: The word "revolution" is commonly used in a number of different ways. If we want to discuss revolution in the literal sense of "armed resistance against a government," my point of view would be that none of us in the US should want it, at this point. My guess is that other panel members will agree on this—although I may be mistaken about that...We don't want to define a world that encourages a small number of multibillionaire "winners" and a majority of [subsistence level] "losers" in a competition that the winners claim will protect all of our best interests.

SKP: I usually think of revolutions as being violent. So it depends on whether you're saying a global revolution or a revolution in politics. A couple of people here know that I'm a physician, so in my case, I'm willing to have a revolution in healthcare, but I don't really want an actual US revolution with everybody being nuked and bombed and thrown in jails. I don't know if a revolution of a thing—a part of society—counts as a whole revolution. I want change—substantial change, meaningful change—but I don't want to totally demolish the system. I don't want to be living in post-war Iraq, you know, with chaos and harm to people and no infrastructure, no food, no electricity, no water. We can get rid of all the money part; we have to keep the society part.

PNH: When we were discussing this panel in advance email I may have gotten us off—at least gotten myself off—on a slightly wrong track because all I had to go on was what I now see as a somewhat misleading title of this panel "Who Wants a Revolution? Will a Reform Do?" so I basically focused on the fact that actual revolutions actually involve lots of actual blood in actual streets and usually wind up being led by really unpleasant people and going sour and so forth. Which doesn't mean that I'm a gradualist by any means. If we just want to continue with this panel using the word "revolution" simply to mean drastic change, punctuated equilibrium, I'm fine with that.

Aud: Question: the fall of the Soviet East German government, would you call that a revolution?

PNH: I would. In fact, probably a justified one. I'm not saying that blood in the streets is never necessary. Obviously it is sometimes.

Aud: He's talking about the recent one, not the 1918...

PNH: I know, it was remarkably successful! It's like the system just went "poof."

LQ: It was successful, but look what we have now in Russia anyway.

PNH: That's true. What we have now in Russia and what we have now, for instance, in Czechoslovakia, is totally different. But anyways…if we want to just talk about gradualism versus drastic change, I want to pre-agree with Ian that, often, drastic immediate comprehensive changes are in fact the most compassionate, humane, and least violent option. When FDR put in social security, it wasn't a series of phased-in, super-gradual over-many-years-and-decades changes; it just basically shoved the system in, built in a constituency for it, and made it strong and made it endure for decades or generations. If I was in charge of reforming healthcare for this country, I'd do something really fast and immediate before the opposition could coalesce.

LQ: I want to come back to that, because I'm not sure that can really happen.

PNH: With healthcare, at this point, I'm not sure anything is possible.

LQ: Lenny, what do you think about this topic?

LB: In the 1960s, I was in favor of a more or less nonviolent revolution or a dramatic change that didn't necessitate violence in terms of the things that were going on before Bush, like the World Trade Organization protests. Basically I believe that we need some kind of fundamental paradigm shift in which we're not living to produce product for a small group of people who become wealthy. We would like for as many people as possible to have a reasonable quality of life, but on the way to that revolution it's kind of like we've encountered a national urgency where our country has been taken over by criminals, and so it basically causes me to re-think what exactly we are talking about. I don't think that things are bad enough in this country that we should even consider a violent kind of response to the criminal takeover that's happened. I think the Declaration of Independence is a pretty good litmus test of when it is necessary to have that kind of violent action against the government.

LQ: Can I poke at that for one second, even though I know it's just your introduction? What exactly does the Declaration of Independence say? It feels to me that it's pretty vague: "When in the course of human events…."

LB: When any form of government becomes destructive to the ends of enjoying the unalienable rights of life, liberty and the pursuit of happiness, it's the right of the people to abolish the government.

LQ: South Dakota has just banned abortion.

IH: Actually if I can sort of jump in, the Declaration of Independence was one of the things that the Black Panther party members were expected to have memorized back in the '70s, just because it really was a quite radical document and also because the Black Panthers needed to get as much legitimacy as they could when they were being pinned down in the streets and in their beds and all that other stuff. Towards that end, one of the first things I wanted to say about revolution that I didn't think about earlier is Malcolm X's statement, which was "Revolution is based on land." There are several different kinds of revolution, and I don't think a revolution has to be violent or fast or fundamental or based on comprehensive analysis. I think that what makes a revolution a revolution is that after the revolution there is no way to think about what happened before it in the same way. Without that fundamental paradigm shift in what I think of as the experiential knowledge of "wow, I wonder what it would be like if…" occurring as lived experience, I don't think it's a revolution. Now, Patrick was quoting something I've heard more recently, and the version I heard was, "What do we want? Incremental change! When do we want it? In due course!" [*laughter*] And that's usually what I think of as reform. And whether something is a reform or a revolution is, in my mind, not related to the methods used for it, or anything else. What makes a reform, in my mind, is whether or not it is a stepwise progression on the same curve.

PNH: Reform leaves the basic players in place. It just improves the efficiency of the system.

IH: Well, in many ways. For example, when Amazon.com got formed it was a revolution in bookstores because all of a sudden you could get any book in print through them. Prior to that, all of the biggest bookstores had about 250,000 titles. All of a sudden, the number was about 2.5 million—that's a jump, after which you can't think about bookstores the same way. Although I don't normally think of businesses as revolutionary, I just want to be clear about that.

LQ: So revolution is a fundamental shift in consciousness; it's not a change in government. Is that the defining characteristic?

IH: I would agree with that. I would say that political revolutions, almost by definition have to have a change in government.

LQ: Was feminism a political revolution? The women's movement of the twentieth century?

Aud: Be *vewwy* careful.

[*laughter*]

IH: I think that some of feminism was a revolution; I think that some of feminism was a reform. I also think that it's a continuing conversation, and I think, like most of the things that are associated with "the '60s" we're losing ground rapidly, and I think the more ground is lost, the less likely the revolution was successful. For me as a black man, to be here in Madison and sharing a room with a white woman, is a revolution that I don't think we can go back on in quite the same way that we seem to be going back on a lot of things. But maybe I'm just optimistic.

LQ: So I'm hearing that revolution is a change in consciousness, that it can be slow and gradual, and this is very different from the traditional kind of vision of revolution versus reform and the assignment we were handed in the initial panel. And I would like to open this up to the audience too to see what you guys think about. Are these your definitions of revolution? What were your expectations when you came to this panel?

PNH: And can we talk about science fiction before we get out of here?

LQ: And let's definitely bring up some science fiction.

Aud [Joe]: I heard the WTO mentioned earlier on and my experience with that protest really ties into this panel because when I was first protesting I thought, "This is not going to be any big deal. I can't just stand by and let my city be a showcase for this capitalism run rampant, so I'm gonna restrain myself." And after four days of being gassed and clubbed and maced, I had a much different outlook on things. So, I think it might be a conceit or an illusion that we get to choose whether it's incremental or it's all at once, that when in the course of human events, we don't get to choose when that moment is. We just become part of the flow.

LB: But we might be able to recognize that that moment has arrived or that moment has not yet arrived.

LQ: So a little bit of resistance can become a revolutionary moment. Is that the point? <snip> I'm curious what science fiction has to tell us about revolution, and I actually have not learned much about revolution from science fiction although I constantly seek out revolutionary science fiction. But one thing I did learn from, I *think*, a little bit, about revolution was Kim Stanley Robinson's Mars Trilogy. And there was not a lot of discussion of the in-the-streets revolution—although somebody thinks there is a little bit more than I remember—but just really talking about these fundamental shifts and people grabbing control when they had the opportunity and taking these different means and engaging in some violence, for example, destroying the chute from the moon to Mars, or actually destroying the moon. And I'm curious to know whether science fiction or fantasy or other kinds of speculative fiction have provided information for us in terms of creating a revolution.

PNH: Not often enough, I think. I think that most political science fiction presents drastically oversimplified pictures of how politics actually works. You have scene after scene of leaders of nations or political units meeting each other in rooms in which there are only two or three other people instead of twenty or thirty other people. I think Stan Robinson's work is a huge exception. His two most recent books, *Forty Signs of Rain* and *Fifty Degrees Below*, which are both set in

Washington DC like fifteen years from now in a world in which global warming is accelerating, are even better because they're hyper-realistic and they're depictions of how people in congressional offices, and government scientists, and people who decide who gets what grant and so forth, actually work. But they're gigantic exceptions. SF is potentially revolutionary in a much more simple way in that it expands our imagination of the extent to which another world is possible. It helps us think of what we can get to; it's not very good at the actual process. If it was so smart, we'd all be rich. If it had actual procedural recommendations for conducting reform or revolution, we'd be in a different world.

LB: Obviously, we've all read lots and lots of thought experiments. We've seen Philip K. Dick dystopias where stoners become political tract writers. We've seen Ken MacLeod futures where nuclear weapons become a market commodity. But more importantly, we all face the existential moral challenge of becoming participants in the political process around us, rather than passive observers. This might be the most critical issue in the panel: how to transform feelings into actions. Global capitalism might work humanely, after all: see Bruce Sterling's *Islands in the Net*. My take: the element in Sterling's vision that makes it succeed in his story, is the development of a strong communal conscience. Community and conscience are at the root of successful opposition to the abuses of global capitalism.

Aud: For an individual, reading science fiction can create a revolution for an individual... So it does open up worlds for people and changes their—

PNH: Science fiction helps people work out in their heads the extent to which the way things are is an arbitrary result of contingent things.

Aud (continuing): And as a child in your youth, you're using that to endure the imprisonment of your childhood sometimes. I'm speaking personally...

PNH: I think most people in this room here know what you mean.

Aud (continuing): It saves lives! It creates that...I also use it as a drug to bring comfort and relief of pain, in order to endure what would otherwise be unendurable.

SKP: Well, two things. Actually, that is kind of interesting because I bet for bunches of us here, sf is our religion of the masses. It keeps us content enough to go on living and not explode. (And that's probably true of me, in a sense). But one of the things science fiction has done for me is make me very very very very very very clear that I don't want a cataclysmic revolution and to be in a dystopia in a *Handmaiden's Tale* or a Suzy McKee Charnas totally destroyed world, even if the women are on top, or any of many nuclear holocaust ruin scenes that were very common when I was reading them (I kind of stopped reading them when I got too depressed). But I read them more in the '80s.

<snip>

Aud [guy with pink hair and beard]: One of the things that is really, for me, one of the biggest issues in terms of talking about the idea of a revolution or having a cataclysmic or contingent locus point is the difference between a revolution and sustained change. Right now, it wouldn't do any good if suddenly a bunch of folks rose up, marched on the sea, and took out the Capitol Building and the White House, and leveled it, and took out every member of the ruling elite because, weeks from then, there would be a whole new set of ruling elite ushered into place. And culturally, I don't think American society is capable or prepared, as 270 million people, to have a society that is different from what it is now. There's too wide of a spectrum, and there's no way, if we got the revolution we wanted, there's no way it would last.

LQ: I totally agree with you but I also totally disagree with you, because you said "capable" and "not prepared," and I heard those words during apartheid, when people were thinking, "Can the South African government be taken by black people?" And people were like, "No, they're not prepared. We need to ease them in." And South Africa now still has huge problems, but has one of the most progressive constitutions in the world and is making huge strides.

PNH: That is a fantastic model for how to deal with your previous oppressive class... without purges.

LQ: The Reconciliation. And the Reconciliation model has been tried elsewhere—

LB: Successfully. We don't actually *need* a revolution, hopefully, to redeem the people who are in Washington, DC. Obviously the point that you are making is that the underlying conditions that would allow that to take place would not be changed simply by removing a rogue president. We have a number of different problems. We need to remove the infection that is poisoning us and hurting us, but we also need to address the underlying conditions that allowed this to occur—a paradigm shift from the acquiescence that permitted these people to take power.

LQ: Yeah, we have to have a paradigm shift, but that may not work if they're stealing the ballots, if they are maintaining control in any conceivable way. Maybe we *do* need a revolution in the system. Maybe we *are* at that point. Patrick, you said we're not at the point where we *need* a revolution, and you said that so confidently. I'm actually not so confident. I sometimes wonder whether we're actually at that point.

PNH: I think marching on the offices of the *New York Times* or the *Washington Post* might be more effective.

LB: The revolution begins with getting the media to do their job, so that the Republicans can't steal the election.

PNH: I actually think the media is the central problem of the current emergency. I mean, there's always been a thuggish business class. There have always been Dick Cheney types. Our political media class at the moment, in my view, is unprecedentedly and morally feckless and corrupt, and despicable. They are the moral equivalent of the late nineteenth century Russian officer corps. They are drug-sodden, decadent, depraved, vicious, meretricious, worthless human beings.

[*audience cheers*]

LQ: Applause for the rant. Applause for the rant.

Aud: Let's get you on *Crossfire*.

SKP: But that didn't happen overnight. That actually was a gradual reform plotted by the Neocon Bushite kind of people back from 1970 or so, on. And it took them thirty—

PNH: Because of the push for corporate media consolidation, and all of us boring *Nation*-reading progressives were whining about this because they were sorta going "yeah, yeah, yeah, let the big dog..."

SKP: And they kept saying how liberal the media was.

PNH: That was a great piece of *mau-mauing*. I popped my cork over this recently because of that most recent, unbelievably stupid thing on *Slate.* I'm no big Hillary Clinton fan; I voted for her against the Republican in New York State, but I'm not enthusiastic about her running for president. But Jacob Weisberg, who is the editor of *Slate*, a supposedly center-liberal web publication, had this unbelievably despicable article about when Hillary was asked what was on her iPod. She said, "Oh, some Beatles, some Rolling Stones, some Aretha Franklin, a U2 song." This entire article is spelling out how this shows that she's a *calculating and cunning* politician; these are *careful* choices, *calibrated to appeal* to her audience, and show her *fundamental dishonesty*. Yeah, somebody who grew up in the '60s and early '70s, that went to college in 1972, likes the Beatles and Aretha Franklin. Holy cow, is that ever calculating! Geez! ("Playlist Politics," Jacob Weisberg, May 24, 2006, *Slate*, at

http://www.slate.com/id/2142359/)

[*laughter*]

Aud [Arthur from Wisconsin Public TV?]: I'm feeling personally attacked here. The problem is that the media, like everybody else in this world, like every other profession, has certain rules and conventions by which we operate. You have to have that if you're going to have any sort of structural edge. If you're running your own little blog, you can do whatever you want to, but if you're part of a larger structure, which most businesses are, you have to have that.

LB: But how did we get to the point—

Aud (continuing): Let me finish. The problem is this: Republicans and, to a lesser degree, Democrats, have learned what those conventions are and they have learned how to subvert them. I'll give you the classic example: the Talking Point. When you're in Journalism School, you're taught to go out and interview as many possible people as you can find and get their collective thoughts together and write a story.

[transcriber: jesus...the testosterone in here...]

PNH: Average them out. This is how you get the classic story, "Administration..."

Aud (continuing): That's right. Now let me finish! So you keep talking to more people. But Republicans very shrewdly have learned, if everybody says the exact same words, reporters keep asking over and over and over again. Jon Stewart—one of his classic shticks is to take fifteen people all saying the same thing. And believe me, you almost have to view them as you did the Soviets. If you got Vladimir Posner's comment, you didn't go out and try to interview another fifteen people because you knew that everyone in the Soviet power structure said exactly the same thing.

Aud [another guy]: I would argue that the Republicans haven't just subverted the rules of journalism; they changed them. I wanna ask how we got to the point where calumny and innuendo trump truth in terms of sales value.

PNH: I wasn't thinking of Wisconsin Public Television as a central and internal organ in the belly of the beast, but it doesn't seem to be particularly convincing defense of the behavior of the modern political pundit...

Aud: What I'm saying is, we have to learn...what I personally think the problem is that at one time in our country, and honestly the rest of the world right now, you have obviously partisan presses.

PNH: But we've had partisan presses before.

Aud: Yes, we have, but at some point we started getting into the idea of this "one objective voice," and that has fallen apart. That's where the internet media come in—

> [transcriber: LQ tries to put a lid on it...guy keeps talking right over her. Oh man...I might as well be teleported into the comments thread of *Daily Kos*. Hello, did we forget the "feminist" as well as the "sf" part of this panel? Overbearing dudes need to shut up a bit.]

LQ: Sir, I'm sorry, I want to open it up a little bit more. So, Anna?

Aud [woman in feathered hat]: Revolution doesn't happen because people decide that there ought be a revolution. Revolution is often thought of as a bad idea. It happens when people have nothing to lose. And I think that in America people are still a long way from having nothing to lose. But the thing is, you are going in the wrong direction, and I don't know how long it will take but it will come to a point when people really have no rational reason not to resort to violence. And that's when revolution happens, and it usually doesn't end well. A reform would be a much nicer idea.

IH: Actually, my understanding is that most revolutions happen when things start getting a little bit better after a long downturn. And if you can organize a long downturn without that little up-kick, then you're a lot less likely to have to worry about revolution.

> [LQ comment: I just have to observe, reading this transcript, that this is also when most suicides occur for people having a major depressive episode: after the depression eases up just a little bit, so they get just enough energy back…]

LQ: Is that what the Republicans have done?

IH: Well, I think that's intentional. To bring it back to science fiction briefly, one thing I do want to emphasize is that science fiction, because it is a literature of ideas, helps people really know what it is they are fighting for. One of the examples that certainly is near and dear to *my* heart, is the notion of responsible non-monogamy. Responsible non-monogamy as a lifestyle was mostly started by science fiction fans, who read about it in science fiction, and then it moved out into the larger culture. And, well, it was something people did to the best of their ability, but it wasn't something that people talked about and it wasn't something that people really thought carefully about. And that's an example of something where I really think without having seen it in action, maybe even in some not terribly well-written works which might or might not have comparatively treated women as good as they might have. Not that I'm keen about anybody in particular.

[*laughter*]

LQ: Is he talking about Heinlein?

[*laughter*]

IH: I know better than to mention certain names on panel!

Aud [woman with ponytail sitting in the back]: Looking at revolution in the United States right now, it seems to me that everyone is trying to fight the battle that's right in front of them. In Wisconsin one of the things we are fighting is gay marriage. I have friends that are going out and knocking on doors and are really passionate about it. The reality is that that's not where the battles are. I mean, it's not that that's not effective, but as far as the long-term war, I don't see it as a physical thing; it's more in the aesthetic of what we're doing, where the great divide is.

PNH: Interestingly enough, this argument is actually being played out inside the Democratic Party. I mean, obviously there are people in this room who regard the Democratic Party as totally bankrupt and illegitimate—there is a reasonable argument to be made for that—but nonetheless, there is this big argument happening between Howard Dean, the Chairman of the Democratic National Committee, and consultants like Paul Begala and so forth over Dean's fifty-state strategy. Dean got elected to the DNC chair by promising all of the state Democratic Parties that he'd raise and spend money to put activists on the ground in all fifty states, no matter how "red." And people like Begala feel that this is foolhardy because Democrats have the best shot this year than in several electoral cycles to gain back at least one house of Congress, and that we shouldn't be spending money having activists knocking on doors in Mississippi when it's really important to get all those narrow, close House races. To the extent that I care about the Democratic Party, which is every other Tuesday, I think Dean is right. What you were talking is that you do have to make long-term investments. The problem in this country is this: there are a lot of people who have economic reason, every statistical practical reason, to sympathize with progressives, with liberals, to vote left-of-center, and yet there are huge swatches in the country in which it's simply *embarrassing* to admit that you're a Democrat or liberal or progressive, and having people knocking on doors in Mississippi and Utah and Idaho and other places where they're not going to win any elections any time soon is one way to counter that. You have to make your existing supporters feel strong. Politics is to some extent a gut game, and I think that radicals should certainly understand that.

Aud [Michael]: Just to make my bias clear, because I'm not going to pretend I'm not biased, I'm a card-carrying IWW member…

LQ: Woohoo!

Aud [Michael]: …and you said, "The media aren't doing their job." Well actually, yes they are. I see this "liberal media…conservative media…liberal media…conservative media." All the media, with very few exceptions, are owned by the rich. The entire purpose of the media is to put on a pantomime to keep people divided into two mutually antagonistic mobs. It requires no great conspiracy theory to expect people to do what is in their obvious self-interest, i.e., expect those with wealth and power to move in such a way to keep themselves wealthy and powerful. Most people in this country don't feel horribly disempowered, and they got their 150 channels of cable, and they think they have something to lose.

LQ: So I actually hear this about the media; I'm down with that. What are we going to do about it?

PNH: I saw your analysis coming. I completely agree with it by and large. On one level, these people who I'm condemning *are* doing their job that their owners want them to, but the purpose of pointing out what a bunch of feckless shitheads they are is to embarrass them and to appeal to what vestigial, fossilized, tiny, withered sense of professionalism and self-respect they may still have. The analysis you put forth was correct though; it could have been put forth at any time in American history. It was certainly true in 1898, when we embarked on our first spasm of imperial idiocy, when the Hearst papers were running rampant.

IH: Actually, that was the second or third. You gotta remember the Native Americans…

LB: There's no such thing as investigative journalism? I'm not sure that newspapers are strictly a puppet show all the time.

Aud: But the owners have amazing influence—perhaps not on a tactical, day-to-day, article by article level—but the owners of newspapers, television stations, etc…

[*multiple interjections*]

LQ: Hold on! We can argue about the media. Is the solution to the media to have a revolution? This is my question. What are we gonna do about people owning the media? And that's one part of the problem, that there are the owners, there is the state. I am actually curious how we are going to get past this problem. *[Pointing out audience members for next questions]* John, and then I've got "pink mustache," and then one, two, three.

[*laughter*]

Aud [John]: I guess I wanna raise the moderate versus radical question to the panel. Now this comes back partly to the fifty-state strategy as far as how will you approach the revolution. Do we go out to the extremes of how we feel, or do we talk to more of the moderates and try to win over the subjects?

LQ: So do we play to the extremes or win the moderates? Pink hair.

Aud [the guy with pink hair]: This ties a few things in. One is, so far in many mentions of revolution, it is this automatic assumption that it's *violent* revolution and/or this physical power overthrow, and to tie in to how to deal with…the idea of cultural revolution. It's slower obviously than taking up arms and burning down centers of power, but the idea that you can reach out to people you know, talk to people. I mean, if one of your coworkers makes a bigoted comment, call them on it. Call them on their shit. Challenge them in everyday life. And rather than having politicians pay people to go door-to-door, where people are going automatically to turn a stranger out, challenge the people in your everyday life who are really a part of the status quo, whose ideas are probably the status quo, and call them on their bullshit, and change people culturally.

Aud [guy in back]: Thirty-five years ago we brought down a monster with substantial help from the media.… Twenty years ago the media said, "*Yessuh, massa*" when told there was nothing happening at El Mozote. That is an obvious change. The question is, what specifically happened then? Where do we reverse it? <snip>

Is it appropriate to attack the media as the weak point, or is it appropriate to attack the fractures that are already showing up in the Republican Party as in that

Richard Vigerie article that Patrick linked to, and to break them far enough apart that they will no longer come up with any talking point that dominates the media paradigm?

LQ: I'd like to hear from some of the women.

<snip>

Aud [woman in black velvet hat sitting in the back]: We are talking about revolution being this violent thing, but the way that things are right now, is violent. People dying because they don't have healthcare is violent. People stealing people's livelihoods through trade agreements is violent. And I think we need to realize that—

Aud [guy in back who brought up El Mozote]: Nobody sees that as violence on the order of mugging or terrorism.

Aud [Liz Henry]: But it is—

PNH: I mean, our overseas presence has become centurions.

LQ: So how can we make people see that that is a level of violence too?

Aud [Cynthia White]: Doesn't that bring in the question of strategy? <snip>

SKP: I have an actual science fiction comment to go with that! So the idea of the people who are actually dying now—poor children without immunizations, without enough food, or in poor health—if you could in fact shine a light on that very visibly, that would be like the story by Ursula K. Le Guin, "The Ones Who Walk Away from Omelas." If you could make everyone look at the misery that actually does happen at the poor—[*interrupted*]

Aud [guy in black who brought up El Mozote]: But can you make that seem like "the poor are us" rather than "the poor are else," which isn't working now.

LQ: I think we could because I think that when people actually see what's real, when they do see humanity, I mean, that was a crucial way in which the media helped us during the Vietnam War, by showing the lives and the dead bodies and the injuries and the harms that we were causing. But my concern with "The Ones Who Walk Away from Omelas" is that some of those people did not walk away from Omelas.

<snip>

SKP: Well—

LB: Well the problem is, I'll tell you—

LQ: I want to hear Susan finish and then you, Lenny.

SKP: People don't believe that the level of poverty that exists in this country exists. People don't believe that we're fourteenth out of the fourteen top industrial nations for healthcare or twenty-seventh *out of the top twenty-seven*! Wherever you cut it, we're at the *bottom*. People don't *believe* that.

<snip>

LB: I'll subside [on this issue] if there's a big show of hands. How many people in this room write letters to newspapers and television stations? Okay, the first thing we need to do in terms of "What are we going to do about the media?" is let them know that we're *here* and that when they parrot outrageous lies, we don't like it, because newspapers are *sensitive* to feedback from readers. [Don't let them get away with the game of averaging lies and truth together without fact checking. Don't let them sell the idea that the real truth must be an average of two opposite statements.]

LQ: I like that, and that's a positive thing. I think it's a little more effective, in *my* opinion, than voting—which is something I actually *do*, but I think that reaching out to other people and other kinds of ways that people absorb media is critical and important.

PNH: It is true, as you were pointing out earlier, that people inside a corporate hierarchical structure *do* get the messages about what they're supposed to be fundamentally doing. Nonetheless, there are handles where you can grab them—it's professional pride, it's a sense of their social status and so forth. You can shame people who have been toadies into behaving a little bit better, and even "a little bit" is a plus.

Aud [Anna—woman in pirate hat]: Isn't the mental narrative in American consciousness that your prime motive for acting is self-interest, and that is ultimately self-defeating in that you can always convince people that their self-interest is ultimately the interest of the hierarchy. And you need to change their narrative so that there's a new morality, so that people don't act in their own interest but on what they think is moral, and I see that as very hard to do.

LQ: That is true. It's shaping the vision of what's going on.

Aud [Larra Clark]: I work with media every day, NPR, for librarians.... I think that, one, it's a problem to say that the media is all one way. I mean, I think we have lots of liberal media, although I think what we see the most of and *hear* of the most of is CNN or Fox or whatever, and I think they have a disproportionate amount of power. But I think that writing letters to the editor is getting published, and if you read the newspapers you probably read letters to the editor. That is a way to also have a voice, as well as telling people about how they're doing their jobs. But I think people also have to engage the media in a very active way, and just like with politics, we become very passive with media. And people don't want to engage; they'd rather just say it's crap and just walk away instead of actively confronting it and looking for ways to engage or create media. And I think that that's a mistake, that we just give up and say, "It's crap. I don't watch television. I'm not engaged in that culture, so it's not for me and I don't care about it"—instead of doing something and engaging it in some active way.

LQ: So creating media I totally see, but what would *engaging* media be? Like, standing in front of Verizon and yelling?

Aud [Larra Clark]: I don't think there's just one way. I think it's about thinking about what the work is that we're doing and who needs to know about it and how can you find an avenue looking for outlets for it, whether it's your community newspaper or community radio station, looking for ways to talk to other people through media and looking at media as a potential way to do that. And it's going to be different if you're in Chicago or New York or LA than if you're in other communities. But I think that we don't *engage* media, that we look at it as something "other" as opposed to something that also can belong to us. We have an obligation to engage, and if we don't, our voices will never be heard. And I think that it's a struggle—you work on a number of pieces, you do a lot of work and end up with nothing to show for it as in the case of the news station—but I think that too often people don't engage media in this way at all.

PNH: I think you're absolutely right. You stated the case extremely politely, but basically—I don't want to make crazy, over-the-top claims for the power of political blogging, but blogs do get read by reporters, by media professionals and by their secretaries, and by the people in the advertising department and so forth. And a sustained, remorseless attack on the conceited self-image of these worthless *popinjays* has an effect. It chips away at their confidence. It makes them defensive. They start their own blogs and then they make even bigger fools of themselves.

Aud [Michael, in front row]: You were saying that we're the fourteenth or twenty-seventh in terms of child death. The problem as I see it is not that people don't know, but that so many people in this country don't care. It's exactly what Anna was saying about self-interest coupled with "the great accomplishment" in quotation marks of Ronald Reagan—that he turned the poor into the enemy. And people bought into that literally by the millions. It's *fun* to kick somebody while they're down because you know they aren't getting back up again. And until we can get people to give a flying *fuck* for the fact that we are twenty-seventh out of twenty seven, it's not gonna change.

LQ: I have a note that says "blue shirt" and I think that might have been you.

Aud [woman sitting in the middle of the room]: It is. Actually, it's just another re-statement of what he was saying, which is that it would appear that people no longer feel any shame for the things that go on, that our government does. When I talk to people at work and I say how many children are dying of malnutrition, they say, "*So*."—

LQ: Where do you work?

Aud: Department of Surgery, University of Minnesota.

LQ: Damn.

Aud: Yeah. And I brought up Abu Ghraib, and they said, "Well, it has nothing to do with *us*."

LQ: They were dark, they were terrorists, they were taxicab drivers.

Aud: It wasn't just that! It was that they didn't have any responsibility. There is no sense of shame anymore about hunger or poverty. There's no sense of public property anymore. I talked to several people who didn't know that libraries belonged to the public.

PNH: You know, this kind of talking about how there's been some ineluctable moral behavior in the public in general—

Aud: That's not what I'm saying. What I'm saying is that there's a shift in the way people *look* at things. I mean, the whole idea of public property is not a theory—

[multiple interjections]

Aud [Avedon Carol]: I still think a lot of it is [that] people don't—I'm amazed that sometimes I'll be talking to somebody who's really worried about their healthcare, and I'll start to say, "Well, yes, that's why it's really nice to have a national health service." "Oh, but it's so terrible!" And I hear so much about how *terrible* it is, and I'm just there going, "You know, I just had a couple of nights in the hospital and some really tricky surgery in *the best eye hospital in the world*, and I never *once* had to ask myself, 'Can I afford this?'" Because I couldn't. I would have just lost the use of my right eye.

LQ: There has been a structured attempt to control information, and corporate mass media has been one part of that. And I think that's why we have a de-funding of public and community media, and education and critical thinking and people's abilities to get into these things have been a real problem.

IH: I wanna get back to the question of paradox, because what I hear is a particular kind of model coming back at me—over and over and over again—about what kind of tactics are necessary for revolution. You know, this sort of "big leader" model, which isn't how any of the revolutions that I know of actually happened. And more and more, I think that a lot of it has to do with that great quote from Goebbels: "If you repeat a lie often enough it becomes the truth." I mean, pick a revolution. My favorite one is the Civil Rights revolution just because, you know, it's the one that affected my life the most. Martin Luther King didn't create the bus boycott. The bus boycott was a whole preexisting solution; that wasn't a woman who stood up one day and decided, "Wow, I think I'm gonna get arrested today." There were a lot of conversations before that happened; there were arguments within that community ahead of time; there was somebody brought in to be a figurehead, who was able to be sacrificed in case it went badly. But there were *hundreds and hundreds and hundreds of hours* of people voluntarily driving other people around the city in order to make that bus boycott work. Part of what made Seattle effective was new tactics. Decentralization. They weren't able to stop the activists because *there wasn't "an activist" to stop.* There wasn't your traditional top-down organizing principle. It was a whole bunch of affinity groups who all got together and said, "We'll take over *this* intersection for *this* period of time."

LQ: That's how we took over the streets of San Francisco when the Iraq War began, too. It was affinity groups and it was damned successful in terms of getting media attention, and I have friends from Iraq who have told me that they didn't think that Americans cared, but when they saw that San Francisco was shut down, it gave them some hope.

IH: Yeah. And the other thing I would say is that the way to start things is to do the right thing because it is the right thing to do. When it comes to journalism, the right thing is to tell the truth. I think it was Upton Sinclair who said, "The most radical form of journalism is to tell the truth."

LB: And start by not putting up with bullshit when you see it in news media. Treat it the same way as if they're shortchanging you on your bank account. Take the time and trouble to call them and tell them that you don't like what they're doing.

Aud [John]: To bring this over to science fiction: We have political science fiction—who do you direct it at, and what do you change their minds about? I guess this sort of relates to the center versus radical thing. We have to speak to red states,—I don't like the term "moderate the voices" because your ends are still there—but we have to speak in a way that's understandable to people who are on the other side.

LQ: Susan, take that [comment].

SKP: I'm a Democratic organizer, as well as being a doctor and a science fiction fan. I think that it's fine to have some workers out on the ground in red states too, and people who live there should certainly speak to their neighbors and their friends. And I don't want South Dakota to have banned abortion. But you could say we want things to get better—clearly, we do—but if you want to keep things from getting worse as well, we can't have a one-party system where one party has two houses of Congress, the executive branch and the judicial. Then it's not any kind of party system, and I think it's important that we work hard to get back one or two of the four institutions so that there is some difference, even if you don't see the Democrats and Republicans as being "real different." Now, of course, we have the Neo-cons in the far Right, and I think they're pretty different from even the moderates as well as from the far Left.

<snip>

Aud [woman in black]: I'm just really frustrated here because we keep focusing on the *media*, we keep focusing on *government*—and what we haven't brought in is where the dollars come from, which are businesses and corporations. And to bring science fiction into it, I'm wondering if there's a relationship between the Left or liberals or us or whatever you wanna call it, and what we see as the "bad guys," the Republicans in the government right now, based on reading science fiction. When you're talking about where the businesses take over space and they take over a planet, and that becomes the business itself and everyone runs by the corporate rules. And what I see in the United States and personal experience is not only that self-interest, but there is a total break between what business morality is and what personal morality is. And individuals can operate on both levels and not see any discrepancy.

LB: I have a quick comment on that. Are we going to continue to go to science fiction conventions held in hotel chains that are the largest corporate donors to the Republican Party? [*Clarification that WisCon's hotel was not what LB was talking about.*] Basically there are things we do in our own lives, and you all have to make the decision on where to draw the line and recognize that "I'm lending economic support to someone who is acting against me. What am I going to do?"

Aud: But also in your working day, you have control over making those decisions.

LB: That's right, I'm an IT manager and I have a few hundred thousand dollars and I have to decide whether I'm going to spend it at a computer company that is one of the Republican Party's greatest contributors.

PNH: You're not getting the question she's asking. Forgive me if I'm misinterpreting, but I saw it pointed out recently that here in the Land of the Free, most working Americans spend most of their time in profoundly authoritarian environments. Our working lives are a million miles away from anything resembling democratic and egalitarian. We spend our lives having authority figures make decisions for us and boss us around. There is an assumption that that's just inevitably how the business working life is going to be, and that is an entirely questionable assumption. That's what she's trying to get at, I think.

LQ: I want to recommend a really good book about revolution [when] your world is run by corporations. *Illicit Passage* by Alice A. Nunn, an Australian writer who has gotten very little attention over here, is a really great book. So "turnkey girl," then "AK Press pink," and then Anna. Turnkey, you have a key in the back, right? You had a key earlier, yes? Different outfit? Different person, but similar outfit.

Aud [girl in white frilly outfit]: No. Oh, I was like, what's the turnkey girl? Talking about what you had said earlier about the Civil Rights movement, I think that part of where, in my mind, the conservatives are so successful right now is that they're not necessarily trying to wage revolution. They're doing very successful reform where, in the case of the Civil Rights movement, you had the Christian church acting in a very significant way to create real change and reform. Now, when we think of the Christian churches, we hardly think of positive change happening or anything remotely leaning toward the Left. In the same way—I'm from Georgia—I bought a wildlife license plate that had an eagle and an American flag on it, and all my friends thought I had gotten some sort of "pro-gun" license plate because the symbols have become so associated with the Conservative Movement, and I felt that they had really beautifully orchestrated a reform system of incremental changes. And I also frighteningly have to come back to your comment on Goebbels, because I think that the Nazi Party did a brilliant job of that as well. And I feel that people who want to move to the Left are not thinking of that kind of game being played. It's either a revolution around a charismatic leader or it's these—sorry about this analogy—but it's like birds pecking at seeds, when you're trying to write letters to someone. I don't feel like that's actually really attacking anything or going for a *real* change. That has the illusion of people having a different kind of power. Like when you want someone to be president or something like that, [as if] the writing of letters would really effect that kind of change. But I'm wondering how the Left can achieve the kind of reforms that the Right is doing very brilliantly right now. [In the] Civil Rights movement, the Christian church acted in a significant way. When most of us think of Christian churches, we hardly think of anything positive. [There's been a] hijacking of symbols.

IH: Well, to answer that question directly I would say that I think the Left needs to do a much better job of dealing with strategic alliances. The right wing managed to pull those feminists, who I thought were absolutely out of their fucking minds, and co-opt them for the anti-pornography movement. And that gave them a lot more legitimacy for all the other stuff they wanted to do because they had formed a strategic alliance. When I watch a Rightist parade, all of the signs are the same. When I watch a Leftist parade, it's like—I actually thought teamsters and turtles was a pretty decent combination in the WTO—but usually it's like "this" group and "that" group and the "other" group and the "other other" group and the "other other other" group.

PNH: Are you suggesting that if we have an anti-Iraq demonstration that perhaps we should shut the fuck up about Mumia [Abu-Jamal]?

IH: Uh, yeah, actually, I am. [*laughter*] I also think that if I, as a Mumia supporter, go to an anti-Iraq demonstration, it would make sense for me to perform strategic alliances with the folks who are organizing that demonstration such that some of *them* can come out and support Mumia.

PNH: That's perfectly reasonable.

LB: About newspapers: if a newspaper is lying about my friend, I believe that if I write to the newspaper and I tell them that they're lying about my friend, they may choose to ignore me and not to publish it. But if they get a hundred letters from people that are telling them the same thing, they may think a little bit more about lying again.

<snip>

Aud [Avedon Carol]: Well let's not forget about what the Republicans actually did. It was a very small number of very rich Republicans that spent thirty-five years putting their money in strategic places. All those think-tanks you hear mentioned all the time now—which aren't real think-tanks, and which didn't exist thirty-five years ago—magazines, all kinds of media infrastructure—that they built from scratch; they put people in place to do stuff. You hear about all these weird places like A[merican] E[nterprise] I[nstitute] and others compared with the RAND Corporation. The RAND Corporation does *actual research*. All these right wing think-tanks—they don't do research. All they do is PR, but they're treated as equal.

PNH: They are, however, an extraordinarily effective career system for young people who want to be professional right-wingers. It's *incredibly* lucrative and *incredibly* easy to get into if you simply want to spend the remainder of your entire life spouting right-wing talking points. We much need to build structures that do this, that support young activists.

Aud [Avedon Carol]: There is no reward for being a liberal or left-wing activist. You can't make money doing it.

<snip>

LQ: <snip> We've had some good suggestions about ways to make incremental but meaningful changes, but we also have a sense that maybe we're in a position where we're holding back the barricades. I mean, is there a real problem here? Is it a time when we actually need to focus on these little elections because the Fascists are coming, and like anything we can do to stem the tide is good? Or, is this a moment to actually say, "Screw it, let's actually go for broke and try to get the revolution now and go for some real change and quit fucking around with the pissant Democrats," and how would we do that?

Aud: What do you mean by "go for real change"?

LQ: I don't know! I throw that out to you guys. How do we know it's time for a revolution? Are we going to be able to hold the barricades if we try to vote for Democrats? Are we going to hold the barricades or are we not?

Aud [Liz Henry]: How do we know when it's time for revolution?

LQ: Yeah, how do we know when it's time for revolution?

Aud [woman sitting in the middle of the room]: My comment was about coalition-building, and I'm probably talking about coalitions that you'd probably rather not talk about. I'm a banker and I spend all my time dealing with business people, and I deal mainly with small-business people. And people on the left have really, really missed the boat with vilifying business in general. I go out and talk to small businesses all the time, "What is the number one issue for small-business owners today?" and I hear the same thing from everyone: "Healthcare." (*others also saying healthcare*) Small businesses want universal healthcare.

Aud [woman in black velvet hat]: You think we've missed the boat; you're wrong. It's them. We've been saying it, why aren't you coming on board? This will save your life. *Do* something.

Aud: But where I see it in my community in a small town, they're not hearing that from *anybody*, where I am.

PNH: Oh I think, as a class, American small business is the biggest bunch of pampered, sissy, whiny crybabies. Every politician at every point in the spectrum—*every* elected politician in the spectrum—

LQ: You said you weren't up for throwing bombs on this panel!

[*laughter*]

PNH: Yeah, well...*Everybody* is in favor of small businesses, because there is no business model that is guaranteed to succeed.

<snip>

Aud [Kathleen]: If I'm repeating something that you said before, please forgive me, but I noticed that when hundreds of thousands of people in the city where I live left their jobs and left their schools and took to the streets to communicate what they felt about immigration reform—the politicians, the media—everybody—went, "Ah yes. Now we're *hearing*."

LQ: Yeah, they paid attention to that (the mass immigration demonstrations of 2006).

Aud: Yeah, but you're in Chicago. I never *noticed*.

Aud [Allen Baum]: The first interesting point is that the Right wing has spent thirty-five years building up something. They've been very very patient. They take the very very long view, and I don't see that here. I see lots of very short-view things but not very many long-view things. *Long*-view things are the things that are *really* going to succeed in the *long* run.

PNH: There's not actually a shortage of money on the Left. There are Left billionaires. I'm agreeing with you. I'm supporting your point. I'm saying that this kind of infrastructure could be built on the Left. We need to shake down our rich people, and we have plenty of them. And think long-term, as you're saying.

LQ: So I'm just going to list the kinds of things that I've heard, and then if we've forgotten any or if anybody has any short, quick points of how we can make this better, tell me. So I've heard: we need strategic, long-term thinking and putting our money in; we need to actually be contributing to the media, writing to the media and responding when we see things that are wrong, right away; we do need to be, some people feel, working on elections where we'll actually make a difference; blogging and actually creating our own media is another thing. What else am I missing, and what other quick ideas do we have?

Aud [Anna]: Courts. General strike.

Aud [Michael]: Ian hit it on the head: building coalitions. The IWW is outnumbered two to one by the National Model Railroad Association for Christ's sake.

[*laughter*] But the good news is most of them are over sixty so in a dust-up…

Aud [John Kim]: Win the culture wars on the moderates; not just focusing narrowly on individual races.

LQ: So focus on the moderates in the red states.

SKP: Universal healthcare. We need to get universal healthcare *very* soon.

Aud [Jasmine]: Meeting things in your everyday community. And identifying and calling people on their bullshit.

Aud: Convincing the middle-class people who voted for Bush in the current administration that what GM is doing to its employees (*bailing on their pensions*) can and will be done if it's allowed to anybody else, and assume you will not have a middle class to be any sort of a buffer to protect the poor.

IH: In just two words, I would say: "celebrate success."

PNH: I'm voting for what she said [*points toward SKP*] because the lack of guaranteed healthcare in this country is probably the single thing that keeps people scared, keeps them from taking creative risks and political risks, keeps them in their foxholes, protecting themselves. We're all scared all the time. And it keeps us in jobs where we're terrified by authoritarians.

LQ: And can I say that we do have a right to *healthcare*. We don't have a right to health insurance. Blue shirt.

Aud [blue shirt]: Violent revolution is not practical; people have too much.

LB: I have one more: read. Stay informed. Think about what you're reading so that you can recognize a good coalition when you see one.

LQ: And I have something to add to "read": talk. And talk to your neighbors and your community and control the media and get the radios back. Get the airwaves back.

IH: Vote with your dollars. I mean, like, *really*.

Aud [Paul]: Put your money into businesses and into things that have the same political viewpoints that you do.

Aud [Jasmine]: You gotta keep your sense of humor rather than being angry. <snip>

SKP: Try and help, and show other people how to do critical thinking. The scariest thing for me is that, not my *own* child but lots of people, fifteen to twenty-five, that I know, don't look at anything critically. And I know a bunch of kids who know they should vote. And they go in and they go "eenie meenie mynie moe."

Aud [Jeff]: I just wanted to that something important is that if you have a 401k or some other kind of diversified investment account, check and make sure you're not accidentally investing in people you don't want to invest in. There *are* socially-conscious 401ks and mutual funds.

LB: Check out the school board in your neighborhood, which takes a little more effort.

Aud [Avedon]: What is the website that has the list of which businesses…?

LB: Oh, Blue America and Red America. I'm not sure. If you search for "Blue America"…

Aud: Check "Act Blue."

IH: Support long attention spans.

[*laughter, applause*]

Georgie Schnobirch

We Aren't Civilized Yet: Reflections From the WisCon 30 Panel on Women Warriors

An Essay in Two Parts

by Nancy Jane Moore

At the end of the WisCon 30 panel "Military Women: Past, Present and Future," my co-panelist David Haseman thanked the audience for letting us skip the question that usually dominates such panels: whether women can be effective soldiers. Instead, we ended up having a lively discussion—at 8:30 AM on Monday morning!—that covered such divergent topics as whether one function of war is the biological goal of genetic mixing and if democracies are indeed less warlike than other forms of government.

Of the many topics we covered that morning, two are close to my heart: self defense and overpopulation. The purpose of this essay is not to recap the discussion at WisCon, but to share my current thoughts on those two subjects.[1]

Part I: There Are No Front Lines in Modern Warfare—or Modern Life

One of the more obvious lessons from the Iraq War is that it's difficult to plan where to put combat troops. Even during the so-called "actual war," there were a number of times when support military units such as cooks and supply troops found themselves under attack. As the war degenerated into an insurgency and the current civil war, this situation multiplied.

The result in a US military that is 14.4 percent female is that women soldiers have sometimes found themselves on the front lines, whether or not they were prepared for them. This situation makes a mockery of the exclusion of women from combat positions, which are also the jobs that provide the greatest opportunities for career advancement in the armed forces. Women are actually serving in combat, but are neither being given sufficient training for it nor receiving professional credit for doing the job. They continue to be treated as second-class soldiers though their lives are on the line.[2] The lack of a clearly defined front line in modern war also creates a good argument for upping the combat readiness training of all soldiers, even those who do paperwork jobs.

Whether a war takes the form of the traditional battle between two trained armies or the now more common form of bombing campaigns against civilian targets and guerrilla-style attacks, the historical truth is that civilian women have always been on the front lines. Although in the past the official combatants may have primarily been men—a few disguised women notwithstanding—battles have rarely been confined to areas that don't overlap with civilian populations.

Now that direct attacks on civilians have become an acknowledged strategy—one not confined to those labeled "terrorists"—the idea that men must protect women and children is exposed as the myth it probably always was. In fact, the discussion at the panel about the value of war in producing genetic mixing comes from the idea that women are a legitimate spoil of war and rape is the privilege of the conqueror. That we now, on occasion, punish soldiers for rape does not mean that this idea has become obsolete.

While too many wars are raging across the earth, much of the human race is not currently in danger of being caught in the crossfire. But all of us are at risk from crime. Everyone—male or female, young or old—is at some risk from violent criminal attack. No matter how many laws we pass, humans have been unable to legislate violence out of existence. While these days we not only punish traditionally defined assaults but also have begun to recognize crimes such as date rape and hazing—activities that were once ignored, if not quietly approved—assaults still occur.

Humans have come up with many systems for protection over the years: walls, locks, and their modern counterpart, the security system; armies in their defensive role; police, private security firms, and even personal bodyguards. But no one wants to stay locked inside all day, and police officers cannot be everywhere at once. Even bodyguards are not a perfect solution (the well-trained Secret Service was not able to prevent the assassination of John Kennedy or the shooting of Ronald Reagan), and given the amount of privacy and money one must sacrifice to be guarded full-time, most would not exercise this option unless their lives were under constant threat.

Our culture operates on the myth that men are, for the most part, able to defend themselves. There's a corollary to that myth: men are expected to put their lives on the line to protect others, particularly women. Classically, this even includes protecting the honor of women. This corollary is well-entrenched: indeed, the story of the unskilled man who attempts to protect a woman from a verbal or physical offense and then finds himself in a fight that is over his head is so common in fiction as to be a cliché. Of course he always wins, or at least gets the girl. But in real life, alas, victory is never assured.

The flip side of the myth is that women need to be protected, can't defend themselves, and shouldn't be expected to; they must, however, defend their children in all circumstances. The corresponding myth involving women is thus that of the mother who gets between her child and the rampaging tiger or wild man with a gun. We often see warm-hearted human-interest stories about women who succeed in protecting their children as well as equally tear-inducing stories about those who die in the attempt.

These stories developed in more primitive times, when the survival of a clan—or indeed, of the human race—was tied to reproduction. Men were expendable, since they can't bear children and aren't equipped to breastfeed, and the next generation was worth more than the current one, so it was worth sacrificing a woman to protect the children. But as I will discuss in the second section of this paper, since we no longer live in a world where every woman must produce as many children as she possibly can to ensure that the human race survives, we need to let go of ideas about defending ourselves that were developed when survival required producing as many children as possible.

We must recognize two important facts. First, the world is not safe. The level of risk may be greater or lesser, depending on where you live and what your resources are, but we are all at some risk of attack from our fellow human beings. While we often use the word "inhuman" to describe particularly awful crimes, the truth is that interpersonal violence is as much a part of the human makeup as love and compassion. In addition, there are numerous other dangers in the world—disease, natural disaster, a vast potential for accidents—that further jeopardize our sense of safety.

Second, women are as capable as men of protecting themselves and protecting others when necessary. That both genders buy into the myth that they are not keeps women at a significant disadvantage, because they must place limitations on themselves, such as traveling with a male companion or avoiding certain neighborhoods. Acting in accordance with this myth not only perpetuates a helpless mindset among the female population, limiting their sense of potential as well as their careers and dreams; it also impels men to take foolish risks, particularly men who really don't know how to protect themselves but feel that they must do something nonetheless.

During the panel, a member of the audience asked if we thought it would change things if most women knew how to defend themselves. According to Quilter's notes, Haseman and I both answered "yes" in unison and with enthusiasm. Once enough women know the basics of self defense, we will no longer be seen automatically as a group of victims, all of us vulnerable to attack on the sole ground of our gender.

Another audience member brought up the Heinlein quote, "An armed society is a polite society." But I'm not arguing that we should revert to a society where everyone carries a gun or a sword—even if everyone includes women. Giving everyone a weapon is a more simplistic response than training everyone in the broad range of skills that provide self defense.

In the first place, while I do believe that people who have seriously studied the arts of war are much less likely than others to fight unless it is absolutely necessary, I question that "armed" leads to "polite." Too many people assume that having a weapon gives them an edge over others, and it's easy enough to learn how to use a gun without learning any of the restraint taught in martial arts or even the military.

In the second place, self defense has very little to do with fighting. Fighting skills can come in handy and learning them is a sure way to build self confidence, but most people will rarely, if ever, need to fight to protect themselves or someone else. In fact, when I teach Aikido, I point out to my students that the most important self defense technique you can learn is how to fall down and get back up. Not only will that help you if you should get attacked, it will also come in handy when you slip on the ice or take a header off a bicycle—things that are much more likely to happen.

Here are some of the other important skills that allow people to protect themselves and others:

- Paying attention: seeing what is going on before what is going on sees you.
- Presenting a confident, but not overaggressive, persona: finding the balance between standing your ground and running roughshod over your adversary.
- Being flexible: changing your route, changing your plans; adapting to the situation.
- Trusting your intuition: if your gut says a situation is dangerous, get out of it, figure out why later.
- Learning what to fear: learning that the things that frighten us the most emotionally—stranger assaults and terrorist attacks—are not nearly as big a risk as more ordinary actions, such as driving a car.

Perhaps most importantly, women and men need to learn something about self defense because it teaches you to accept risk in your life and to understand and deal with your own capacity for anger and violence.

On the whole, I'd say a society in which people have learned to pay attention to what is happening around them and come to terms with their own anger will be a polite society—perhaps even a civilized one.

Part II: We Have Too Damned Many People in the World—And It May Damn Us All

When I took biology as a freshman in college, my professor, Michael Menaker, took great pains to teach us—the leading edge of the baby boom—about the problems presented by overpopulation. He once drew a map of India on the blackboard and then crossed it out. "It's already too late for India," he said. I remember being horrified but convinced we could do something to save India.

The world population has increased by three billion since I took biology. The population of India has doubled to over a billion people. I find myself wondering what other countries Dr. Menaker would strike off the map today.

Virtually every major problem faced by the human race today is caused by—or at the very least aggravated by—the overwhelming size of world population. Global warming might not be a significant issue if there were three billion people in the world instead of six and a half billion, even if the same percentage of the population was living high on the hog. With a smaller population, it would be possible, both economically and environmentally, for every person on this planet to enjoy a decent life. Perhaps humans would be less inclined to kill each other if everyone had more space, housing, food, education, health care, and work.

Yet here we are at a time of population crisis, still fighting for the right to birth control and abortion in the most powerful country in the world—a country whose government is more interested in protecting embryos in fertility clinics than it is in assuring good lives for the already born. Instead of taking the lead in promoting family planning worldwide, the US government has promoted abstinence—a project that would be laughable at best if the results weren't so tragic.

While I am appalled at such foolishness in a wealthy country with a supposedly educated populace, antiquated religious attitudes about family planning—the US campaigns against birth control come from the increasingly out-of-touch Roman Catholics and fundamentalist Protestant Christian sects—are only one piece of the overpopulation puzzle. The heart of the problem is that the world has gone through a period of incredibly rapid change in the past 150 years. While many of us have adapted intellectually to living in the modern world, with its amazing communication technologies, medical treatments that extend so many lives, and scientific advances that require fewer and fewer people to live on the land, the human body itself has not changed much. Evolution doesn't work that quickly. Physically, we don't differ much from the hunter/gatherer societies that were our initial forms of civilization. And we certainly haven't evolved much since the agrarian cultures that dominated the world up to the twentieth century.

Our genetic code still programs us to act in ways that are not constructive to modern life. Even though we are developing the ability to tinker with genes and may take significant charge of our evolution at some point (a possibility I find equally exciting and alarming), we can't change our genes quickly enough to have any effect on our current lives or those of our grandchildren. But we can make cultural adaptations. After all, it is not only our biology, but also our cultural baggage that is driving our population explosion, generating climate changes, and causing other problems that we confront daily.

What is the biggest problem created by that cultural baggage? The overwhelming importance placed on contemporary ideas of "the family" and raising children.

For many thousands of years, human survival was tied to having lots of children. Children were the "retirement plan" for their parents: have enough children and there would be someone to take care of you when you got old. They were also the way to get rich: have enough children and you could farm more land. In addition, they were a way to gain power: have enough children and your village or country could grow large and strong.

While humans have many times throughout history overpopulated particular geographical areas (some of the current deserts are apparently the result of overusing a delicate ecosystem), these instances did not affect the planet as a whole. Having lots of children paid off for most of us, most of the time.

But that's no longer true.

Most reports on population growth talk about how it took all of human history up to 1830 for the world population to hit one billion, 100 years to hit the next billion, 30 years for the next billion, 15 for the next, and so on up to our current 6.5 billion. This is a scary sequence of numbers, but it doesn't provide much of an explanation for why the population got out of hand so fast, outside of the basic Malthusian answer of geometric progression.

So what has changed? Well, one clear answer is scientific progress: the industrial revolution, modern medicine, and all those other things that make our lives very different from those of people living a couple of hundred years ago.

Or, in other words: oil.

The rapid growth of population (the world population is five times as great as it was in 1850) and modern oil extraction and refining both had their origins in the mid-1800s. Because we were unable to foresee how much oil would change our lives, we continued to reproduce as we always had.

Predicting the future is not something humans do well, and I doubt that many could see the amazing changes that advances in science and technology were going to bring us. The automobile alone redefined the world landscape over the past 100 years But we are now way past the point where those changes became obvious, way past the point where we should have taken serious steps to change our way of life. We are, in fact, at the point at which we could well destroy ourselves. Who knows whether we can make sufficient changes to counteract the effect of global warming that is already underway?

Of course, we may only go through a difficult period that reduces our population back to what the planet can handle—a time that will be painful, but survivable. If significant family planning can be pushed worldwide and coupled with obvious economic advantages for those who have fewer children, we may be able to slowly drop the population back to a level that allows us all to live comfortably on the Earth.

Or we could go through a dark age. Jane Jacobs in her last book before her death, *Dark Age Ahead*,[3] warned of this possibility. Instead of making it possible for all the human beings on our planet to live in the reasonable comfort we in the West take for granted, we could have hundreds, even thousands of years in which the amazing technological feats of our current life—worldwide instantaneous communication, human beings on the Moon—become myths, as everyone on Earth once again struggles simply to survive.

We've all read plenty of science fiction about that.

But there's something else that came along in the mid-1800s, along with oil and population growth; something that gives me a bit of hope that we will be able to adapt and survive: feminism.

Feminist thought has been intermittently with us from earlier times, but in the US, modern feminism dates from the mid-nineteenth century; the Seneca Falls Convention was held in the US in 1848. Although feminism is related to other movements for human rights such as the democratic revolutions and the abolition of slavery, I do not think it's a coincidence that a philosophy advocating more roles for women in the world grew up at a time of unprecedented population growth and technological change.

That is, modern feminism began as the world started changing into a place where we needed to bring fewer children into the world. We no longer need for every woman to give birth. In fact, at this point, we desperately need for many women to forego having any children and for those who do to have only one or two.

Feminism addresses the problem of overpopulation by offering women other purposes in life besides childrearing. To bring this back to the warriorship discussion: Women are free to choose the dangerous life of the soldier (or the explorer) because the human race doesn't need to reserve them for childbearing, as universal reproduction is no longer crucial to humankind's aggregate survival. And, to go one step further, we need for women to choose other roles besides motherhood, because our survival as a planet now depends on slowing population growth and, ideally, on reducing the population to a sustainable number and stabilizing it there.

In the recent court decisions rejecting gay marriage, judges have wasted a great deal of paper on the idea that states recognize marriages between a man and a woman because they want to promote procreation. If that is true, it's time we had a shift in priorities. We should be discouraging procreation, not encouraging it.

I'm not arguing for the oppressive rules of bleak totalitarian future science fiction in which everyone is sterilized and only a lucky (and obedient) few are permitted to have children, or even China's one-child policy (though given China's population crush, it's easy to understand why they adopted it). But we can make changes both cultural and legal that will discourage people from having children. Here are a few suggestions of things that can be done in the US:

- Provide tax breaks for singles who don't have children.
- Abolish dependent tax deductions for children beyond two.
- Provide easy and affordable access to birth control, including Plan B and abortion.
- Adequately fund family planning programs worldwide.
- Educate children on population issues along with sex education.
- Give tax breaks and other government assistance for adoption.
- Prohibit insurance coverage for fertility treatments or artificial insemination.
- Legalize gay marriage as a symbol that the purpose of marriage is to unite two people who love each other, not to produce children.

- Revitalize feminism, so that women are encouraged to develop serious careers and to consider foregoing childrearing.
- Devalue the cultural myth that the most important thing a person—and particularly a woman—can do is bring the next generation into the world.

Some demographers have come up with scary statistics pointing out that educated elites in Western countries are not having many children, while immigrants and/or fundamentalist Christians are reproducing like rabbits. They foretell a future overrun by those who do not respect our way of life. Both Japan and France grapple with these issues. Japan, of course, is an island, making the pressures of population obvious. But its population is graying, and it still discourages immigration. In France, the birth rate is much lower among those of traditional French heritage than it is among those whose families originally came from parts of Africa. Many of those of African descent are also Muslim, which has led to the rise of anti-Muslim actions by fascist groups and significant unrest among young and unemployed Muslims. Here in the US, it also appears that population growth owes more to immigrant birth rates than it does to native-born births, and our current debates over immigration are becoming increasingly xenophobic. A wall is being planned between the US and Mexico, and vigilantes who call themselves "Minutemen" are "helping" the Border Patrol by hunting undocumented immigrants. Despite all this, many large employers are still hiring those who enter this country illegally.

Other demographers worry about who will do the work to take care of the elderly if the population is declining. In the US (and France and Japan), the short-term answer to that second worry is immigration. A longer-term answer is encouraging people to stay in the workforce for more years—upping the age for Social Security, which we have already started to do, and recognizing that people need not retire at some automatic fixed age. A third, and more painful, answer is that reduction of the world's population will cause suffering, thus making our task one of minimizing that suffering as much as we can.

One concern of overpopulation—that the "wrong" people are having children—is frequently a racist one. I reject it out of hand. However, I do worry about the influence of fundamentalist religious groups. The influence of the radical Christian right in the US produced the Bush administration, whose mistakes could bring about the downfall of the country and certainly will haunt us for generations to come. Similarly radical Muslim fundamentalists have turned to terrorism. The amount of warfare on this planet due, at least in part, to the powerful religious conviction that "our" group is the true religion, is staggering and painful to contemplate.

Nevertheless, in an overpopulated world, a reproduction "arms race" isn't going to solve anything. Liberals can't resolve their differences with the religious right by having more children any more than France can address the issues raised by its Muslim population by encouraging those of Christian backgrounds to increase their birth rates. In fact, a "reproduction arms race" will merely create more conflict.

The solution is making sure that every child born in the world receives the opportunity to get a thorough education—not just basic reading and writing, but enough skills to survive in the modern world—and the other things we in the West take for granted: a home, meaningful work, health care, enough food. Statistics show that educated women bear fewer children, but I'm going for something more basic than that.

We need to start seeing all the children of the world as our future. Right now, the middle and upper classes in the US are obsessed with showering advantages on their children. Parents make themselves into nervous wrecks trying to get their kids into the "right" college. In some cases, mothers who should be pursuing careers stay home with the children—sometimes even going so far as to homeschool them. Children of the upper classes are given the latest in computer equipment and exposed to a vast array of extracurricular activities. In areas known for their poor public schools, most parents who can afford it send their children to private schools.

Meanwhile, every local election in every major city in the US focuses on how bad the public schools are. Every politician promises to do something about it, and very few of them succeed in doing anything constructive. Further, in the latest anti-immigrant hysteria, many states have passed laws that make college educations—sometimes even public schooling—unavailable to immigrants whose papers are not in order, and the children of families that don't have the resources to educate them elsewhere are stuck in inadequate schools, or receive no education at all.

If we shift our priorities to see *all* children as our future, instead of just the few in our immediate families, we can ensure that the next generations will provide us with competent workers and educated leaders while still making the effort to reduce population. This will take money, of course—always a problem in our tax-averse society. But more than money, it will demand cultural change: a recognition that the future of the human race doesn't just belong to "our" children, but to all the children of all the people of the Earth.

It is no longer useful for every woman to have children, or even for most women to do so. But it's absolutely imperative that human society nurture and educate every child. And we need to think about quality, rather than quantity: we need to bring no more children into the world than we can nurture and educate.

This would have been a lot easier to accomplish even fifty years ago, when the world population was under three billion. Maintaining the population is difficult enough to do in a world that values growth; reducing it will require most people to make some sacrifices. I do not underestimate the difficulties. And, of course, there is the elitist approach to the problem—the one represented by the current growing gap between rich and poor in the US: protect the elites and screw everyone else. Let AIDS, tsunamis, pandemics, and warfare deal with the population problems.

Such a position may be immoral, even reprehensible, but it's tempting for those who see themselves as part of the elite or who at least have a foot in the door. But consider: like everyone else, elites will jettison even their own for survival, and those on the fringes are usually the first to go. More importantly, the problems we face are substantial enough that even the wealthiest may not be able to protect themselves and their offspring if climate change alters our coastlines or a particularly virulent flu virus spreads around the world.

We're all in this together; it's time we started to act like it.

Conclusion: We Aren't Civilized Yet

The other night I happened to catch the radio version of "The Day the Earth Stood Still" on a program featuring shows from the "Golden Age" of radio. In this story—as those who have seen the movie know—an alien representing other intelligent civilizations in the universe comes to Earth to warn us that if we don't stop being so violent, they will be forced to annihilate us.

This movie, based on the 1940s short story "Farewell to the Master" by Harry Bates, was made during the Cold War, at the height of the fear over the atomic bomb. Movie-making of the time lacked realistic special effects, but this film remains one of the best science fiction movies ever made because it does one of the things science fiction does best: offers a new perspective on the problems of the day.

However, outside of the irony that the aliens threatened violence to stop violence (an example of just how limited the human imagination can be), "The Day the Earth Stood Still" has one other major flaw, one that came to me while listening to it on the radio: it assumes that the human race is advanced enough to be able to correct our dangerous shortcomings once we are made aware of them. That is, it assumes that we are civilized.

And we aren't—not by a long shot.

Most people believe that those of us alive today (and especially those of us in the US) are the pinnacle of civilization. Those practices and mindsets in our history that embarrass us—slavery, for example, or believing that the Earth is flat and that the Sun revolves around it—were the product of primitive times. We, now, are truly civilized, and though those who come after us will be more technologically advanced, they'll be no more civilized.

In truth, we have only reached that point in our evolution where we may be able to begin to understand what a truly civilized human race might look like. Consider this: we barely know our own history. Printing has only been around for a few hundred years; writing for a few thousand. And much of what actually got written down of our history has been destroyed. We are learning more about ourselves through science—for instance, through DNA analysis, geology, and archeology—but huge gaps remain. A substantial civilization lived in the US southwest up until about 1400 AD and then disappeared, yet we know nothing about how they lived and can only speculate about why the culture died. Shakespeare's plays are considered among the greatest works ever created, but we aren't even sure who Shakespeare was. There are a thousand such examples of our ignorance of our history.

One thing we do know from human history: war and violence have been with us for a very long time. Today we are as embroiled in war as ever. While the engine of our wars is distribution of natural resources—i.e., economics—religion remains a prominent factor. We are, in a so-called scientific age, continuing to fight over religious beliefs that are tied to an archaic, supernatural view of the universe. And despite substantial evidence suggesting that we all descended from one group of people in Africa, we persist in emphasizing our racial differences, with each group believing that they are truly the "chosen" people.

These are not the hallmarks of civilization.

To become civilized, human beings must learn to take the long view. This isn't easy; as individuals, we don't live long enough to learn everything we need to know from personal experience, although personal experience is usually the best teacher. But history, science, and science fiction can help. History can show us the past; science can provide us with better tools; and science fiction can help us develop the imaginative thinking required to plan for a long-term future.

We must learn to think outside of our short lifetimes. Perhaps then we will become civilized.

Endnotes

1 For those who would like to know what else the panel discussed, Laura Quilter has posted notes at: http://wiki.feministsf.net/index.php?title=Military_Women:_Past%2C_Present%2C_Future_(WisCon_30_Panel).

2 For a detailed discussion of how inadequate training of women in the military is both limiting their careers and putting them at risk, see Erin Solaro's excellent book *Women in the Line of Fire: What You Should Know About Women in the Military*. 2006. Emeryville, CA: Seal Press.

3 Jacobs, Jane, *Dark Age Ahead*, Random House 2004

Nancy Jane Moore's novella *Changeling* is one of the Conversation Pieces from Aqueduct Press. A collection of her stories is forthcoming in 2008 from PS Publishing. She is on the board of Broad Universe and a member of SFWA. In addition to writing fiction, she works as a legal editor and trains in the martial art of Aikido.

http://home.earthlink.net/~nancyjane

"A Man is Like a Nut": Gender and Magic in Ursula K. Le Guin's Later Earthsea Novels

Sylvia Kelso

The construction of masculinity(ies) in fantasy film and fiction has been attracting some critical attention of late. Here I'll be looking at the relation of gender to magic in the Earthsea novels, and the way that Le Guin's construction of masculinity, in particular, is first predicated on traditional oppositions, including gender, but also follows traditional narrative patterns for the male magician, or mage. With *Tehanu* (1990) and *The Other Wind* (2001), I'll try to bring out the ways that Le Guin resists or modifies these patterns after the original trilogy.

Early in *Tehanu* the witch Moss distinguishes men and women through images of their power/magic. A man is "like a nut in its shell...hard and strong, and...full of...grand man-meat... And that's all." When a wizard loses his power, "he's gone. Empty" (56). In contrast, a woman's power is "all roots...like an old blackberry thicket" (110). "No one can say...what a woman is, a woman of power, deeper than the roots of trees...older than the Moon.... Who'll ask the dark its name?" (57).

Here "man" becomes equivalent to "mage" while "woman" blurs into "witch," and the whole recalls popularist publications like *Men are from Mars, Women are from Venus*. That is, gender essentialism. Le Guin herself has leant to the feminist version of essentialism in both fiction and criticism, as with *The Eye of the Heron* (1978), "Sur" (1982), and "The Carrier Bag Theory of Fiction" (1986). Empowering in its recuperation of women's history, the re-vision of myth, and the valorizing of "feminine" attributes such as pacifism and nurturance, such essentialism culminated in Mary Daly's monolithic construction of Woman in *Gyn/Ecology* (1978). But though it did empower women and went a good way toward making men theoretically visible, essentialism precludes differentiation among men or women. Just as late '70s and '80s feminists almost instantly splintered Daly's Woman into Women of different race, color, class, culture, and sexuality, masculinity theorists like Lynne Segal, Bob Connell, and Michael Kimmel have moved to distinguish nuanced, inflected, and historicized masculinities.

Foremost of these inflections is the concept of hegemonic masculinity, accepted as fundamentally white, middle-aged, and middle-class (Carrigan, Connell, and Lee, 110-12), resting first on women's subordination (Connell, 74) and then (78) on what Adrienne Rich originally called the heterosexual imperative. Ellen Jordan and Angela Cowan document the imposition of such masculinity in kindergartens, where boys learn to renounce "warrior narratives" of individual violence for acceptance in "civil society." Jordan and Cowan see such society in terms of Carol Pateman's post-Enlightenment fratriarchy, a brotherly hegemony controlling a rational, bureaucratic public world, with violence either the province of the state or banished to the private world of fantasy and desire (Pateman, 125-29).

Fantasy texts, as I discovered when analyzing Patricia McKillip's novels, also reveal this imposition of hegemonic masculinity, most obviously in the story of the male protagonist who learns to become king. As Chantal Bourgault demonstrates for Robert Silverberg's Valentine in *Lord Valentine's Castle* (1980, 6-8), becoming king also means learning to keep the "civil" status quo: to restrain heroic, individual violence, accept counsel, avoid tyranny. Like countless fairy-stories, *The Lord of the Rings*, the core modern fantasy text (Attebery, 13-14), makes the cornerstone of such kingship the symbolic and practical demonstration of heterosexuality: once crowned, the good king marries and sires an heir. The equally central story of Arthur shows the consequences when a king's (hetero)sexuality fails.

In fantasy, however, a second narrative of power runs in uneasy juxtaposition to these stories. Beside the kings stand figures who lack military force and civil authority, but whose unhuman power outdoes both kings and armies, and whose presence reveals a lasting blind-spot about the nature and consequence of magic, which equates with more than human power.

The Arthurian story offers the best-known example: Merlin is a wizard. He is at best only half-human, but his magic's power is implicitly supreme. So why does Merlin never consider taking the throne? Instead, in the medieval versions, he engineers Arthur's kingship. In modern versions like *The Once and Future King* he plays Arthur's mentor as well. In Mary Stewart's *Crystal Cave* sequence he has an equal blood-claim, but again, never thinks of competing with Arthur. In every version, having installed the king, Merlin is eased off-stage, to end in fettered and/or enspelled obscurity.

This division may expose a deep-seated naturalization of the historical split between church and state. Or the wizard's story may be another of hegemonic masculinity's teaching narratives, aimed at the lower status but white upperclass male: the maverick strong enough to overthrow a social order learns to use his forces for that order and then to remain content without its supreme prize. Given that surveys show 50% or more of fantasy readers are males under twenty-five (Kerr, 1-2), already in danger of being considered geeks or nerds because of their increasingly atypical reading habit, this narrative seems tailor-made to reconcile them to an outsider's life. Suspect narrative logic then makes fine ideological sense.

Le Guin's original Earthsea trilogy follows the traditional masculine story arc. Though a wizard replaces the king as protagonist, like Merlin or Prospero, Ged learns to use his power by the same rules as kings: to eschew violence, to be "civil," to protect the status quo. He rises to become Archmage; he uses and loses his power to install a king. But while, like Arthur, the king goes on to rule in glory, Ged is now "done with doing" (Le Guin, *Farthest,* 213) and will presumably retire to low-status obscurity.

Much of Earthsea's impact springs from Le Guin's use of Taoist oppositions and Jungian archetypes, most obvious in the ongoing rhythms of light and dark, from Ged's double in *A Wizard of Earthsea* (1968), to the underground labyrinth in *The Tombs of Atuan* (1972), to the lands of death and life in *The Farthest Shore* (1973). Again, the first book deploys the powerful motif of the doppelganger, the dark within the individual soul. Yet with the Tao and Jung, as Jewell Parker Rhodes pointed out a good while ago, come the equally traditional hierarchical binary oppositions that align man with the superior light and woman with the inferior dark. This is most obvious in *Tombs of Atuan*. It is less obvious in the most striking gender imbalance of the trilogy. Ged is male. There never are female mages in Earthsea, but in the original trilogy, it is never noticed that magic belongs exclusively to men.

Le Guin's lasting attraction to the Tao and Jung may explain why it took till 1990 for her to publish a fantasy text that attempts to resist such gendered essentialism. *Tehanu* begins this attempt by breaking the traditional wizard's story arc. Rather than close it where he gives up magic, it asks, What happens when a mage is done with doing? *After* he loses power?

The answers move the text into a gritty, almost overtly politicized exploration not merely of magic, but of power's gendered, authorized, everyday, again, usually male form. Abandoning the small casts of the trilogy novels, Le Guin traces power's use and abuse through a gallery of male and female characters that may be further divided between those with and without magic, and those with or without civil authority.

At the bottom of the magicless but civilly powerful range of male characters appear the king's messengers who come to Gont seeking Ged. They are kindly, polite, and almost comprehend Tenar's standing as the bringer of the Ring of Akbar. But though they recognize Ogion's wine as "Andrades" (*Tehanu,* 99) and they do not mistreat Tenar or Tehanu, they fail the test of what we may call gender insight: not "seeing" Tenar for what she really is, they cannot discover Ged.

A fuller version of this lack is Tenar's son Flint, who deploys harsh civil authority. Tradition makes him inheritor of his father's farm, but he is neither loving nor sympathetic, having, "Nothing to offer, and...unable to accept." He simply comes home expecting to take over, without consideration, even to saying how long he will stay (229). Eventually his personality is so "flinty" that he drives out Tenar, Tehanu, and Ged. Unlike the messengers, Flint does appear to reach some sense of his shortcomings before Tenar leaves (235-36).

Up the scale in power but right down in authority are Handy and his cronies, the men who kill Tehanu's mother, abuse the child, pursue her, and eventually try to break in at

Tenar's farm. Handy and Co. are an extreme version of male violence and abuse of women that at times reduces both Tehanu and Tenar to mindless terror. They never learn their faults, though they are eventually defeated—by "good" male violence—and then removed from society by renascent civil—male—authority. As the central illustration of *Tehanu*'s recurrent question: Why are things as they are? (meaning in particular: Why do men treat women like this?) these men also embody the residual essentialism of feminist writers like Andrea Dworkin and Sheila Jeffreys, the hardline portrayal of men as brutes and women as victims, that alienated not merely outsiders but many feminists.

In direct and deliberate contrast to Handy's crew stands the young king, Lebannen, who personally rescues Tenar and Tehanu from Handy in Gontport. Lebannen is young, handsome, just, not merely gender-insightful but able to empathize with the terrified women. To Tenar he seems a "dear" son (162). He is also re-establishing royal authority, putting down pirates, appointing local law-keepers. But he cannot protect Tenar and Tehanu from Handy's final attack. And his authority has no magic to back its power.

Among those with magic, the most peripheral male characters are also the highest in rank, the Masters of Roke. Yet though they have both magic's power and its authority, in gender they are blinder than the king's messengers. Sexist, conservative, they cannot even manage to question the traditional exclusion of women from magic. When the Master Patterner, their nearest approach to perception, is asked a name for the new Archmage, he says, "A woman on Gont." The Masters can only assume such a woman is a way to the Archmage, not herself the end of the search (157-58).

In contrast, Ged's teacher Ogion sees and welcomes the coming "change" (26). Though only adumbrated in this book, the change will bring a revolution in the practice of magic, which seems to symbolize our own gendered structure of power, and by the end of *The Other Wind* it has consequently altered Earthsea's whole way of life and death. But though Ogion foresees, though he has both welcomed and taught Tenar like a mage, he could not give her magic, and he dies at *Tehanu*'s opening, thus abdicating his power in the traditional male mage's way.

In stark contrast, the mage Ash is young, orthodox, gender-blind, and more dangerous than Handy. Like Handy, Ash embodies the worst characteristics of essentialist male portraits, but his verbal attacks echo the visceral gender loathing of some Christian patriarchs. To him "'a woman's tongue [is] worse than any thief'" (127). His spell steals Tenar's own words, making her cry out "shrilly," "'fool, halfwit, imbecile, woman!'" (137). Nor does his hostility stop at words. His first spell almost destroys her ability to think (136-39), and his second enslaves both her and Ged (239-43). Having made them crawl like beasts, he is about to throw them off the Gont cliffs when he is physically destroyed by the dragon Kalessin (247).

So far in this range, masculinity does not come off well in relation to power. Civil authority may be kind or cruel to women, but its supreme example, Lebannen, is still a boy. Nor does lack of authority preclude abusive use of male power, as with Handy's group. But nor does the possession of magic guarantee either insight or kindness. In fact, women's and men's deadliest foe is an established but hostile wizard.

Straddling both character ranges stands Ged, remembered as archmage, now deprived of magic and with it civil power. But when *Tehanu* moves beyond the traditional mage's story, an important aspect of magic that went unseen in the original trilogy becomes overt. Unlike witches, the mages are all celibate. They trade sexuality for magic (107). The corollary is that while they can "call the sun out of the sky," they cannot achieve sexual maturity. With his magic gone, as Moss points out, Ged has suddenly become "a boy of fifteen" again (106).

For Ged the novel then becomes a wry revision of a *Bildungsroman*. He has first to recover from almost literal death, then accept his loss of magic—being unable to summon birds, for instance (83). Then he has to find a living, as a goat-herd. But to be counted fully adult he must first fight—skewering one of Handy's group with a pitchfork when they attack the farm—and then have sex. Tenar mocks this traditional rite of passage: "'Now you're a man indeed. Stuck another man full of holes, first, and lain with a woman, second'" (212). But mockery does not alter the events. Making Ged and Tenar lovers breaks the traditional mage's story as well as the Earthsea limits on a male mage's sexuality. Yet at the same time, it plays into the hands of an older tradition: making Ged fight to attain love replaces the hegemonic story of a king or wizard with an orthodox warrior narrative, which endorses sex and violence as the markers of maturity.

By the end of *Tehanu*, good magic/power has become non-human, as with the dragon Kalessin, or non-human and/or female, as with Tehanu herself. Good male authority and power appear as masculine but immature, with Lebannen. And though bad male power with or without authority or magic has been suppressed, "good" male mages apparently face a choice of retaining magic or attaining "human" maturity—which, again, appears to equate with sex and individual violence.

While *Tehanu* reviews the male mage and highlights the gender imbalance in the original trilogy, it has to leave women's power as the indescribable, the excess of the Symbolic Order sketched by Moss. This, too, can be traced from the nature of traditional story lines. But though the king/enchanter opposition may expose one facet of hegemonic masculinity, it suppresses power's other gendered configuration. The equally long-lived opposition of king/enchantress aligns fantasy narratives with deep-seated reinforcements of gender inequality that feminists have traced everywhere from Christian dogma to the works of Donne and Poe (Bassein). With king vs. enchantress, femininity is again positioned as the inhuman, evil, and inferior side of the power split, and in these stories, there is no ambiguity. Inhumanly powerful enchantresses don't help to install kings. And when they oppose royal masculine authority, they lose.

At least, they do in what may justifiably be called pre-feminist narratives. Again, Arthurian legend offers the prime medieval example. Merlin may be ambiguously good, but Morgan/Morgaine/Morgause is unequivocally evil, and in the pre-Lancelot versions, it is she who brings Arthur down. In the romance of "Gawaine and the Green Knight," it is Morgan who orchestrates Gawain's fall from grace. Feminine versions of unhuman evil recur into twenty-first-century fantasy, often using the traditional figure of the "Queen of Air and Darkness," as, again, in T.H. White, Emma Bull's *War for the Oaks* (1987), and Laurell Hamilton's current Meredith Gentry series.

This tradition changed most noticeably from the late '70s, when feminist theory was infiltrating women's practice in so many fields. In 1976 C.J. Cherryh began remodeling Morgaine, five years before Marion Zimmer Bradley's version in the better known *Mists of Avalon* (1981). Such a change often has to be worked through in the fiction rather than taken as a fait accompli. So it takes Cherryh three books to give Morgaine subjectivity, make her sympathetic, and to show her as less wicked than explicably ruthless, in the manner of a king. But by 1990, in *The Fire's Stone*, Tanya Huff can imagine a young supremely powerful female wizard who is also a princess, and who re-writes both traditional stories: she accepts her royal role, she gets married—if to two men at once—but she keeps her power as well.

Such female power does not exist in the original Earthsea trilogy. Indeed, *Tehanu* shows Le Guin, like Cherryh, still working toward imagining a woman anywhere like Huff's wizard. The female characters in *Tehanu* rather offer a spectrum of traditional female positions, from victim to the marginal imaginings of women who might possess more than human power.

As Handy's crew represent the worst vision of masculinity, Tehanu's mother, their victim, represents the worst, perhaps the extreme feminist view of female helplessness. She is not merely abused, perhaps abducted, raped, and eventually murdered, but she appears to have no agency of her own, even to attempt an escape, and she lacks even a name. She is only "the woman" (Le Guin, *Tehanu*, 3) until she disappears from the text.

Far more important versions of the victim are Tenar and of course, Tehanu herself. Tehanu appears first as the archetypal figure of the female child victim, damaged physically and emotionally and scarred for life (3-5; 7). Nor is she entirely safe, until firstly Handy's crew are removed at the climactic violence and action of the text, and then Ash is destroyed by Kalessin. Unlike her mother, however, Tehanu's status and role change through the story. She acquires a name; a new mother (8); a home (33); a new dress (121). She learns to play (37), and to acquire lore (183). Eventually, her scar becomes a badge of something more than abuse, and in the final phases of the novel, it is her agency that saves Ged and Tenar both.

Tenar offers the adult version of Tehanu's progress. Unlike Tehanu, who is always depicted in alterity, we get inside Tenar's head. Consequently we get not only her emotional responses to the entire story, but the novel's higher ponderings, in her thoughts on the misuse of power and the problem of defining gender: what is man? What is woman? What is magic? (59; 67; 76) It is Tenar who asks these questions, though in *Tehanu*, for women at least, nobody can satisfactorily answer them. And by the end of the story Tenar, like Tehanu, has made a voyage of development, from potential victim and at the least, woman in stagnation, to a woman fulfilled with her true love and her life of choice.

Except for Tenar, however, these women are magicless. The next group are the women of possible power, the witches, Moss and Ivy. Here again, at first, tradition dominates. The witches are depicted in the old hostile manner: they are supposedly weak in magic, ignorant, dirty, and probably malicious (35-38). Though shown only briefly, Ivy fits this pattern. She has some form of power, but her attitude to Tenar and Tehanu is either hostile or patronizing.

In contrast, Moss at first appears equally traditional, but Moss is also the actual voice of change in this text: it is she who spells out the mages' celibacy, and who sets up the traditional oppositions of men and women. But it is also Moss who begins to contest the original picture of witches. Women's power may not be men's, but it is not weak. It is deeper rooted than bramble bushes, and it is stronger than men's knowledge: who'll ask the dark its name?

And Moss herself, for all her dirt and ignorance, has not only the sexual maturity the mages lack, but sexual choice, and sexual power. She can call a man she wants, and he will come. She has called such men, in her time, and in telling Tenar she takes this freedom and agency for granted (108-10). With Moss, Le Guin begins the process not merely of deconstructing male power, but of constructing a women's power that also resists the traditional forms.

In *Tehanu* this power can appear only on the margins, as in the embedded story of the Old Woman of Kenay, who was both dragon and woman (9-14), or the final deed of Tehanu, who calls a dragon at the end of the text. Since dragons will speak to Tenar, she is technically a dragon lord (68), but she has neither magic nor non-human power. Le Guin first centers a story around a woman with such power in "Dragonfly," from *Tales of Earthsea* (2002). But though Irian can find her way into the Mages' house on Roke ("Dragonfly" 242) and confound the Masters, she never becomes a mage. Instead, she realizes her second, dragon nature. Though she can then manifest as woman or dragon, at the story's end she has left both Roke and human life (279).

In *The Other Wind*, the story's central concern is the step beyond the exploration of gendered inequity in the processes of power: *Wind* imagines an actual redress of this inequity, at a level that will reshape both the cosmology and the magic of Earthsea. Central to this change are not only male mages, but women, both those like Irian with nonhuman power and those with presence in the human scale. As a result, formidable women also take highly visible social roles. In *Wind*, in contrast to *Tehanu*, there are no large galleries of male and female characters.

The most marginal woman is perhaps Alder's wife Lily, who dies before the story opens yet remains central to its action. Though she has been silenced, though she appears a victim, her portrait as it appears in Alder's story shows a woman with agency, a witch of some power, and, unlike Moss or Alder's mother Blackberry (*Wind*, 14) also beloved and beautiful (16-17).

The living woman most briefly glimpsed is the "pale-eyed, hard-handed woman," "notable" even among the worker guilds' "flexible and canny bargainers," who represents the miners of Osskil at the king's council (137). In contrast, Tenar has a large role in the action. But though she remains a "small, very light-skinned" woman with "grey hair and large grey eyes," (91) she is no longer the "widow Goha" on Gont. She is "Tenar of the Ring" (91), honored by both king and court, and it is she, not Ged, who travels to Havnor and acts as the king's councilor.

Even more imposing physically is the Kargish princess Seserakh. Brought to Havnor as a political bride for Lebannen, she appears first as a veiled "red column or pillar, cylindrical, featureless, motionless, silent" (69). She is gagged by lack of language and knowledge, which makes her terrified of her new people. But contact with Tenar, who speaks Kargish, transforms her first to an imperious ruler, and then to an intelligent, courageous woman who not only dares to change her customs, meeting Lebannen unveiled, but also supplies a vital piece of knowledge to the overall story. Now she is "a tall young woman" in "soft white trousers, a long shirt of dull red" with a "very thin red veil over her face and head" (200). As she speaks to Lebannen she becomes passionate, her eyes are "like blue fire," she moves gracefully but regally, and when she goes, "lithe and sure-footed," Lebannen stood as if "last night's lightning had struck him at last" (204).

The flamboyance of red and gold reappears with Tehanu and Irian, the women with power, who take an even more central role. Thus, despite her initial reluctance to become involved in any way, it is Tehanu who first speaks to the dragons invading the islands and persuades them to a truce (108-09). It is Irian, appearing at once "a young, tall, strongly built, dark, dark-haired woman" (147) and a "vast shimmer of smoky gold that dwarfed king and throne" (151) who explains the invasion from the dragons' side. Later, Irian and Tehanu both accompany the king's ambassadors to Roke. There Tehanu takes her dragon form, "a creature all of flame, blazing, beautiful" (238) with "bright mail" and "wings of gold" (240) when she and Irian help to overthrow the wall set up by male magic, and release the dead. At the end of *The Other Wind*, however, both Tehanu and Irian have left the human world, if with a hope of return (240-42). There is no comfortable assimilation into the equivalent of the social or the Symbolic order, as with the female mages in Barbara Hambly's *Sisters of the Raven* (2002). Though central to the story, these magnificently envisioned wielders of female power remain, as in Moss's original description, in excess of womanhood and finally of humanity itself.

As Corrigan, Connell, and Lee pointed out back in 1985, however warm and fuzzy the ideal of gender equality, it is naïve not to realize that "the liberation of women must mean a *loss* of power for most men" (107). Thus, though women or power appear in *The Other Wind*'s reduced gallery, there is a dearth of magicless male characters. Instead we have Ged, who, completely reversing his role in the original trilogy, is now marginalized to the beginning and end of the story and indeed feminized as the stay-at-home reward of Tenar's travels and object of her desire. Moreover, he keeps house in stringent poverty (41-42), while Tenar and Tehanu take the heroic male mage's role as travelers and councilors to the king.

Lebannen himself is the only other developed male character without magic, and he is now being pushed to fulfill the king's hegemonic trajectory by marrying and producing an heir. Again, like Ged, Lebannen has been perhaps unwittingly feminized. His reluctance, and his rage at being offered "A pig in a poke," thus himself being equated, like the bride offered him, with "'A piece of goods,'" (70) aligns him with the resisting but eventually persuaded romance heroine.

On the voyage to Roke all the women begin to appear as a unit, siting the reader in a conspiracy of friends bent on overcoming what now appears as Lebannen's prejudice against Seserakh. But as with the love of Ged and Tenar, the outcome of the story is both a win and a loss in terms of traditional fantasy. On the one hand, Seserakh and Lebannen's love is an idealized royal marriage. On the other, though it ensures Lebannen, unlike the mages, will actually mature, it is also the final step on the king's road to orthodox, hegemonic masculinity.

Males with magic are more numerous in *Wind* but get off more poorly than in *Tehanu*. The Masters of Roke, the most marginal, appear only near the climax and retain their conservative, now dated attitude to women with power. They also retain taints of evil in the Summoner, the most hostile to Irian and Tehanu (210-13), as was his predecessor in Irian's story. The Summoner does partly redeem himself when he moves first after Tehanu and Irian to help pull down the wall (237-38), and the Patterner remains the most insightful and sympathetic of the others. But at the end of the novel they are all presumably left on Roke, either marooned in or not yet freed from their traditional roles and traditional celibacy. Even though the Patterner has fallen in love with Irian (245), a passion for a dragon hardly augurs well for the attainment of human sexual maturity.

As differences of race and culture appear among women in *Wind*, with Seserakh, Tenar, Irian, and Tehanu, the one Kargish, the others from different islands in the Havnorian empire, the novel also begins to differentiate among mages and magic. The counterparts of Ash, the mages off Roke, include Onyx, the orthodox traveling mage: he councils the king and goes to Roke. He is polite, civilized, and respectful of both Tehanu and Tenar, but he is largely impotent either to foresee or to deal with the changes now in train, and once the party reaches Roke, he is largely a bystander.

In contrast to Onyx, the "School" mage, Seppel, the other traveling mage, uses the Earth powers of Paln, an equivocal and dubious form of magic. Summoning, the most dangerous form of magic, is drawn from Pelnish magic, and Seppel is presented as something of a foreigner as well as conscious of his art's shady reputation. Unlike Onyx, he can help Alder escape his dreams, but the help comes from Earth itself, and its price is the loss of Alder's own magic (172-73).

Alder, the center of the story, the one who eventually sees how to "mend the world" (236), is another differentiation among mages, both Ged's successor as male protagonist and his complete opposite. Where in the traditional pattern Ged's power was extraordinary and made him Archmage, Alder is a hedge-mage, the male equivalent of Moss. This is a new figure in the Earthsea world. He has almost no learning and a very small gift, for mending things. In further contrast, he is not merely weak in magic but a kind, gentle, and above all, grieving man, for he has already lost Lily, his life's love. And though the narrative deliberately makes him parallel with Elfarran, the great king and legendary lover (38), Alder is beset by the terror of his dreams, which draw him to the wall of the dead. He does lead the demolition of the wall, the final step in the great change in Earthsea, but to do so he must lose not only his love and his magic, but his actual life.

Alder thus appears as the feminized antithesis of the traditional mage, and *Wind* offers male mages a choice of not very palatable fates: to attain humanity, without either magic or secular power, as Ged does, or to lose magic and life to "save the world," as Alder does. Or, like the Masters of Roke, to keep magic and authority, but in a sterile, celibate stasis that never becomes fully human, because it never reaches sexual/physical maturity.

The novels' final conclusions about the relation of humanity to magic are relatively somber, if ironically true to tradition. Modern fantasy as a genre has been based on the allure of magic to its audience. The sensawunda it is expected to provoke appears in the Windrose trilogy, when Barbara Hambly's wizard Antryg makes light in his palm. At her twentieth century character's expression, Antryg grins "like a pleased imp," and she realizes "she had…just seen magic" (Hambly, *Tower* 142). Yet most wizards' story arcs are also highly conservative. Fantasy softens their descent from status and power, making it appear "natural." Built into *The Lord of the Rings* is the premise that beating Sauron will entail the loss of magic: Gandalf and the Elves will leave Middle-Earth. In her Darwath series Hambly's wizards also set kings on their thrones, but are then content with their total lack of secular power. In the Hound and the Falcon series Judith Tarr leaves her Kindred magic, but sends them out of the world. Yet all these wizards are restrained by morality alone from claiming thrones. The glitch's over-pasting emerges most clearly in Patricia McKillip's *In the Forests of Serre* (2003) where the wizard who tried for a throne and princess is assured by the prince that "'You wouldn't have liked my life'" (McKillip, 288). He leaves, content to resume his power and wandering. But, the safely re-established prince wonders, "where was home for Gyre?" (287).

The later Earthsea novels do not offer such a softening. Lebannen may submit to the dictates of kingship, for which read hegemonic masculinity, and having reached a throne, find love as well as maturity. Ged, however, "grows up" and finds love, but loses magic and ends in abject poverty. Alder not only loses magic and love but dies as well. The mages of Roke are left in stasis, and the mages off Roke must deal with a change that may not merely alter but remove male magic from the world. On the women's side, Tehanu and Irian have achieved nonhuman power but have given humanity as its price. The later Earthsea novels demonstrate far more bluntly than usual the central paradox evaded in most modern fantasy: that though the genre is built on and based around the appeal of "magic," in the final event, using magic and being human, in the fullest sense, as a mature sexual subject within the Symbolic Order, remain, with whatever regret or nostalgia, incompatible.

Works Cited

Attebery, B. 1992.*Strategies of Fantasy*. Bloomington: Indiana UP.

Bourgault, C. 27 September, 2002. "The Return of the King: Masculinity and Power in Genre Fantasy." Paper delivered at the Fantasy Symposium, Sydney University.

Connell, R. W. 1995. *Masculinities*. Cambridge: Polity Press.

Corrigan, T., B. Connell, and J. Lee. 1987. "Toward a New Sociology of Masculinity." Reprinted in *The Masculinity Studies Reader.* eds. R. Adams and D. Savran. London: Blackwell, 2002, 99-118.

Daly, M. 1978. *Gyn/Ecology: The Metaethics of Radical Feminism*. Boston: Beacon Press.

Hambly, B. 1987. *The Silent Tower.* London: Unwin.

———. 2002. *Sisters of the Raven.* New York: Warner.

Jordan, E., and A. Cowan. 1998. "Warrior Narratives in the Kindergarten Classroom: Renegotiating the Social Contract?" In *Men's Lives.* 4th Edition. eds. M. S. Kimmel, and M. A. Messner. London: Allyn and Bacon, 127-40.

Kelso, S. January 2006. "The King and the Enchanter: Gender, Power and Authority in Patricia McKillip's Fantasy Novels." *New York Review of Science Fiction.*

Le Guin, U. K. 1990. "The Carrier Bag Theory of Fiction." 1986. In *Dancing at the Edge of the World: Thoughts On Words, Women, Places*. 1989. New York: Harper and Row, 165-170.

———. 1997."Dragonfly." In *Tales of Earthsea.* New York: Ace, 2002. 209-79.

———. 1978. "The Eye of the Heron." In *The Eye of the Heron and Other Stories.* ed. V. Kidd. St. Albans: Panther, 1980. 209-51.

———. 1973. *The Farthest Shore.* London: Puffin, 1975.

———. 2001. *The Other Wind.* London: Orion.

———. 1982. "Sur." In *The Compass Rose.* London: Granada, 1984. 265-84.

——— 1990. *Tehanu.*New York: Bantam, 1991.

———. 1972. *The Tombs of Atuan.* London: Puffin, 1976.

———. 1968. *A Wizard of Earthsea.* London: Puffin, 1976.

McKillip, P. 2003. *In the Forests of Serre*. New York: Ace, 2004.

Pateman, C. 1989. "The Fraternal Social Contract." Reprinted in *The Masculinity Studies Reader.* Eds. R. Adams and D. Savran. London: Blackwell, 2002. 119-134.

Rhodes, J. P. 1983. "Ursula Le Guin's *The Left Hand of Darkness*: Androgyny and the Feminist Utopia." In *Women and Utopia: Critical Interpretations*. eds. M. S. Barr and N. D. Smith. New York: UP of America, 108-20.

Sylvia Kelso teaches part-time at James Cook University in Australia. Her PhD was on Feminism, SF, and the Gothic, with articles in NYRSF and *Science Fiction Studies*. In 2005 she published a fantasy novel, *Everran's Bane*, and hopes to have a sequel accepted soon.

http://members.optusnet.com.au/~sakelso/

Georgie Schnobirch

The Legendary Joanna Russ

Interviewed by Samuel R. Delany

(Transcribed by Lettie Prell)

Samuel R. Delany is an accomplished writer whose work became impressed forever into the science fiction collective memory with back-to-back Nebula awards in 1966 (for his novel, *Babel-17*) and 1967 (for his novel, *The Einstein Intersection* and short story, "Aye, and Gomorrah"). He has not stopped since. Delany and Octavia Butler have been lauded as African American writers who rank among the top science fiction authors, and Delany has been cited as one of the best contemporary African American novelists. His work often explores race and social issues, and the nature of language. His latest novel, *Dark Reflections*, is coming out in May 2007.

[Note: What follows is excerpted from a telephone interview with Ms. Russ at WisCon 30, in May 2006, and is printed with the permission of WisCon, Ms. Russ, and Mr. Delany. Any inadvertent misrepresentation of their spoken words is my fault, and I apologize in advance for any such errors. In a few instances, titles of works were corrected for the benefit of those seeking recommended reading. —LP]

Samuel R. Delany: In my humble opinion Joanna Russ is simply one of the most important writers who has written in the United States in the last fifty years. This is a writer who has produced works on the level of Willa Cather, James Joyce, and William Gass. She writes, among other things, sentences that are absolutely spectacular. A description of a spaceship which I quote endlessly to my writing students at Temple University, where she's describing a star-liner: "The big one was the platonic idea of a pebble turned inside out, born of a computer and aspiring to the condition of mechanical opera." That is such a luscious sentence I don't think I will ever be the same.

Also there's a range and intensity of concern for the problems of women. Feminism works for Joanna Russ the way Marxism works for the great German writer Bertolt Brecht. It is something innate to the concerns, not something that can be dismissed. It already is of course an incredibly important aspect of the world—possibly one of *the* most important aspects of the world—but she foregrounds that importance, makes us understand it in terms of the social portraits that she creates in her work. Her first story, "Nor Custom Stale," appeared in *F&SF* in 1959 I believe, and she went on to produce many other wonderful stories: "My Dear Emily," "I Thought She Was Afeared Till She Stroked My Beard" (such a wonderful title that it had to be changed to "…I Gave Her Sack and Sherry"), "Adventures of Alyx" (which Joanna calls pre-feminist and I call a spectacular story), "We Who Are About To" (one of my personal favorites), and more, [including the novels] *The Two of Them* and *On Strike Against God.*

So Joanna, what are some of the things you've been thinking about lately?

JR: I don't know if I can tell you. I'm still basking in all your praise.

SD: You deserve to bask. Tell us a little bit about where you're living. What is Tucson like?

JR: Tucson is getting to be a rather sprawling small city. Desert. Very hot in the summer. I just love it. Not the city so much, but the location and the skies. Oh the skies, my friend: Yes, Tucson specializes in that.

SD: [Asks about the "double bind situation"—the economic realities of a writer trying to make a living writing.]

JR: Yes that's awful. It's not the writers' fault. It's the economics of publishing now. What I've seen again and again is that a writer will do very fine early stuff—really good stuff—and say, "Okay, I can make a living writing." But they then find themselves having to work too fast. Words should not only be thought, they should be felt through, and there just isn't enough time. People in that bind never do great stuff again. And if you don't do that, if you say, "Okay, I will keep my day job (as they used to say in the theater), and I will just write what I damn well please," you end up working too hard.

SD: Yes, I can remember my first five books in three years, and I ended up in a mental hospital. Any thoughts on changing it?

JR: No. I don't know, I think it is an industrial capitalist problem. It didn't use to be true. There were niche markets, eighty-five different little magazines all doing something different. A young man wrote to me and said he had read *Alyx* and liked it, and he read another book of mine and he was shocked and horrified to discover that it wasn't the same thing. I know that's funny but it's like *Gor*, the fifty-sixth book of the series, and people will buy these things because they're familiar.

SD: What are some of the authors you find yourself returning to and reading whether fantasy/sf or other journals?

JR: It's a mixed bag. In sf when I was younger I loved Heinlein because he was always doing something different, and the sf didn't disappear after the beginning of the book; it was carried through all the way. I go back to some of Clarke's short stories, and Chaucer, frankly.

SD: Yes, you've always talked about Chaucer; he comes up again and again. What interests you about a classical writer like Geoffrey Chaucer?

JR: He has written some of the most perfect short stories in English, if you can think of Middle English as English. The three men who go out to kill Death is absolutely a smashing thing; the shape of the story is perfect. The pardoner's tale.

SD: I'll go back and take a look at that one. Any other writers you find yourself returning to, to give you solace or what have you?

JR: Well, some of the feminists. *The Chalice and the Blade* which has marvelous early Christian writing in it. Actually I don't read nearly as much as I used to. It's very annoying to have to get up every twenty minutes, and...wait a minute, there's a punch line. I found that, after having a VCR for several years, you can treat TV just as a book. And now I have a DVD player. I have been going mad about Buffy. [*much applause from audience*]

SD: You have a lot of friends.

JR: I'm glad of that. Even though "Buffy" was created by a guy, it was one of those TV shows aimed directly at women, and it is not domestic, but adventurous, and horror fiction, and comedy, and it's very well written, I'll say. A feminist friend of mine wrote me from Philadelphia and said, "You have to watch this." And I did and I loved it. I collected them on VHS tapes and now I've bought them on DVD. And some of the things they talk about are extremely funny.

SD: When we were talking about things to talk about, you mentioned general problems of growing older as something we all do.

JR: That struck me among other things because I have arthritis and chronic fatigue syndrome, and I have begun to understand the kind of writers who write about limitations and mortality. I don't have the books with me—I forgot to bring them into the bedroom—but there are at least two for writers. One of them was Sarah Orne Jewett.

SD: *The Country of the Pointed Firs.*

JR: She has this sense of characters, she does not condescend to them, which I love. Just when you think you can look down on them, they are smarter than you are. She wrote one story called "The Hiltons' Holiday" which is almost heartbreaking because it's such a perfect day and it will never be repeated. I can't tell you the story because I will gobble if I do.

SD: Are you particularly interested in Jewett, because of how she deals with age?

JR: Not just age. She deals with limitations of all kinds—mortality in particular.

SD: How do you experience limitations of old age? I'm sixty-four and can't do what I did before.

JR: I'm sixty-nine and can't do what I used to do before. I thought I would put up signs around the house that said "You are seventy. Stop it!'"

[*audience laughs*]

SD: What about some of the fantasy stories that you have, you mentioned Terri Windling's fantasy collection and some thoughts you had about that.

JR: I think there's a lot of very fine fantasy being written. I don't mean unicorns and warlocks, but fantasy that comes into ordinary life...a kind of vitality there that I don't know is in science fiction. See, I have been out of the loop for a long time, but I know that some of these fantasy stories are just thrilling.

SD: Yes, there is a feeling that some of the energy that was in sf for a long time may have moved over to fantasy. It makes it a very interesting field.

JR: Yes, thinking about your tales of Neveryona. Boy, does that resemble Tolkien.

SD: What else has been going on in your life of interest?

JR: Mostly I have to keep about taking care of my body and keeping it functional and so forth—something I didn't used to have to do. I do trunk exercises in the morning and hip exercises in the afternoon. Ah, very boring, they really are, but they work, they do good things, so I keep doing them. There gets to be a point in your social life...is much more with doctors than anyone else.

SD: I gather you're not doing much writing.

JR: Not doing any—haven't been doing any for ten years.

SD: Talk about the transition from someone doing writing to not.

JR: I found out once I got CFS [chronic fatigue syndrome] that writing takes an enormous amount of energy. It takes concentration, and this is a physical thing. I always used to wonder why when I finished writing I was so tired. I was only sitting down and writing. But now I can't concentrate long enough to do this, and I can't keep a whole thing in my head at the same time. If you're writing a novel, you're keeping stuff in the back of your head for a year or two, and it's very difficult to find suddenly you can't do that. It took about—oh let's see—eight or nine years for me to live with that comfortably.

SD: It's something that one way or another every writer will eventually have to go through.

JR: I find that the real solution is to be very self-indulgent. Really. Go to thrift shops, read books, watch TV, talk to your friends.

SD: Do all those fun things that you weren't doing.

JR: Yes, when you were too busy.

SD: At one point you said sf was a religious literature. Can you comment on that?

JR: Well, there's the old phrase—I don't know if it's still current—sense of wonder. The sense of wonder or awe of the hugeness of the universe. It comes up in all sorts of places. *The Nine Billion Names of God* by Arthur C. Clarke, or *2001*. The protagonists tended to turn into the new messiah on the last page.

SD: Yes that's a fairly common trope I think we call it in sf.

JR: Yes, it was a feeling of awe and wonder and gorgeousness and complexity.

SD: There are many moments in your own fiction when this kind of thing happens, certainly spectacularly presented in language. Toward the end of *We Who Are About To* when the protagonist is starving herself to death and she has a vision of agape, hears the music of the spheres—she's never experienced them at that intensity.

Thinking of comments from your writing that stuck with me, one of them, related to "Souls," that extraordinary novella about a medieval convent which is run by the abbess Radagunda, which is besieged by Norse Vikings, and she saves the place more or less, or makes several attempts to save the people. And the abbess is an alien getting in touch with her inner alien. One night she's musing in her inner monologue, the people want religion that gives and gives but the true god is gods who take and take until there is nothing left but god. This was very powerful when I first read it, and it remains powerful for me even today. I think in terms of the ending of *We Who Are About To*.

JR: I'm temperamentally atheistic, no religion. One of the things I loved when I found it in college was information about Taoism. They are mystics. When I was in my thirties and I was teaching at the University of Seattle one summer—the science fiction course you know, the writing course—I got to talking to one of the students who was also very much into this kind of thing, and we drove several people nuts because we were saying things that were paradoxes, contradictions, and one of them said that cannot be. And I got him in a corner and pulled his hair.

SD: Sometimes you have to do that.

JR: But mystics have always talked in contradictions. A man Asiatic who wanted to be a shooter of golden arrows went to see the greatest of these, [and went to see him where he lived at] the top of a mountain. He was told first you must look at very very big things until they seem small, and then you must look at very very small things until they seem big. And coming back to the guy's hut, the guy who wanted to be a great bowman or whatever, had left his arrows leaning against the hut, and the old man looks at this and says, "Oh! What are those?" It always gives me chills. It's the part where you know something so well and so completely, but in an odd way you can't even talk about it. This is what was driving him nuts. Science fiction does this so well—the end of [Arthur C. Clarke's] *Childhood's End,* mystics do so well. The whole earth becomes light in the end.

SD: I think it was Willa Cather who said that most literary writers get all the material that they're going to write about by the time they are eight years old. And I've always thought that this is one of those things that alternate between seeming absurd, and seeming insanely true. Do you have any thoughts about that? Do you think the same age range applies to science fiction?

JR: No. You learn a great deal by eight or nine, but you're always putting other things in as you get older. I don't know if this happens in other literature, but it does happen in sf.

SD: If all literature is in a sense the literature of childhood, then I think that sf is the literature of adolescence.

JR: Yes, I've heard that from you before.

SD: You were a Westinghouse winner in high school. Can you tell us about the project?

JR: My dad built a long box for me with lights at the top and I grew a fungus in each compartment. And each compartment light had a different gel with colors red, blue, white, and completely dark. The fungus produced different kinds of spores and produced them in different patterns, depending on the light. *Aspergillis janus,* Janus being the two-faced, ancient Roman god of the beginning of the year—two faces, one of future and one of past.

SD: Did you ever use that sort of thing in stories?

JR: I didn't. By the time I finished I thought it was terribly boring.

SD: A story of yours I've always been very fond of, a story called "Gleepsite." Basically a large winged creature hovers outside a window, made of—do we learn what gleepsite actually is in the story?

JR: No it's not in the story, it's the title of the story. And it's an imaginary material made up by a Cornell architect. Whenever you had a problem you couldn't solve, we said make it a gleepsite and change whatever variable you had. The story is in a way about fantasy in which fantasy becomes real.

SD: “Gleepsite” is a great story and a great title. Any of yours you find yourself still particularly fond of?

JR: It’s hard to say—things change as time goes by. I will say this, I read most of them, and I think they were pretty good. I have a few of those and think, “Did I write that?” I have a few of those but not very many.

SD: I think they’re pretty good too, because you’re one of the writers I go back to read. Can we talk about your novels? You don’t talk about *And Chaos Died* much.

JR: Yes. I’m embarrassed. Lots of stereotyped ideas about gay men. That didn’t come to me until later. Marge Piercy put her finger on it when she said if you think of the gay man as a woman, it makes sense.

SD: Those things don’t bother me personally nearly as much as they did when the book came out.

JR: Yes, because the whole social surround has changed so much.

SD: The result is that there are just spectacular passages, just pell-mell one after another through the book, despite anything you might raise an eyebrow at, all sorts of wonderful things. You say it embarrassed you. Are there any parts you like?

JR: Yes. I think the protagonist and one of the women are walking through the countryside—and I think the description of the countryside is very good.

SD: Yes, some of the transition scenes, I read them and my jaw drops even if I’m not in agreement with what he’s transitioning from and to. It’s great writing. It’s also a poignant sympathy for the young that manifests itself in many stories. But in particular, “The Second Inquisition,” the story of the young lesbian girl in *The Female Man*, just wring your heart out. They certainly wring my heart out. Is there any special relationship in terms of your own life?

JR: Yes I think so. I was discovering maybe a little later than that, but also in that time, discovering what they call the child within. And I discovered that I have one. I think everybody does. This is not a separate personality, it’s a kind of different personality, and she insists that she is the empress of the universe. Then if she gets in trouble she comes and hides behind me, and I have to take care of it.

SD: Your descriptions of the young woman in “The Second Inquisition”...I’m trying to remember the epigraph in that story...something like if you can survive the opinions of the people in the small town in which you live, you can survive anything...is what I took away from it.

JR: I put a lot of autobiographical detail in that story: the town, the backyard, the little sort of couch or swing they sit on, stuff like that. The dance. All comes from stuff I’ve seen or lived through.

SD: And stuff that feels incredibly real and has that ring of truth, or as once I described it in critical writing, it's not the ring of truth, it's a whole gong of truth.

JR: I felt very bad about not writing when I got sick and couldn't. The only thing I could do was finish the book *What Are We Fighting For?* that I'd started much earlier.

SD: You did a great job.

JR: Well, I'm beginning to be self-indulgent as I said. I like it.

SD: I don't know why I found myself rereading of all people Plato recently, and discovering that his idea of what education was for, was to make your own world interesting to you.

JR: The more education you get, the more interesting everything becomes. I don't know how long it took me or you to decide that the double-bind in science fiction was economic, but I didn't know that in my twenties. I hadn't had that experience.

SD: But there is the one you did go through. Maybe you can give me some advice because I haven't figured it out. How do you write and teach at the same time?

JR: You write and teach at same time by getting very tired. In a way I did do it and in a way I didn't. In my twenties I was a junior teacher, I was an instructor, and that meant that I didn't go to meetings and didn't have any voice in the department, but it was great because I had lots of time and energy. But as I got older and my rank increased, I had less time. In my fifties, if I got an idea for a story or a novel I'd say, "Oh god, not again. I can't." [But she would write, and the consequences were people remarking she was…] not coming to meetings, not having enough honor students or advisees. I would just look sort of pathetic and say, "Oh yes, I'm trying." But I wouldn't do it.

SD: That's probably what you have to do. You have to break down and take the time for yourself, which is hard to do if you're a labile, friendly, genial sort of person.

JR: Which I was not. I think what I did very self-consciously was teach the same kinds of classes all the time—creative writing classes all the time—so I didn't have to develop from scratch.

SD: My greatest failing is that I do want to teach new things all the time. Now I just want to think.

Question from the Audience: You mentioned that your opinions of gay men used to be very different and traditional. I was wondering if your opinions of transsexual women have changed since you wrote *The Female Man*.

JR: Oh yes, oh yes, it's almost as if my life has arranged itself to disabuse me of one prejudice after another. And all of these have gone because none of them were real, really.

AUD Q: Would you comment on the state of feminism today?

JR: I don't really know enough about it to comment. I've been out of the loop, except for Buffy, for about ten years at least now, so I probably shouldn't say anything.

SD: I've been pushing your books at various people for many years. Which book would you like me to push first? How would you like your works to be introduced to people?

JR: I think you would have to decide what kind of people they are and what would not repel people, but would pull them in.

SD: I think that's what any writer would say. May I offer my own prejudices as someone who teaches Joanna's work again and again? I'd say younger and less sophisticated readers really enjoy *The Adventures of Alyx*; more sophisticated readers like more sophisticated books like *We Who Are About To*, *The Female Man*, *The Two of Them*, and don't forget *On Strike Against God*, which is just as good.

AUD Q: What do you think of the progression of the situation you described in *How to Suppress Women's Writing*, and do you think it's getting better?

JR: Oh boy. Again, I really have been out of touch. I have the impression that yes, it's getting better.

SD: Let me offer my two cents as someone in academe. What seems to be happening is that to make room for women writers is that notion of "Great Writer" itself is dismantled.

JR: Well that's a great thing.... It takes at least two generations to make an artist. In my case, maybe three.

Joanna Russ is the Hugo- and Nebula-award winning author of several novels, dozens of short stories, and a substantial body of essays and criticism. She lives in Tucson, Arizona.

Jeanne Gomoll & Georgie Schnobirch

Jeanne Gomoll

Q: Anything surprising happen this year?

A: Do you mean surprising like when your friends jump out from behind the furniture and shout "happy birthday," or when your partner sneaks up on you, shouts "oooga-booga!," and hugs you?

In that case there wasn't much surprising about WisCon 30. Cumulatively, the ConCom put in thousands of planning hours during the last couple years—more if you start counting at WisCon 24, when Jim Hudson and Diane Martin offered to chair WisCon 25 if Scott Custis and I would commit to chairing WisCon 30.

We did a good job. The huge event came off without any major hitches, or few noticeable ones. By May 21, the Sunday before WisCon 30, I could tell you how each program space in and outside the hotel would be used in any given hour of the week to come. I confess that I tend toward micro-management, but even I resisted the urge to provide a wardrobe plan for a newbie attendee who sent us an email asking for advice ("How should I dress to attend WisCon 30? Formal businesswear? Business casual? Jeans? Costume?").

Nevertheless, there were a lot of details crammed into my head when it all began. The question of whether or not we could afford the daunting cost of bringing back so many of our past guests of honor had been happily answered several months earlier; several grant applications were approved, and we no longer worried that we'd bitten off more than we could chew. We reached our 1,000-membership limit but cancellations were offset by waitlisters, so we continued registering attendees up to the last moment. The program committee submitted a brilliant schedule of events. Publications were printed and delivered on time. We found a way to seat everyone who purchased tickets to the dessert salon on Sunday night and turned no parents away from child care. All the guests had plane and hotel reservations. And several logistical challenges were handled gracefully by incredibly competent ConCom members.

By May 23, I'd checked off almost every item on my massive to-do list. Everything was ready for the first official event to start (the Center for Humanities' program on Wednesday night, "A Feminist Utopia in Madison?"). And with the exception of a torrential downpour that night, events occurred as planned. No big surprises.

From a different perspective, WisCon 30 was nothing BUT a surprise. Looking at WisCon as part of the forest of the science fiction and feminist communities, rather than an event seen through the trees of ConCom logistics, it's actually a surprising thing that WisCon even exists.

WisCon is the opposite of a typical general-interest convention. Where worldcons and most regional sf conventions tend to annex diverse interest groups under an ever-expanding sf community umbrella, WisCon has narrowed its focus and gradually cut loose elements perceived as tangential to its core focus of feminist and politically progressive science fiction. Thirty years ago it would have been impossible for a small group to reach members of this niche that has no geographic center. Today, with the Internet, it's possible for like-minded people to communicate with one another across state and national boundaries and to perceive themselves as a community.

Though it was crowded, WisCon 30 was able to accommodate almost everyone in the world who includes themselves in the feminist sf community and was able to travel to Madison WisConsin on Memorial Day weekend. Guests of Honor Jane Yolen and Kate Wilhelm, plus forty former WisCon guests of honor attended and celebrated WisCon's thirtieth year. The fifteenth annual Tiptree Award (for gender-bending fiction) and the first Carl Brandon Society Awards (for fiction by writers of color or dealing with race and ethnicity) were presented at WisCon 30. Both these awards incubated at WisCon, as did Broad Universe, a networking organization for women writers of sf, fantasy, and horror. We have come to know about one another, made connections with one another, are creating institutions together, and now we are affecting the very shape of the science fiction field. Now *that's* a wonderful surprise!

P.S. from Eileen Gunn:

Jeanne is omitting what would have been a major surprise for me, but it occurred the day after the convention, so maybe she isn't including it in the tally. The convention ended on Monday afternoon, and on Tuesday morning at 8 AM., Jeanne was back at work, finishing a design project for a freelance client. At noon, she and Scott hosted a spur-of-the-moment luncheon for (if I recall correctly) twelve people, including former GOHs Vonda McIntyre and Ursula Le Guin. During a major thunderstorm, we all feasted at Jeanne and Scott's groaning board on morels and local cheeses and charcuterie and who knows what-all. Later, we admired the substantial ant population of Jeanne and Scott's driveway. (I was, or course, reminded of Ursula's superb story, "The Author of the Acacia Seeds.") After that, Jeanne drove Vonda and Ursula through the rainy countryside to the distant station for the Amtrak Empire Builder. An awesome impromptu afternoon, but not even on Jeanne's radar, after chairing WisCon 30….

Jeanne Gomoll, a WisCon founder, Tiptree judge, and Motherboard officer, served as WisCon 30 co-chair with Scott Custis, designed the pocket program book, and owns a graphic design business, Union Street Design, LLC. WisCon 7 GoH.

http://www.unionstreetdesign.com

A Forty-Year-Old Con-Virgin Goes to WisCon

by Stephen Gold

I became an sf fan when I was about ten. My brother and I discovered the genre on TV: Star Trek reruns and shows like The Bionic Woman. We both fell in love, but in different ways. His innocence was fleeting. During his teens, he published a fanzine and ran off to fool around at local cons. I, being the shy one, stayed naïve: a zealous creator of stories and artwork for his fanzine, but reliant on him to show me what was new and "cool."

A generation passed. I took classes, watched movies, and read books, but stopped thinking of myself as a fan. I married, had a son, and resumed writing. About the time my boy discovered Harry Potter, I reconnected with sf, eager to catch up on all I'd missed. I joined a writers' circle and sent stories to several zines, but felt no urge to attend a con. That changed, however, after a summer writing workshop put me in touch with seventeen sf writers from around the country. As soon as the workshop ended, we started planning to rendezvous at a con.

I'm unsure why we chose WisCon. Duchamp was one of our instructors; she might have planted the idea. We discussed Potlatch, World Fantasy, and WorldCon, too, but WisCon just seemed to fall into place. The timing was right, and Wisconsin's central location was likely a factor. The opportunity to visit my brother (who lived in nearby Middleton) helped me decide. In the end, eleven of my classmates attended WisCon 30, giving it the feel of a class reunion.

As I downloaded the registration form, I fretted over the con's feminist theme. While ashamed of injustice and supportive of efforts to improve women's status, I didn't think of myself as a feminist and doubted I could pass muster. Would I feel welcome? As I committed five days and $800 to the trip, I crossed my fingers and hoped my classmates knew what they were getting me into.

One of the workshoppers proposed a group reading and urged us all to participate. Tempted by the opportunity, I signed myself up. My anxiety grew. I was no longer a spectator who could fade away if I disliked the con. I was on the program, committed to read one of my intimate creations to a crowd of strangers. Even the choice of story daunted me; I wanted to present my best work, but wondered how it would go over with a feminist audience.

As I limped off the bus in Madison, I knew I was on an adventure. Overhearing a fellow passenger ask the driver for directions to the Concourse, I overcame my shyness and offered to help her find the hotel. Despite our heavy suitcases, we had a pleasant walk, but the moment we entered the lobby, we parted ways, swallowed up in a sea of strangers.

Years of professional and social events had taught me that volunteering is a fun way to meet people, so I plunged into the packet assembly party. I found it easy to join, but hectic. The process demanded so much of my attention that it made casual conversation difficult. I was glad to spot some of my workshop buddies. As the process wound down, we made plans to attend a reading together.

I spent the weekend torn between hanging out with my clique and exploring the con on my own. I kept hoping to meet people and make friends. In fact, I was obsessed with the idea, and it gave me nothing but stress. I seldom saw men alone, and I worried that an attempt to start conversation with a woman would be construed as a "pick up" attempt. Luckily, I found the program itself enjoyable.

Guided by the easy-to-use program booklet, I sought out panels that looked interesting—mostly ones on reading and writing sf. While the panelists' insights seldom impressed me, I found the panels themselves inspiring. Listening to a serious discussion of world building, small presses, cultural appropriation, or the boundaries of "hard" science fiction made me itch to participate. In hindsight, I wish I'd volunteered to be on some of those panels.

On Friday night, my classmates and I read our stories—short ones, as nine of us had to fit into a standard seventy-five-minute slot. Propelled by high spirits and plenty of chocolate, the readings went smoothly. Enough people came to keep me from feeling I was wasting my time, yet not so many as to give me stage fright. The experience left me hungry to do longer public readings.

Then came the parties—an entire floor of free food and drink. As long as I was with people I knew, I enjoyed myself, but each time I found myself among strangers, an urge to hurry elsewhere overwhelmed me. My most successful interaction took place at a reading group party, where a pair of zealots cornered me and preached for half an hour, oblivious to the fact that I didn't share their politics and lived 2,000 miles from their meeting place.

There was more, of course—much more. After a slow start, the opening ceremonies proved far more entertaining than I'd expected. I got to hold a baby who'd been a bulging belly the last time I'd seen her. I ate "Pork Ginger with Apple"—my first taste of Midwestern-Japanese fusion cuisine. Over melt-in-the-mouth croissants from Café Soleil, I met a Canadian author/illustrator who told me all about herself. And I learned which sexual behaviors are now "cool" and which remain subject to ridicule.

I bought far more than I'd intended. The artwork, books, and magazines proved surprisingly affordable, and items seemed to jump out at me as I wandered the busy dealers room and the crowded art show. I wound up strapped for cash and wishing I'd brought more.

I also learned some useful tricks, such as the existence of a "con suite" stocked with snacks and bored guests, and I put faces to authors and editors who'd previously been mere names, including Chip Delany. He was the one who, at the Fundamentals of Feminism panel, finally gave me the straight dope: men can't be feminists. I guess I'll have to settle for being a sympathizer.

Overall, WisCon proved an excellent adventure, and I left with a new goal: to read all the books I'd bought—before my next con!

Stephen Gold is a divorced dad who enjoys playing the piano. He left Silicon Valley to build an intentional community and write fiction.

http://sgold.members.sonic.net/

Sympathy and Power

L. Timmel Duchamp Asks Samuel R. Delany a Question

> In his "A Forty-Year-old Con-Virgin Goes to WisCon," Stephen Gold notes that "Chip Delany…was the one who, at the Fundamentals of Feminism panel, finally gave me the straight dope: men can't be feminists. I guess I'll have to settle for being a sympathizer." I can think of more than a score of men who attend WisCon every year without fail; there's no question in my mind that they feel comfortable hanging out in a specifically feminist venue. I haven't asked any of them whether they would characterize themselves as "feminist sympathizers," but I suspect that in 2007 there may well be a valid distinction to be drawn between being comfortable in the company of feminists and being a sympathizer that could not have been drawn back in, say, the 1970s or even in the early '80s. Do you think such a distinction can be drawn, and if so, what does that signify to you?
>
> —L. Timmel Duchamp

A sexually active gay man of nineteen, I was married, August 1961, to an eighteen-year-old woman, who had been my best friend since soon after we'd met in the Bronx High School of Science in 1956. Eight months younger than I, she was a year ahead of me in school and went to college at NYU as an early admission student of fifteen. Within a year of that marriage, largely under her tutelage and after many hours of discussion with her and her women friends, I decided that the reapportionment of power between the sexes—women and men—was the most politically important job of all the possible liberatory projects one might take up. The unfair and widely abused power discrepancies between all groups—nonwhites and whites, homosexuals and straight people, children and adults—were all based on the first; and they were fully understandable in its terms and only in its terms.

I believe that today, still—though most of my personal energies now go into addressing the power imbalances between gay men and straight society: living and working in the social niches that I do, those are the conflicts I have the most day-to-day experience with. Those are the ones where I feel I can do the most local good. But I try to keep all my efforts to that end in line with what I still see as the greater political imbalance.

Power imbalances are contingent social constructions. They can be changed; they do change: each handful of years reveals more and more changes in them all. Not everyone is happy with these changes. Nor do many people who are basically pleased by them necessarily understand them.

One of the most confusing aspects of all socially constructed power differentials is power itself. What is it and how does it work? Provisionally the best way to begin understanding power is to realize that, practically speaking, power is different from strength. There are two general approaches to power—or better, axioms about power—one of which is fairly easy for most people to grasp. The problem with it as an axiom is that it isn't particularly useful in changing power structures. It might be expressed:

"Power is the social generalization of strength."

Certainly this has its truth. Because some men are stronger than some women, we generally go through our lives, men and women, assuming most men are stronger than most women. And I have seen that argument generalized to a simple statement that men are stronger than women—and, on occasions, have even heard some men generalize it to "all men are stronger than all women." Whether these generalizations are true or not, most of us can understand how these generalizations work or come about.

I had a friend once—Sunny—a fat, extremely strong, brutal, and violent (but also charming) man. Regularly he got into fights—some of which, when he reached his thirties, he was hired to get in to by criminals, who paid for his services. He almost always won. He had spent several years in jail. He was over two hundred-fifty pounds. By his own admission he had killed at least five people, two accidentally, one for personal revenge. The others were "work." He had been caught for none of them.

The generalization of power can actually undo the extant power structure: "I don't get in fights with women no more—never. Strongest person I ever fought with was a woman. I was at the movie theater, the old Academy of Music up on Fourteenth Street," Sunny once told me. "With some of my friends—we was just sittin' there, watchin' the film, and there was this couple in the row ahead of us. So we decided to fuck with 'em. I began makin' these comments about his woman, and suddenly the guy stands up, angry, and turns around. And I see it's not a guy at all—it's another woman, only she's got short hair like a man. And she's dressed like a guy. She ain't even that big, either—not like me. Or one of my sisters." (Sunny was the only boy and youngest child in a family of twelve siblings. His father, physically even bigger than he was, had spent twelve years in a Canadian jail.) "So I figure, it's just some scrawny dyke. I stand up—and this woman hauls back and socks me in the jaw. I went out, like that! I didn't come to for ten, fifteen minutes. I lost two teeth—man, that's the hardest I was ever hit in my life! And I been hit a lotta times by a lotta guys, who were fuckin' serious about it, too! Don't tell me a woman can't hit as hard as men. The hardest I ever got hit, that's was a woman. So I don't fuck with none of 'em, no more. You do that, and you gonna get your head handed to you. I mean it, 'cause it happened to me."

For Sunny, from a single experience that ran counter to the general wisdom, he had generalized to the assigning of greater physical power to women. Quite possibly some earlier experiences with his older sisters (several of whom had also spent years in jail) when he was a child may have contributed to it.

But the problem with the concept of power as the generalization of strength is that—in general—it doesn't locate the most useful socially effective intervention points.

The other approach-cum-axiom about power does:

"Power (unlike strength) is always assigned by an Other."

Sunny himself is the Other who, from the point of generalization, reassigned power to women so that he "no longer fucks with 'em." Is that enough to change the balance of power? There was a period, certainly, starting in the middle '60s, when physically competent women actually became a staple of adventure movies, comics, TV, and science fiction, and as physical training for women grew much more widespread, which began only shortly after Sunny had his movie theater encounter, incidents of this sort certainly couldn't have hurt the reassignment of physical power to women. But it seems to me, today, reflected in films like *Million Dollar Baby* and *The Road to Terabithia* (where the strong or competent female is killed off by the film's end), that this period is fast petering out.

Holding on to where the other makes his or her move in the assignment process is still very necessary. In the early '90s, I was invited to spend a term as Coles Honors Professor at the Honors College of the State University of Michigan at East Lansing. I and my life-partner, Dennis, went out and, while I taught for a term at the university, lived together on campus.

For a number of reasons, Dennis and I were housed in a faculty apartment on the ground floor of Yakely Hall, a large building, basically a women's dorm, which faced out on the university's main thoroughfare. To its back was a forested area through which a number of short cuts ran to other classroom buildings.

I am a short (five-eight), pudgy adult, with a beard. I was in my early fifties and just beginning to walk with a cane. I have—and had at the time—many visual cues about me of an "older man." Dennis, my life-partner of three or four years at the time, was (and is) a slim, tall (six-one) man, who had been homeless and lived on the street for six years before we met and had an animal vitality and a body that was all muscle. Twelve years younger than I, Dennis was then thirty-nine or forty, but he carried himself like someone as much as ten years younger.

On several occasions, either when collecting our mail with the young women who shared our building, or going to chamber music concerts that were sometimes held in the lounge, or political debates (in the same space), we found ourselves walking through the dorm halls—which were lined with blackboards. Their repeated messages and warnings had an overriding theme:

"Every six minutes, somewhere a woman is raped!"

"Keep yourself safe. Travel with a friend or friends after dark!"

"The best weapon against rape? Use your head!"

Across all of these hung hand-printed flyers about individual cases of sexual molestation on various parts of the campus. (Once I looked carefully at a couple of them to discover they were dated three and four years ago, and had not yet been taken down!) The blackboards were covered with the addresses and phone numbers of rape counseling centers and rape crisis centers. There were emergency phone numbers for battered women shelters and numbers to volunteer for work with displaced and homeless women who had been abused by husbands or boyfriends.

As we were walking, looking at all this, Dennis voiced what I was feeling myself: "That's gotta be kinda weird—living someplace where you're threatened with rape every time you step out of your room."

"It probably is," I said. "But then, it's also probably necessary. You remember, the school paper had an article about a rape on campus just two weeks ago…"

"Oh, yeah. That's right."

A few evenings later, Dennis went out to see some friends, and I went to a program about gay studies. I got home early and retired to bed. A bit after eleven, Dennis came in.

He was visibly upset—so I got up and asked him what was the matter.

A light snow had stopped earlier in the evening. Dennis had been walking home through the back wooded section, when he'd seen a pair of young black women, some ways away, but both clearly—as was he—headed toward Yakely. He wasn't really thinking about them, but he noticed that, now and then, they stopped and looked at him. Then they would whisper together, and hurry on—sometimes moving toward the hall, sometimes away. In fact, he was fairly sure he recognized one of the women as someone he'd seen around the dorm before—and now also realized they were nervous.

The back entrance to the hall was only thirty or thirty-five feet away. Dennis decided to wave and maybe call out something friendly, but the moment he did—he said—he also took a step forward. Perhaps that was interpreted as his starting to run. The two women took off, pell-mell, toward the door—Dennis thought he was involved in some sort of joke, and took a couple of quicker steps after them, to get into the light, and even called, "Hey—it's all right…"

At that point, the women reached the door, which had a light above it. One—after yanking open the door—turned to pull her friend inside…and Dennis saw that the look on her face was, as he said, one of absolute terror!

He stopped dead.

The door slammed behind the two. They had gone inside. Dennis realized that they had thought he was pursuing them. He was very upset. He wanted to go looking for them and explain that he was just coming back to his room, as were they. He alternated between being deeply distressed—and very angry. He was not exactly sure who he was angry at—sometimes it was at who'd ever put up all the frightening backboard notices. Sometimes it was at the women for being "stupid" and thinking an ordinary gay man was a potential rapist. Sometimes it was at himself, for not making clearer that he was harmless before they'd started to run; or for being so silly as to think that they were taking it all as a joke in the first place—or, indeed, that he had been stupid enough to take it that way.

The point here is simply that, because "power is always assigned by an Other," you—if you are male—can't get rid of it just by "being a nice guy" or being personally "harmless" as you walk around in the world.

I (and Dennis; and every other male in this society) exercise my male power and prerogatives (which includes the power of a rapist over his victim) just by walking around in the street. The fact that I—personally—believe the reapportionment of power between the sexes (notice I do not use the word gender) is so overwhelmingly important has nothing to do with the power that is assigned me by every male and female who happens to register my presence as I move through this society. This is why changing the power structure is so difficult. The power never starts with the one who has it. It is assigned by an Other; and effective change is always a matter of changing the assigner, not the assignee.

(In my ideal world, there is one gender with infinite variations; not two with the variations limited to what lies between them. If there are two, they will be assigned unequal power, because—sad as the news may be—unequal power differentials are the only socially meaningful differences that exist. That is, therefore, what two genders means. If they weren't of unequal power, they wouldn't be two.)

This bring us to your question about being a male "feminist" or a feminist sympathizer at WisCon.

But there's a limit case to all this that I wish I could simply skip over—and I would, had I not had to deal with it directly in the first few years that I was teaching at the University of Massachusetts at Amherst. In my third year, 1990, I drew up a course description of a continuing graduate seminar in the history of the novel called "Male Sexuality and the Modern Novel," which, that term, included works such as Joyce's *Portrait of the Artist as a Young Man*, D. H. Lawrence's *Sons and Lovers*, *The Rainbow*, and *Women in Love*, Musil's *Young Törless*, and Gide's *The Immoralist* and *Strait is the Gate*. The course description mentioned that we would be looking at some of these texts from a position "sympathetic to feminism." But the secretary who typed up the description for the course catalogue made a mistake and accidentally the course appeared as "Sexuality and the

Modern Novel." The result was that a number of young women applied to take the course, thinking it was a course in feminism per se. Among the men who registered, one was an auditor, of twenty-three, named Bill, whom I had already met in town, where he worked in Amherst's local comic book store.

Bill was a blond, strapping young man who lifted weights. He was notably better looking than average, and knew it. He was quite intelligent, and during the first class session, when I was telling my dozen students about the focus of the course—and the titling error—and, as I often do in such classes, I asked the students to say a few words about why they had taken the course and what they hoped to get out of it, Bill was the only one who said he had read several of my books already and was therefore interested to hear what I had to say on the topic. He confessed that he too had made the expected mistake, however, and had registered to take the course because he felt "the position of women in the society" was an interesting question.

When the first meeting was over and we had adjourned, however, Bill attached himself to me for the bus ride back into Amherst and, in the course of our chat, said, "You know, I'm not really into all this feminist stuff. But I figured it would be a good way to meet chicks. And even with the mistake corrected, there're still a couple of cute ones in your class. But I guess you have to talk the talk in order to get anywhere with chicks like these."

Needless to say, I was not very happy with this as his opening move—though I chuckled and said, "Who knows. You may even have to learn to walk the walk."

His response: "I don't think there's much chance of that. Believe me—I already know how to handle chicks."

And, indeed, though Bill was often deferential, as our class discussions progressed, it became clear that he had neither any understanding of—nor sympathy with—feminism and that he thought all of us in the class were basically out of our minds. He made two or three efforts to date some of the women students, then, at the two-thirds point—which he could do because he was auditing—dropped out.

It's always been my practice to teach anyone who will show up. But since Bill could be both obtuse and even, sometimes, disruptive, I don't think anyone missed him. In the class meeting before he left, however, one of the women who had long ago lost patience with Bill challenged him: "You're in this class. Do you think of yourself as a feminist?"

Bill had answered, "Sure, I do. I'm a feminist. I like women. I like spending time with them, talking to them. They make me feel good. I just don't think they're generally as smart as men, that's all. And I don't particularly even want them to be—doesn't that mean I'm for women, as they are and as they should be?"

This was, of course, fifteen years ago. But here we are at the inescapable brink of "male feminists" and the power deployment between the sexes.

I don't think we have to spend time discussing whether those men (and women: often the women self-identify as "post-feminist"), who believe that the status quo is fine as it is and that a power reapportionment is neither desirable nor necessary, should call themselves feminists. The point is that some, like Bill, if not many, do.

Please forgive all this contextual elaboration before I turn to your question directly, which is about comfort vs. discomfort, feminists vs. sympathizers, and the change in the relationship between the early '70s, early '80s, and now, in a venue such as WisCon.

Let me start by saying that when power is reassigned, nobody is comfortable with it, at least at the beginning—neither men nor women. Some folks—men and women—who have taken part in a careful intellectual analysis of the situation are possibly more likely to put up with that discomfort in the name of something like "tough love." But while there are certainly joys to be experienced from the reassignment of power, they are interlarded with new rights and new responsibilities that are simply difficult to negotiate.

Also, when power is reassigned to one person, that means it is taken away from someone else—and that is always going to be men. Invariably that is experienced as the taking away of former privileges. Nobody likes or enjoys that. And if they say they do, they're lying. But it's still amazing what you can acclimate to. Nevertheless, the comfort of men that you talk about at WisCon, is, I'm afraid, basically an index that, while WisCon well may be a gathering of women and men who are highly aware that reassignment is necessary, the comfort most feel there—again, men and women—is because that reassignment has not yet taken place.

When now and again in the '70s, I would encounter social experiments where precisely such reassignments were taking place, I remember how uncomfortable I felt with them. Once I visited an English Commune where the back wall carried a large banner, "MOTHER IS A JOB." A condition of my entering and visiting for three days, eating there, and sleeping, was that I had to agree to do a certain amount of child care. And when I said, kind of lightly, "Well, all right. I'll try. But I don't know how good I am at this," the young man who was showing me around didn't return a supportive smile, and say, "Oh, you'll get used to it. And we'll try to make it easy on you and show you what to do." Rather, the look he gave me said: "What's the matter with you? Are you nuts?"

That's the effect of the reassignment of power. And it isn't comfortable. For what it's worth, they did help me. I learned a number of techniques that I used with my own daughter (and that led, I'm sure, directly to the wonderfully warm relationship I have with her today, thirty years later, now that she's an adult in medical school). After three days I was a better parent because of the time I'd spent there.

Then there was the Grayrabbit, a collective that ran a bus back and forth from New York to San Francisco in the late '60s and early '70s. The bus was restroom-equipped, but among the free-wheeling young people, especially the young men, on a shaky vehicle with dubious springs, the restroom quickly became un-usably foul, to the distress of the women passengers. The driver happened to be a woman, however, and she was also handy as a carpenter. After the next run, she sawed off a couple of lengths of two-by-four and positioned them across the john space, one just inside the door, one further in, so that it was impossible to approach the commode standing. You had to back in and sit.

She accompanied it with a sign:

You don't sit,

You don't piss!

That's the reassignment of power—and most of the guys on the bus were pretty uncomfortable on the first day of the three-day run. At the end, however, even they appreciated the much cleaner space. And the rear third of the bus no longer smelled like a stopped-up urinal.

The benefits of reassignment, even in so small a taste as I got at the British commune, were huge.

But no one should approach them looking for comfort. It isn't there. Indeed, the sign that they have taken place is initial discomfort.

As far as the changes over time from the '70s through the '80s, it's always difficult for me to distinguish the changes that age itself brings—the kinds of experiences that age precludes me from (or, suddenly, includes me in)—and the changes that are transculturally there.

At dinner only last week, a young gay studies professor told me, "Oh, today all the queers are the straight kids. The gay kids don't want anything to do with 'queer' any more. It's been completely co-opted." And, indeed, I'd noticed only last term when I taught a class in gay studies here at Temple, all the men who registered for the class were straight—and the one who most vociferously self-identified as "queer" also most vociferously self-identified as "heterosexual."

I also noticed something else, though. The class was half men and half women, but the women dominated the discussion. They were extremely comfortable with our progression from Kinsey and Kenneth (*Scorpio Rising*) Anger to the Derek (*Sebastiane, Edward II*) Jarman films we screened and our readings of everything from Foucault and Freud and Henry (*Deep Gossip*) Abelove on homosexuality to "Chapter V" of Philip Aries' *Centuries of Childhood* (in today's atmosphere of hysteria over child abuse and childhood sexuality certainly one of the most "shocking" pieces of scholarship, in its findings, I know of) to my own *Times Square Red, Times Square Blue*. To support one abstract point or another they offered anecdotes about their own bodies freely and intelligently, in a way that, twenty years ago, I'd only found among older gay men and women, while the men in the class... what can I say, still sounded like boys—and not what I, at least, think of as adults. (Many of them reminded me simply of quieter and less hide-bound Bills.) Some reassignment of discursive power, at least, had clearly taken place, though whether it was permanent or larger than the accidental fall of the class roster, I have no way to know. Nevertheless, the constantly reiterated message from the young men in the class was, "I never even knew people did things like that—ever. Wow...that's just so weird," (sometimes said to me in class, sometimes said wonderingly outside in the halls), while the women seemed to find it wholly non-threatening and interesting for the ways it suggested the world might one day be rearranged. This seems to represent a change that is palpable over the last seven years since I first came to Temple.

Do any of these attitudes, to the extent they are indexes of comfort or discomfort before the social reassignment of power, mirror anything that you have seen at recent WisCons? And that question, really, is about as far as I can go.

I feel as through I have not answered you with any sort of directness. But perhaps I have given someone younger than I (and someone who has been to WisCon more than twice in twenty years—my own situation) a tool or two that might be useful in working toward an answer. Or, perhaps, I have only displayed some tools, the value of whose inspection is precisely that they have no particular relevance or use to the question. But all intellectual work is a gamble.

I wish you the best of things and the best of words and thoughts
to stabilize their best order for you—

—Chip Delany

Rob Hanson & Jeanne Gomoll

Samuel R. Delany is a novelist and critic who lives in New York and teaches at Temple University in Philadelphia. His most recent book is *Dark Reflections*, from Carroll and Graf. WisCon 11 GoH.

Dry Eyes

by Nisi Shawl

WisCon 30 hosted the first presentation of the Carl Brandon Society's dual literary awards—and I was there. Already somewhat dewy-eyed after speeches by Guests of Honor Kate Wilhelm and Jane Yolen, many in the audience wept openly during the ceremony's stunning climax. I'm crying now as I write about it.

The Carl Brandon Society was founded in 1999 at WisCon 23, and the creation of our two literary awards was first announced at WisCon 29. The Parallax Award is given annually to the author of color who has published the year's best new work of speculative fiction; and the Kindred Award is given annually to the author of any racial background who has published the year's best new work of speculative fiction dealing with issues of race and ethnicity. In keeping with the tradition of the Tiptree, we announce short and long lists of noteworthy nominees along with award winners, weeks prior to the actual ceremony. Each award comes with a $1000 check.

Founders of the CBS see a strong connection between the struggles for gender and racial equity, and from the beginning we've fostered ties between the Society and both WisCon and the Tiptree. The first Tiptree was awarded at WisCon 16; the CBS Steering Committee and the awards' two juries struggled with all our might to present the first Parallax and Kindred Awards at WisCon 30, and our struggles were successful. On top of the usual contentions and casualties any award jury is prone to, we had to cope with the organizational equivalent of opening-night jitters. Additionally, while we looked to organizers of the Tiptree Award for examples of how to accomplish our tasks, we still had to do them: pick winners, write statements about why they won, arrange plane tickets and other perks for winning authors, select and purchase the physical awards and then get them engraved with our newly created logo… And when we reached Madison, we still had to write and choreograph the ceremony itself.

One nominee, Octavia E. Butler, had died while the juries were in the process of deciding who'd receive the awards. Octavia's death affected all of us at the Carl Brandon Society, affected many of us deeply enough that persevering with the awards process became simultaneously easier and harder. Easier because we knew we were doing work she had endorsed, furthering the cause of multiracial representation in the genre. Harder because the very name of one of the awards, the Kindred, reminded us of her novel of the same name, making her absence that much more obvious.

But we managed to get almost everything done before arriving in Madison. Then, between chairing WisCon 30 panels and giving readings, in hotel rooms and busy hallways, two of us wrote a script that we felt reflected the Society's consensus operating structure. We made sure everyone present had something to say, and that what they said reflected their input from earlier conversations. For instance, we had Ian K Hagemann, Parallax Award juror and Carl Brandon Society Treasurer, note the jury's difficulty in finding appropriate work, saying that "These awards wouldn't be needed if such work were being published daily, or even monthly." And we included a line from Kindred Award juror and Carl Brandon Society Steering Committee member MJ Hardman in which she pointed out that "many young adult novels were nominated, which gives us hope for bringing more young people into the genre."

However, we were still going over the ceremony's logistics as the line for the Dessert Banquet, where it was scheduled to take place, began to move ominously forward, past the room where we'd met to iron out final details. Would we be seated together? Did we have a photographer to capture this momentous moment for posterity? Where had the box of programs printed that afternoon gotten to?

Somehow, it all worked out. Lisa Cohen snagged us a table, and we found the programs under a chair. We handed them out, made our prepared statements, moved smoothly onto, around, and about the stage and off of it again, exactly as planned. Since Walter Mosley, first recipient of the Parallax Award for his novel *47* was unable to attend WisCon 30 in person, Nalo Hopkinson read a letter he'd written expressing his appreciation.

Then Susan Vaught, winner of the Kindred Award for *Stormwitch*, made her move: it was totally unchoreographed and not only unexpected but also beyond the boundaries of any possibility of expectation. Acknowledging her debt to Octavia E. Butler in the development of her own writing, she announced, "It is with great pleasure that I sign this check back to the Carl Brandon Society for their Octavia E. Butler Memorial Scholarship Fund."

Near the opening of this essay I wrote that "…many audience members wept openly…." I only know this, however, because other people who were present told me so later. I was there, but I didn't see the audience reaction. I had covered my face with my hands. What Susan Vaught had done was terrible in its beauty. There was no way to encompass it in the same step-by-step mindset involved with pulling off an awards presentation. "Stop, stop," I muttered under my breath. "Stop." My lover stroked my shoulders, trying to comfort me.

There was no comfort. Octavia was dead. Is dead. All we have left are her books and these tremendously powerful acts committed in her name.

This act, in particular, remains a topic of conversation months after the first Carl Brandon Society Parallax and Kindred Awards were presented; like the influence of the awards themselves, its effect may be felt for years. The scholarship fund will enable writers of color to attend a Clarion Writers Workshop using the same format as the one that gave Octavia her professional start. The worlds that scholarship recipients will create will carry her legacy forward—and that of Susan Vaught's amazingly generous donation. It will help bring "more young people into the genre" and ensure that works fit to be nominated for the awards are at least written, if not published.

But all this is hindsight. It's all a retrospective view of what happened on Sunday night, May 28, 2006. It's all aftermath, now. Like the words of the woman who told me days later, miles away, that there couldn't have been a dry eye in the house.

My eyes were dry. Then. Blinded, but dry. Seared by a truth I didn't want to see, a truth Susan Vaught's actions made unavoidable.

Here is the truth Susan Vaught taught to me: Octavia-as-we-knew-her is gone. What lives and breathes and moves is something more, and it hurts to see it, and I have to keep on looking. Even through the tears when, like now, they come.

Nisi Shawl is a coauthor, with Cynthia Ward, of *Writing the Other: A Practical Approach*. Her work has appeared in *Asimov's* and in anthologies including *Dark Matter* and *Mojo: Conjure Stories*. Her reviews and essays have appeared regularly in the *Seattle Times* since the turn of the millennium, and she is a contributor to *The Encyclopedia of Themes in Science Fiction and Fantasy* and to *The Internet Review of Science Fiction*. A Clarion West board member, she likes to relax by pretending she lives in other people's houses.

http://www.sfwa.org/members/shawl/

Robert Kellough

Carl Brandon Society

Candra K. Gill

Octavia E. Butler (1947-2006) was the first black woman to come to international prominence as a science fiction writer. Incorporating powerful, spare language and rich, well-developed characters, her work tackles race, gender, religion, poverty, power, politics, and science in a way that has touched readers of all backgrounds. A critical force, she was a MacArthur Fellow and received numerous awards, including both the Hugo® and Nebula® Awards, the Langston Hughes Medal, and a PEN West Lifetime Achievement Award.

The Octavia E. Butler Memorial Scholarship Fund is administered by The Carl Brandon Society. The goal is to raise $100,000 to endow the scholarship permanently.

http://www.carlbrandon.org.

No Man's Land

by Rosaleen Love

We didn't have long to wait to meet our first man.

It was Grandmama Belle who found him and marched him down to our firm.

We'd seen the spaceship crash, on our screens, and the flash of four escape pods as they ejected. It's happened before, the crashes. But this time it was different. This time, there were survivors.

I shall never forget how terrible that first man looked. Not surprising, I suppose, because of the crash, and the escape, and then, when he came to, he found himself in the middle of Blackwater Swamp, and the first person he met was our Grandmama Belle.

Our Grandmama. She'd gone off to live by herself in a shack by the swamp, the way old people do, and she preferred talking to the tangle-trees rather than us. That's how she made first contact.

I was there, the day it happened, the day the space-liner crashed.

They've all crashed, the spaceships that tried to land on Namon. Nice to know they didn't forget us, back on the mother planet. Then, after a while, the ships stopped coming. It's been a thousand years since the first people came to this planet and set up their settlements, and a thousand years since spaceships could land without crashing. The Veil in the sky let the first ship through, then learned what we were up to, or thought it did, and stood by to repel all boarders. Until now.

"Name's Jaco," said Grandmama Belle, pushing the space man along. She walked behind him, poking him in the middle of the back with a long black piece of metal that I'd never seen before.

Jaco stumbled forward, clumsy in spacesuit and helmet, but glorious with it, that first man, glowing in the soft light of the evening sun.

Mother Calypte rushed up to Grandmama Belle. "Where'd you get that thing?"

Jaco shivered and shrank down a bit within his helmet, but Mother Calypte didn't mean him. She meant…

"She's got a gun!" Mother Calypte shrieked.

Jaco gave a low moan.

The small kids circled round, and Marianova, my twin sister.

"Of course it's a gun. It's a good thing I kept this from my own Grandmama's time," said Grandmama Belle.

Mother Calypte shrieked even louder, and the three other Mothers came running. Sometimes it takes all four mothers to talk Grandmama Belle down from where she's at, but I'd never seen so much excitement before, over a…?

"What's a gun?" I asked. Marianova didn't know either.

"Give that gun to me." Mother Veita spoke in a calm insistent voice, and I'd have given her what she wanted, for sure, hearing her speak.

Grandmama Belle got that stubborn look.

"What about bullets?" asked Mother Barbastella. "Aha, you don't have any bullets, do you?"

Grandmama Belle got that crafty look.

Mother Barbastella gave the nod to Mother Vieta, who circled round behind Grandmama Belle, ready to pounce.

"What's bullets?" Marianova asked.

"Of course it's got bullets," yelled Grandmama Belle, pointing the gun in the air above her head.

There was a loud bang. A branch of the lily tree crashed down and hit the spaceman on his head. He fell forward, smashing his faceplate into the ground. He lay motionless.

"I practice," said Grandmama Belle. "You never can tell when shooting someone will come in handy."

The mothers crowded round Grandmama Belle, taking more care this time.

The rest of us crowded round the spaceman.

"Now look what you've done," Mother Calypte said, with low, sorrowful voice, "Grandmama Belle, you've killed him."

"He's gone, is he?" Grandmama Belle lowered her weapon.

"Sure, he's gone."

Grandmama Callie grabbed the gun and spilled out all the bullets. Like she'd been there, done that, before.

"I brought you a man," said Grandmama Belle. "What have you ever done for me?"

The spaceman moved his head.

The littlies crowded closer, behind Marianova and me.

The spaceman opened his eyes and looked at us. He shuddered at what he saw, and shut his eyes once more.

I now know why he was so upset. There are eight of us, and four mothers, see. It's the way of our world, and in our world, the children come two by two. Twins. Identical. I now realize he thought he was seeing things wrong, seeing double, but he was really seeing things right. It was the start of him learning to see things our way, and I now know why he gave that sad moan and closed his eyes, and opened them again, and looked at us, but we were all happy and smiling, and I think he could see we were delighted to see him, and we meant him no harm.

We're the oldest, Marianova and me, at eighteen years of age, and about to join the mothers ourselves. The littlies saw we weren't frightened, not by the spaceman, though Grandmama Belle and that gun was something else.

"I'm so sorry," said Mother Veita, extending a hand to the spaceman and helping him to sit up. "I do hope you're not hurt? You are a traveler and you must be tired. You mustn't mind Grandmama Belle."

"I do so mind her. I told you, Calypte, that Granny is a danger to herself and others. A gun? Whoever's seen a gun for the past hundred years? What do you need a gun for?"

"To kill him," said, Grandmama Belle. "We killed all the other men, so let's kill this one."

"Grandmama, you know that's only a story. They didn't kill all the men"; Mother Calypte smiled at Jaco. "Of course they didn't kill all the men. The men just died."

Jaco suddenly looked a whole lot worse.

"Of a virus," Mother Calypte explained.

"That's why he's got his helmet on," Marianova whispered. "He doesn't want to breathe in the man germs."

Grandmama Belle broke free of the mothers and stormed up to Jaco, "Go away!"

Mother Calypte pulled her back and tried to shush her.

"If we don't shoot him, can't we just breathe on him? Kill him off the slow way?"

"Man germs," said Grandmama Callie, explaining to Jaco. "When our ancestors first arrived, a thousand years back, there were men, but they died from a virus or something."

"Kill him off and eat him! He'll taste real good with tangle-tree roots, and ginger." But Mother Calypte had pulled Grandmama Belle away by then, and her words floated in from a distance, and it's just as well Jaco didn't really take it in.

Jaco looked round at us all, seeing, for the first time, that he was the only man. He shuddered and lay back on the ground.

"Why's he all yellow?" asked Marianova.

"It's called a space suit," I told her. "Remember? From the old days?"

"You can take off your helmet," said Grandmama Callie. "Those stories about man germs—they're just not true. No, the old days, the men? They just went away one day on a hunting trip and they never came back. They've got their own world on the other side of the planet. Men's Country."

We looked at each other. Everyone knows Men's Country is only a story.

Jaco didn't know what to believe then, and he still doesn't. Every place has its own stories of origins. I suppose where he comes from it's the same, but it must be a bit different on Namon. I expect he's not used to people talking about men like they're an extinct species.

✳✳✳

Then the second man turned up. He came out of the jungle by himself and found our settlement. He had instruments with him, and the chatterers showed him the way to our village, though he wouldn't have known about the chatterers back then. I think he thought he found us all by himself.

His name was Ferec. He'd analyzed the air, and found it good, and he took his helmet off.

When Jaco first saw him, he yelled, "Put it back on! Your helmet! At once!"

Ferec took no notice. "Hey, nothing's wrong with the air here. Smells good to me."

"No, no!" Jaco yelled, "'Look, around you! No men! Not one! All dead! There's a virus!"

That stopped Ferec for a moment. "But hey, look at me. I'm alive."

Jaco kept his helmet on till his air ran out. It took a whole day before he got to breathe our air.

Jaco told Ferec, "We've arrived at No Man's Land." Jaco saw us as a kind of Woman Problem, whatever.

Ferec, from the start, saw us as more of an opportunity. I liked his business-like approach—though he was, of course, deluded.

⁕⁕⁕

"There were four of us," said Ferec when we'd made our introductions. "Four of us were in the ship, and four of us got out. We need to find the others."

News of the first men spread through the village by the usual chattering routes, and people gathered to stare.

"We can look it up, we've got our own firm," Mother Calypte explained, though you could see Jaco wasn't really taking anything in, and Ferec was so busy trying to take everything in that he couldn't process nearly the half of it. "When we saw you coming, we knew you were going to crash. Everyone does, all the space ships that have tried to land on Namon. After the first people. They got through all right. Otherwise, we wouldn't be here, would we?"

It's too hard, you see, to get through the Veil. The Veil is up there, in the sky, in a layer round the whole of Namon. It's active, alive, and learning. It's not quite omnipotent and omniscient, not yet, but flexing its powers, doing its best, learning from previous experience, and it worked out a bit better, this time, for the survivors.

We got Jaco and Ferec away from the crowds and into our instrument room. We played them the records from the monitors.

"See, four flashes of light? Four trajectories? That one must be you, and this one must be Jaco, and these other two… I'll just get on the bug and find out." Mother Calypte reached into a terrarium and selected a good bug, the one bristling with the most static, and raring to go.

Jaco totally freaked out when he saw what she did with it. Ferec gave a bit of a jump, but kept his cool. Just.

Bugs. Chatterers. They're what our firm is famous for. We breed them, and adapt them, and sell them to all the other settlements all over all over Namon. They're in your head, yes, and they're a bug, the kind of bug we have on Namon, a species of chatterer that's really good at long-distance communication.

"OK," said Mother Calypte after some transmits, "You don't need to worry about that one." She pointed to one splash of light. "That pod fell in the ocean."

"But that's Eldred!" Jaco cried, "He's our geologist! We have to get to him!"

Mother Calypte explained a bit, how the ocean is our mother, and he'll be safe there. "Of course, he may come out wearing gills but that's all for the best, really, if he's in the ocean. And they may take a bit of time bringing him out. There's the big Pan-Oceanic Congress happening now."

Mother Calypte took in Jaco's concern. "Oh, believe me, it's much better than trying to look in the ocean all by ourselves. The water world goes its own way. He's already been found. Like we found you. Someone, some thing, entity, whatever, perhaps a creature he's not met before, perhaps, will take him in hand, fin, or flipper, and show him friendliness and all."

"Just like Grandmama Belle?" said Jaco.

Mother Calypte gave him a look.

"He's a geologist, you said?" Mother Veita prompted. "What would you be wanting a geologist for, then?"

But they didn't reply, the men, not just then. Jaco shrieked as the instrument panel began its mid-morning ooze. The instrument panel was kind of organized, but not totally. The trouble with organics, the metals make their own shapes round the frames, and we don't like to fuss too much, because well, the metals on Namon are a lowly form of life, but they've got feelings, just like us. They have an innate aesthetic sense of how an instrument panel should look, from their point of view, and it's just one of those things you have to work around.

Ferec jumped back, but quickly regained his composure. He congratulated us on the fine state of our instrument room, and our clear mastery of new materials technologies.

✳✳✳

"Men!" Mother Calypte said, and we're with the mothers, Marianova and me, learning by listening. "Four of them! What are we going to do?"

"What we used to do, I expect," said Mother Veita.

"You don't mean, kill them all off, like Grandmama said?"

"Shoot them? I could never do that."

"No, let's find another virus. We must have done it once, if that's what happened."

"I don't want to kill anybody, virus, gun, no way. Let's just tell them to go away."

"Shhh, the littlies are listening."

✳✳✳

"What are men for, Lydda?" Marianova asked.

"In the old days," I told her, "Men used to open doors for women. That was one of the things they did."

"Doors open all by themselves," said Marianova. "What else can men be for?"

"There are those stories of knights in shining armor. Remember, Jaco really shone, that first day we saw him?"

"He shines. So?"

"I think the women were supposed to be the damsels in distress, but really, it was the knights who were having a hard time of it, keeping their armor shining, going forth into battle, and so on. Women stayed home and got on with more important things."

"What else can men be for?"

"I think I once knew, but I've forgotten."

✳✳✳

"Don't you see, they'll kill us?" Jaco said to Ferec.

"I rather think she fancies me," Ferec said to Jaco.

"The planet will kill us. It's alive. Everything here's alive! It's creeping. It's crawling. Did you see what they do with those bugs?"

"Lydda. Or Marianova. One of them fancies me."

"The virus will kill us. It's in the air, the food, the water."

"Both of them fancy me, more like it."

"Or if it isn't the planet, or the virus, it'll be mad old granny who'll lie in wait and gets us with her gun."

"Hard to tell. Both? One? Lydda? Marianova? Lydda and Marianova? Twins, isn't it amazing when you think of it?"

"Look at them. Why are those women laughing?"

"Women, they like to laugh."

"I think those women are laughing at us."

"Four mothers, eight children. No men! How do they do it?"

"Shhh, Ferec. They're listening."

✳✳✳

The fourth man posed a different problem.

"That's Bertil," said Ferec.

Mother Calypte did her best to explain. "Bertil, now, looks as if he's come down over here." She pointed her finger into the screen, and the colors flowed out and over her hand. The words, "Bad sector" hovered in the air.

Jaco shuddered.

"Just what did you say you'd be needing a geologist for?" Mother Veita asked, but Ferec didn't reply, not then.

Bad sector. Badlands. Mother Calypte didn't tell them, not at first, not everything. She was a bit evasive, and I think that was wise of her.

"Lydda," said Mother Calypte, "We're going to need you to come, and Goliath." For the Badlands, we'd need Goliath, an old ore-miner with a shovel, for the shoveling. We may have to shovel this Bertil out. After all, he's not come walking out, all by himself, not yet, like the others. If the chatterers had found him, they'd have sent him our way.

"I expect a geologist might come in handy for the sand-pools," said Mother Veita. "Did you know, there are sand-pools in the Bad Sector? One mistake, and you're in trouble."

"Kind of like quicksand," Mother Calypte explained, "Only slower. A problem, but not too bad a problem, not if you're quick."

It was then I came to realize something important about the relationships between men and women, what they might have been like in the old days. Women took over some of the worrying for the men, to keep them from worrying too much for themselves.

Mother Calypte kept things positive. "Here's what we'll do. First light tomorrow, we'll take the sand-skippers, and a few days rations, and we'll find your friend. I'm sure of it."

"Your friend, the geologist," said Mother Veita.

"Oh," said Ferec, "No, Bertil's not a geologist. That's Eldred, who's in the ocean."

"What's Bertil then?" Mother Veita asked, but Ferec didn't tell her, not then.

✳✳✳

Jaco and Ferec balked when they saw the sand-skippers.

"They're perfectly tame," I told them, "They're just babies, really." I patted them to show I wasn't scared.

The men stayed on the safe side of the fence.

Sand-skippers are like round frisky balls, big ones, and you have to sit in a loose fold of skin on their backs and communicate with them through bugs, yours and theirs, and I could see that bugs were a bit of a problem for the men.

"What's with them, those men?" asked Marianova.

"They said men were the weaker sex, back on the mother planet. They had to be looked after, and protected, and we're doing that, here, to make them feel more at home."

The men asked if they could leave the sand-skippers to more experienced hands, and perhaps they might perhaps ride in Goliath's scoop?

✳✳✳

The ore-miner, Goliath, was a thousand years old and came with the first people. Goliath had a shovel-nose, two side arm-extensors, four trundle legs, and four wheeled feet. It wasn't fast, but it was dependable. Goliath was made with metals from the mother planet, and metals on Namon are different. There's been a process of learning on both sides, and Goliath survived where the other ore miners have rusted away, the huge ones from the old days. There's only this small one left, more adaptable to new circumstances and new ways of being. We've kept it working. That's been my job. I'm the driver.

A long time ago we discovered that mining ore is a delicate business on Namon. Our metals have a lowly level of life. The ore must agree to being mined, and that involves a lot of negotiation about the end to which it will be put. Our ancestors, the first people, mustn't have known this. They just ripped into the earth and didn't listen to the voices of the chatterers.

When our ancestors came, they thought they could just do as they pleased. It took them a while to realize things are different here.

Next morning, we rose early and set off together, our small team, the two men, Mother Calypte, Mother Veita, me (because I know Goliath and its ways), and Marianova, my twin.

✳✳✳

As Mother Calypte told it, the Bad Sector is bad because of what happened back in the early days.

A thousand years ago, our ancestors came to Namon. They came in a star-liner to mine the planet and send the metals home. They planned to terraform what was left, changing the planet to suit the people, because the planet was there before the people, and we hadn't evolved with it. Terraforming, we now know, would never work on Namon, where everything, from dust to us, has a place and a contribution to make. Relationship is all. Namon is a planet in the process of becoming. It was essentially different from Earth, the planet from which our ancestors once came.

There's something in the air of Namon, something the first settlers didn't know.

We give it a name: the entelechy.

Because of the entelechy, the mining ventures were doomed, and the mines were abandoned.

That was why, when the ore-miners first came, there was going to be trouble, because they did not consult with the metals about the uses to which they would be put, and the metals did not like it. Their preference is for peace, and we have to respect that.

Not only did the first people never ask, they didn't listen, either, when the ore bodies whispered amongst themselves and used the chatterers to initiate the process of communication, through the normal geo-bio-neuro channels.

Over time, people on Namon changed to fit the planet. We had to, that's for sure. Before we used to have men, and then, suddenly, for whatever reason, we didn't have men any more—which goes part of the way towards explaining how we changed. For reproducing the species, we don't need men, just four mothers and the bark of the lily tree and the... But I'll tell you all about that later.

✳✳✳

At first the sand-skippers skipped ahead, and Goliath trundled after, creating a path away from over-hanging branches. As we climbed the rocky path to the plateau, the lush jungle round Blackwater made way for the stunted heath of the high country.

Up on the plateau the plants are quite different. They form a *maquis*, a heathland of small bushes and stunted trees. Tough stems push their way through layers of shiny brown pebbles. Here the chatterers take the form of insects and small lizards and act as go-betweens, plugging us into the slow mineral consciousness of the local ores.

After a few hours travel, we took a break.

"Bonsai," said Ferec, getting down on the ground and looking closely at the plants, the monkey puzzles, the parasitic pines, the palms, the cactus flowers.

The Aurum plants grow where the gold is richest. They're like spiky cactus and they poke out of holes in the rock. Some places there's nothing but gold plants.

Ferec and Jaco wanted to know more.

"It's not just gold," we said, "The plants are like that here because of all the metals in the rocks. There's nickel and chromium and…"

"So much gold," said Ferec.

"It's the gold you're after then?" asked Mother Veita. "That's why you need the geologist? The man in the ocean?"

Mother Calypte caught a small brown lizard, "A chatterer," she said, "Let's see what the locals are saying." She held it to her head and deftly inserted it.

Ferec smiled a steely smile.

Jaco shuddered and shut his eyes.

"He must be close," said Mother Calypte after a couple of transmits. Ferec's instruments showed the same. They worked out what direction to take.

By nightfall, we reached the edge of the Badlands and set up camp in preparation for the next day's search. That night, the Veil revealed its full splendor to us. We lay on the ground and watched the green lights play through the shifting veils. As the night-bugs buzzed in an excited swarm outside the shelter shield, we tried to explain to Ferec and Jaco where things had gone wrong on Namon, and that it was all the fault of the gold.

"What use is gold, anyway?" asked Mother Calypte. "It's a stupid, dumb metal, the least lively on any scale of consciousness, useless for interspecies communication."

"Why did you come here?" Mother Veita asked. "It was for the gold, wasn't it?"

"We wanted to find the lost colony," said Ferec. "And we did."

"*We* found *you*," said Mother Veita. "What do you want gold for?"

"Once there were men on Namon," said Mother Calypte. "We really don't know what happened to them all, but we do know what happened to some of them."

That got Ferec's attention, and Jaco's.

"Each year, people assembled here, at this place, and they went over to Clearwater Lake, out there, beyond the horizon. It was some kind of ritual, to bring the gold, because gold, you know, like all other metals, grows in the earth of Namon, and perhaps that's why they did what they did."

"To the men," said Mother Veita.

"To one man. The settlers by then must have known they'd never leave Namon, that the ships that came after were crashing and there'd be no going back home. So they adapted themselves to changing circumstances in a way that made sense to them, but not so much to us."

"They chose one man, and they took him to the shores of Clearwater Lake. They fêted him, dressed him in fine clothes, and the festivities lasted a week. At the end of the week, and he'd known the day was coming, his fine clothes were taken away. He was covered with mud from the shores of the lake, and then gold dust was pressed into the mud until he was covered in gold and shining with it in the light of the sun."

Ferec and Jaco listened intently, the glint of gold dust in their eyes.

"They built a raft from the bark of the lily tree, and they piled it high with chunks of the gold they washed from the gravel, and he was pushed out from the shore into the middle of the lake. There, he stood up and threw the gold rocks into the lake, and then, he jumped into the middle of the lake. All golden."

"And he was lost forever."

"And so, we ran out of men," said Mother Veita.

After a pause, Ferec asked, "How deep is the lake?"

This is one of our stories about how Namon lost its men, but maybe it's a story about something else. It's more about how people can lose their way, if they go looking for stuff that's no use to anybody, if they devote their lives to it, and then, when they find it, they throw it to the bottom of the lake and jump in afterwards.

✻✻✻

Next morning, with Ferec guiding us from the signals he picked up from the pod, and Mother Calypte with the information she got from the chatterers, we traveled further into the Badlands. We passed from the firm ground of the heathlands into the sandy wallows of the old mines. The Badlands are visible relics of the old days. They are in the process of changing themselves into something new, doing it their way, and mostly we respect them for it and leave them alone.

We followed the beeps until we found the source. Except there was nothing there. But both Ferec and Mother Calypte agreed we were right on top of the signals.

Right on top of the signals! Ferec gave a shout, "It's coming from underneath the sand! Bertil's been swallowed in a sand-pool!"

Mother Calypte said, "There is someone down there, the chatterers tell me, and..." She frowned and adjusted the lizard, where you could see the tip of its tail.

Jaco looked away. Ferec stared, his mouth sagging.

"You can get down from the shovel," said Mother Veita. "There's no sand pool here. We'd know if there was. We'd have been sucked under by now."

We set Goliath to work digging. It trundled out the dirt and scooped out the gravel and made a tunnel to the signal. We found the pod where it was buried under the sand.

"I don't understand," said Ferec. "Those pods, they're supposed to glide to earth, like we did."

"He must have done it himself," said Jaco. "The pod must have dug itself down, under the earth."

"He's landed in a bad place. Perhaps it was guiding him away from danger," said Ferec.

"Or taking him somewhere?" Jaco looked down the tunnel, to where Goliath was busy clearing the path to the pod.

"Gold?" Ferec whispered.

I could feel Goliath, under the controls, getting skittish, and the chatterers were excited, and the Veil itself lit up in the light of day. It was the most exciting thing we'd ever done, Goliath and me. I could feel we were onto something big.

Goliath exposed the pod completely, and something else, as well.

What emerged from the sands was something we'd never known was there, the remnants of an old spaceship, an IC-3 starlifter.

Bertil's pod had found the docking area. Bertil had left the pod. We found him, after a while, in the ruins of the ship. He was really confused. "Why is everything so wrong? Why is our ship full of dust and dirt?"

"It's OK, Bertil, you're safe." Ferec said.

"We left on an ICAP-2 starlifter. This is an IC-3. Pile of junk."

"It's O.K., Bertil, we can explain."

"Nothing works. Look, these instruments! The panel is oozing!"

"Things do ooze in this place."

"Hear the voices?" Bertil asked, "Do you hear all those voices?"

"No," said Jaco.

"Yes," said Bertil, "Things chatter here, you wouldn't believe."

"I'm going crazy. You're going crazy too."

"Bertil, it's all OK."

"We crashed, didn't we?"

"We did."

"It's like our spaceliner, but it isn't," said Bertil.

"Bertil, there's an explanation for all this."

"Look, Jaco, Ferec, the storeroom's been plundered."

"Bertil, come away."

"The toilets are filled with sand. A starliner, with toilets filled with sand?"

"Come outside and see where we are."

"It isn't our ship."

"No, it isn't," said Mother Calypte. "You know what I think this is? It's *our* ship, the first ship to come to Namon. It's the ship of our ancestors. They didn't crash. They got through. But then…that was when it changed. This has been here, buried, all along, and we never knew."

"Women!" Bertil saw us for the first time. "Women on a spaceliner? Women in space? What are they doing here?"

"We've landed, Bertil, we're not in space."

"Women, they're history. Who needs women when you've got womb-pods?"

"He's raving," Jaco explained, "You've got them too, like Grandmama Belle."

"True enough," said Mother Calypte, but she was certainly paying attention. Who needs women? How crazy is that? Who needs men, more likely.

✳✳✳

Once Bertil recovered, he stayed with the ship, wandering its rooms, coaxing it back to life, restoring it to its former glory. He wants it to fly again, perhaps take off through the Veil and return home. He might just manage it, with the co-operation of this planet. Just as Goliath changed and adapted to the planet through a kind of unnatural selection, a techno-geo-neuro adaptation, a co-evolution of starliner and planet might just work.

The men must have come for gold, but after a while, they realized the futility of that particular dream. Gold? Useless on Namon, where gold is merely one element among many, striving to achieve its own inner potential, not that of its users.

As for Ferec, when he forgot about the gold, he tried to get us to see things more his way. He's trying to persuade us to try sexual reproduction they way they do it on his planet. He's persuasive, and persistent, and really quite charming with it, and when I feel like it, I may look into what he's on about. It may be it happens only when Grandmama Belle has passed from us.

I said I'm willing to give it a go, but I want to on my terms, in conjunction with the proper ends of being human on Namon and the unfurling of our species. Namon is our new mother planet, and we are her offspring.

Reproducing the species—it's where the entelechy helped us, showing us that we all have the end within ourselves, and that each of us, like each and very other thing, entity, whatever, exists in a state of being in which things work, actively, to be themselves. They don't just sit in themselves, so to speak, and take what fate hands out to them. They unfurl from within with an energy that propels them to be what they are, which offers resilience to chaos, and which works towards, in our case, human ends.

We didn't want human life on Namon to end with us. Imagine what it would be like, the person who is last to die, alone, remembering in sorrow all the other deaths, without the sharp consoling joy of new life coming into being.

On Namon, we get together, four mothers, eight children. Later, I'll go traveling with Ferec, and we'll find some potential mothers in the other settlements away from Blackwater, because that's the way we do things on Namon, and we'll travel together and see the world. We'll show him the lake of the golden boy, and the western ocean.

Some say, Men's Country is at the bottom of Clearwater Lake, but I think it must be on the far shore, and it's populated by generations of golden boys, who've worked out their own ways to reproduce the species. As we did.

The man who landed in the sea? Eldred? We never did get to meet him, but from time to time we hear he's safe, and adapting, which means what it means in the context of life in the sea

As for Jaco, one day he just left, and we assume he went to find Men's Country.

My future lies with Ferec and the other mothers I shall choose, and we'll all have fun together, selecting the chatterers we want, those specialized for the task, and don't forget the bark of the lily tree, which gives our complexions its distinctive orange glow. This time, we'll include Ferec, and when the time comes, we'll know what to do with him.

I have great faith in Namon, in its capacity to change and learn, its innate sense of planetary responsibility. I think the planet Earth, from which we came, did not really have a duty of care towards its inhabitants. The Earth shook, and the tides rose up over the land in earthquake and tsunami. The air raged in typhoon and tornado. Old Mother Earth was a planet in the process of decay.

Our planet is in the process of becoming.

Jeanne Gomoll

L. Timmel Duchamp is the author of *Love's Body, Dancing in Time*, a collection of short fiction; *The Grand Conversation: Essays*; *The Red Rose Rages (Bleeding)*, a short novel; and *Alanya to Alanya*, *Renegade*, and *Tsunami*, the first three novels of the five-volume Marq'ssan Cycle. She is also the editor of *Talking Back: Epistolary Fantasies*. She has been a finalist for the Nebula and Sturgeon awards and short-listed several times for the Tiptree Award. Her stories have appeared in a variety of venues, including *Asimov's SF* and the Full Spectrum, Leviathan, ParaSpheres, and Bending the Landscape anthology series; and her critical essays have appeared in *The New York Review of Science Fiction*, *Extrapolation*, *Foundation*, and *Lady Churchill's Rosebud Wristlet*. In 2004 she founded Aqueduct Press, which publishes feminist science fiction. A selection of her stories and essays can be found on her website: <http://ltimmel.home.mindspring.com>. She lives in Seattle.